D1006388

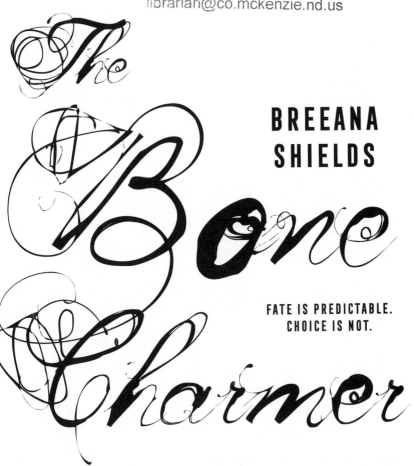

The Bone Charmer

BREEANA SHIELDS

FATE IS PREDICTABLE.
CHOICE IS NOT.

PAGE STREET
PUBLISHING CO.

PAGE STREET
PUBLISHING CO.

First published in 2019 by
Page Street Publishing Co.
27 Congress Street, Suite 105
Salem, MA 01970
www.pagestreetpublishing.com

Distributed by Macmillan, sales in Canada by The Canadian Manda Group.

23   22   21   20   19   1   2   3   4   5

ISBN-13: 978-1-62414-737-1
ISBN-10: 1-62414-737-2

Library of Congress Control Number: 2018958702

Cover and book design by Kylie Alexander for Page Street Publishing Co.
Cover illustration by Mina Price

Printed and bound in the United States

FOR MY MOM, WHO IS STRONGER THAN SHE KNOWS
AND FOR MY DAD, WHO I MISS EVERY DAY

Saskia

Tomorrow my future will be decided by my dead gran's finger bones. It's how my whole life has been determined—with bones and blood and snapping flames. When I was five days old, my mother dangled me over a stone basin that was heavy with the shoulder blades of an ox and pierced my heel with a sewing needle. I'm not sure how many drops of blood splashed into the basin. One? Two? Ten? It doesn't matter. It was enough blood to infuse the bones with my essence. Enough blood to tell my mother anything she wanted to know about the next few years of my life.

It's always been a prickly thing between us, her insight and my ignorance. And the other way around, too. The bones can't show her my heart.

I creep down the stairs toward the sharp scent of sage incense, a sure sign my mother is consulting the bones about one thing or another. It's almost impossible to sneak up on her, but I can't resist trying. Maybe if I know what she's up to, I'll have some hint about what the morning will bring.

The deep voice that resonates from below surprises me so much that I nearly forget to avoid the creaky fifth step. My mother isn't alone—one of the townsfolk must have arrived for a last-minute reading before the kenning tomorrow. I sag against the wall, disappointed. I don't care about knowing any future except my own.

Yet the sound of bone scraping against stone propels my feet forward. When I reach the bottom of the staircase, I peek around the corner.

My mother sits in the center of the room across from one of Midwood's most prominent farmers, Mikkel Hemming. A stone basin rests on the floor between them, filled with a handful of animal bones that, from the looks of them, are probably cheaply prepared and not especially powerful. A casual reading then. Nothing like the ceremony and solemnity that always permeates the kenning. My mother isn't even wearing her Bone Charmer robes.

"Thank you for seeing me on short notice," Mikkel says. "The moment I touched the soil this morning, I knew I better come see you. I'm worried it's too wet for planting asparagus."

"It's no trouble at all," my mother says. She pricks Mikkel's index finger with a needle and squeezes a few drops of blood onto the bones. Then she uses a bit of flint and a stone to light a small fire in the basin.

2

The room tilts and I squeeze my eyes shut. Minutes seem to pass and then, beneath my closed eyelids, I see Mikkel at the door, his hat clutched in one hand. I startle as I hear his voice in my head, thanking my mother for her time. My eyes fly open, but to my horror my mother is still at the beginning of the reading—tipping the bones onto the rug in front of her.

My throat closes.

This hasn't happened in years—this unsteadiness around the bones, as if the magic is like a dog on a lead, determined to reach me whether I want it or not.

And I don't.

Dread sits in my stomach like soured milk. An image of sharp black tattoos shaped like arrowheads rises in the back of my mind and I shove it away. Gran said once that in families with long lines of bone magic—families like ours—power is like a fire that burns hotter with each new generation. She meant it to be encouraging, and she had pride in her eyes when she said it, but by then I already knew the truth—the stronger the blaze, the harder it is to control. And the faster it destroys.

Bone magic would be dangerous in my hands.

I press my knuckles to my mouth. Mikkel is still sitting silently across from my mother. Picturing anything else was only the result of an overactive imagination. Still, I don't want to be matched as a Bone Charmer tomorrow. Surely, there's a path more appealing for me than the constant risk of hurting someone I'm supposed to help.

"You're right, Mikkel." My mother's voice snaps my attention back to the present. "If you plant asparagus, you'll have an outbreak of purple spot that will cost you most of the crop. I'd recommend something else this year—perhaps corn."

Mikkel sighs and rakes a hand through his hair. "That's what I was afraid of."

She gives him an apologetic smile. "Sorry to be the bearer of bad news."

He climbs to his feet. "Better to know now," he says. "Thank you, Della."

I push my back against the wall as she walks him to the door and closes it softly behind him. I edge slowly up the staircase.

"I know you're there, Saskia. Don't bother trying to slink away."

My cheeks suffuse with heat. I descend the rest of the stairs two at a time and round the corner to find my mother with her hands on her hips and a reproachful expression on her face. "You know better than to spy on a reading. I take confidentiality very seriously."

"I hardly think Mr. Hemming's choice of crops is a secret."

Her lips press together in a pale line. "Would you want someone sitting in on your reading tomorrow?"

At the mention of the kenning, my stomach twists. "I don't want to be a Bone Charmer," I tell her. "You know that, right?"

She shakes her head and walks away. I follow her to the kitchen, where she picks up an apple from the bowl on the table and slices off a section with a knife.

"Mother?"

"The kenning isn't for determining what you want, Saskia. It's for determining what's best for you. And for the country."

She pops a piece of the fruit into her mouth.

"What's best for me is to have some measure of happiness," I tell her.

She chews maddeningly slowly and swallows before she answers. "First Sight causes more heartache than the others. Your gran's visions always came too late to make a difference in anyone's happiness. But maybe the bones will reveal one of the other Sights for you."

Gran had First Sight—the ability to see the past. My mother has Third Sight—the ability to see the future—but I wish she had one of the other two Sights instead. Then I could get my kenning from a different Bone Charmer, one who wasn't concerned with preserving the family legacy.

I open my mouth to tell her that she's misread my concerns entirely. I'm not worried about having too little power. I already know that there's more heartache in having too much. But if I go down this road with her, she'll ask for explanations that I'm not willing to give.

Knowing what I want my life to look like should be enough for her.

"I don't want a bone-matched partner, either," I tell her. "Unless it's . . ."

Her eyes narrow, and the rest of the sentence dies on my lips. "The bones don't take requests." Her voice is clipped, impatient. The knife moves deftly through her hands as she cuts another slice of her apple. "I should think you'd want to know as much about your future as possible. Not everyone is privileged enough to start a relationship on such sure footing."

"I know we can afford it, but what if I disagree with whomever the bones choose? I don't want to be stuck with someone I don't love for my whole life."

"Don't be melodramatic, Saskia. No one is stuck with someone they don't love. Bone-matched or not."

Anger flares in my chest at her cavalier dismissal of my worries. It's true that no one is forced to accept a bone-matched partner, but it's that or a life spent alone. No one wants a mate who was fated for another.

I slam a fist down on the table and my mother startles. Good. At least it's an expression besides the calm mask of certainty she usually wears.

"Can't you just *consider* my wishes tomorrow?" I ask her. "Please?"

"And what are you wishing for, exactly?"

"It might be nice to be matched as a tutor."

All the tutors I've ever known have outlived both their hearing and their eyesight. Even when they've made mistakes, none of them have ever hurt their pupils with anything more than a sharp tongue or unrelenting high standards. It's the safest vocation I can think of.

"That's an interesting choice," my mother says. "And certainly something worth considering." She slices off another piece of apple and offers it to me. It's a poor substitute for a promise, but it's the most she's willing to give.

The next morning dawns bright and cold.

The townsfolk are gathering in the square, shoulders hunched against the chilly bite of the early spring morning. Those of us turning seventeen this year are milling around the Marrow—the circular stone hut where my mother waits with the velvet-lined boxes that hold our futures.

There are eighty-three candidates this year—forty-one boys and forty-two girls—and a box for each of us. I counted them myself, fingers trailing over silver scrollwork and polished wood, all while a cord of anxiety cinched tighter and tighter around my neck. All of us will at least have a chance to be matched with an apprenticeship today. Not like several years back, when one box was missing and Callum Elliot didn't show up to the kenning. He was the youngest of ten children, and by the time he turned seventeen, his family couldn't afford anything more than mouse bones. My mother offered to waive her fees, but it wasn't enough. Between the hefty cost of bone preparation and the kenning tax charged by the council, the family couldn't scrape together enough coin.

In the end, it probably wouldn't have made a difference. Mouse bones were unlikely to work well for such an intricate reading. But even the most expensive, well-prepared bones can sometimes fail to produce a clear kenning.

The possibility is a weight on every heart—no one wants to be a leftover.

I have the opposite problem as Callum. Affording a bone reading—any bone reading—has never been a concern for me. But my worry is useless now. I won't get another chance to appeal to my mother before my reading, so I try to focus on something else instead—the hundreds of brightly colored paper lanterns hanging from spindly branches; the giant bonfire in the distance; the children with arms full of snowy-white blankets, bouncing on their toes from either cold or excitement.

"Saskia." A familiar voice sends a thrill racing up my spine.

Declan's breath dances against my neck. He probably shouldn't be standing so close to me. Not yet. What if one of us is bone-matched with someone else? The thought opens a pit in my stomach. My mother wouldn't dare. Not when she knows how we feel about each other.

I step out of Declan's reach before I spin to face him. A wide grin notches a dimple on his left cheek, and his vibrant green eyes spark with mischief. He has combed his normally unruly hair into submission, save for a disobedient whorl just above his forehead that makes him look like a kitten that's been freshly groomed by its mother.

"Morning," I say. He lets his gaze hold mine for a beat too long, and my cheeks flush. Another slow smile creeps over his face like drizzling honey.

"I'll be waiting for you over there." He winks at me before he walks away. I glance at the other girls to see if anyone noticed the brief impropriety, but no one is paying any attention to me. It's the kind of day where our thoughts are only of ourselves.

I watch Declan until he is swallowed up by the crowd of boys, my heart swelling before worry shrinks it again. I should know better than to love anyone before the bones have spoken. But there's something about Declan—his easy smile, his full-bodied laugh, the carefree way he approaches life, as if he has no doubt that fate will always work in his favor. If anyone is confident about the results of the kenning, it should be me. But I'm not. Not at all.

Movement at the edge of the courtyard catches my attention. A lone figure strolls toward the throng of candidates. Bram Wilberg.

Late to the kenning.

He stops short of the Marrow and settles beneath the shade of a giant oak tree, right where a wide expanse of grass borders the cobbles. He closes his eyes and tips his face toward the sky, resting his mop of chestnut hair against the tree trunk and folding his muscular arms over his stomach. No one approaches him. When it comes to Bram, everyone steers clear.

Especially me.

A breeze trembles through the cherry blossom trees and petals drift onto my hair and shoulders like pale pink snow. I close my eyes and breathe them in. The subtle fragrance has always been intertwined in my mind with springtime and new beginnings and the kenning day.

I never imagined being this nervous.

A hand falls on my shoulder and I turn to find Ami, her eyes shining with excitement. The muscles in my back unwind, and I pull her into a quick embrace. "You're late," I say, my voice muffled against her collar. "I was starting to worry I'd have to do this alone."

The bones chose Ami as my friend before either of us could walk. Our lives are woven together like the strands of a rope.

Ami pulls away. "Sorry," she says, circling her hand in the air near her head. "Mama wouldn't stop fussing." Her dark hair is swept away from her face and pulled into a twist, and her cheeks are pink from the cold. She wears a lemon-yellow cloak that flatters her complexion. I finger the ends of my hair. It hadn't occurred to me to do something special with it today. Then again, my mother wasn't at home to help me get ready. She left before dawn to prepare for the kenning. I wonder what it must be like—to have a mother invested in your present instead of your future. A mother whose only task on a morning like this is to braid your hair and hope for a result that will make you happy.

"Has your mother given you any hints about what's going to happen?" Ami asks, as if she can read my thoughts. The question bumps into something raw inside me.

"No," I say. "She won't tell me anything."

Ami squeezes my fingers. "I guess we'll find out soon enough."

As if on cue, the bugle horn sounds and a hush falls over the square. It's time. All the candidates start moving closer to the Marrow. I can almost feel the anticipation rolling off Ami. She has nothing to worry about because she will be happy with any outcome. *What's meant to be will be,* she always says. But my stomach feels like a clenched fist.

"Good luck, Saskia." Ami plants a quick kiss on my cheek before taking her place in line. It's an ironic wish, considering that luck is the very thing we're trying to outfox. But I return the sentiment anyway.

I look around for Declan and when I find him, his eyes are

already trained on me. I offer him a shaky smile, but his grin is unfaltering. I try to remember if he was always this certain of the future. For the past year he has been, I know that much. He has whispered it against my ear in stolen moments, promised it to my fingers in fleeting touches. His confidence is like a shelter against the storm that rages inside me. I can envision a life—a safe life—by his side. And it doesn't hurt that the sight of him hurries the blood through my veins.

The first girl in line—Meisha—disappears into the cottage. We watch her go, a thousand pairs of eyes glued to the closed door, afraid we might miss something if we blink. Silence hangs over the square for a few minutes, but soon the expectation of a quick answer fizzles away. Children begin shuffling their feet. Mothers and fathers whisper to each other, no doubt fretting about the pairings. Some of the candidates dress up their worry in banter—elbows nudging ribs, heads thrown back in exaggerated laughter. But others don't speak. Some of us won't have a clear enough result to be matched with an apprenticeship today; others won't be happy with their reading.

Meisha is probably only gone for ten minutes, but it feels like days. She steps out of the Marrow with her eyes cast down, and at first I think she's crying. But then she looks up and a shy smile spills across her face. Good news, then.

Instead of heading toward the bonfire, she walks to where the boys are standing with abruptly stony expressions. A chorus of gasps ripples over the crowd. Meisha's parents must have paid handsomely to secure a matchmaking reading along with her kenning. Most of the townsfolk save for years just to afford a bone match for an apprenticeship. Only the wealthiest can pay for a bone-matched partner, too.

Meisha holds out her hand to Bunta and the square erupts in applause. A love match is always cause for celebration.

Watching the new couple walk toward the bonfire hand in hand fills me with bittersweet longing. What a gift to have so much confidence in fate. I hope my own reading won't include a matchmaking—I want to be chosen because I'm loved, not because fate decrees it—but I'm not optimistic. My mother has never been able to resist knowing my future, no matter the cost. I wrap my pale, unmarked arms around my middle. I wonder how long it will take for the slender red tattoo to etch itself around Meisha's wrist. I wonder if it already has.

One of the children races forward with a teetering stack of pale blankets. Bunta plucks one from the top of the stack, and he and Meisha settle in front of the snapping fire to have their first conversation as intendeds. I sneak a look at Declan, but he's not watching me this time.

Several more candidates come and go—apprenticed as bakers, craftsmen, merchants, farmers. A few of them are apprenticed to one of the bone magics—as Masons or Healers. But so far, no Bone Charmers. The line is shrinking and my courage along with it.

I drag the toe of my boot along the edge of the path that leads to the Marrow. The cobblestones are still shimmering and rain-slicked from last night's storm. I think of my mother's creamy, soft hands, of the way she used to take my face in her palms after she'd tucked me in at night. "You have a hundred possible futures, my love," she always said.

But of those hundred possibilities, my mother can only pick one. And unfortunately for me, she's always cared more about what the bones tell her than what her daughter does.

Saskia

The morning inches along like a river of syrup and yet, when it's finally my turn, I don't feel ready.

The door to the Marrow opens and the smell of sandalwood incense hits me full in the face. A girl with curly black hair and copper skin steps into the sunlight. "How did it go?" I ask.

She gives me a tremulous smile. "I've been apprenticed as a tailor," she says, "which is close to what I hoped for." Her smile falters. "I really wanted to work as a seamstress, but"—she shrugs—"at least I get to work with fabrics." She's trying to put on a brave face, but it's clear she's disappointed in her match. A surge of anger rises in my chest. Why should she have to spend her life doing something she didn't choose? But saying it won't do either of us any good.

"I hope it brings you joy," I tell her.

"Thank you," she says. "I hope so too." She squeezes my arm before turning away. "Good luck."

I watch her as she makes her way down the path. As she marches toward a future she's only half-excited about.

The impulse to run rises inside me like a wave. I lay a palm flat against my stomach and pull in a deep breath. My father's face floats to the surface of my memory. *Trying to escape your fate is like trying to make a toad croon like a songbird,* he used to say. *No matter how good your intentions, you're just wasting your time.* And he was right.

The bones said he would die young, and he did.

Death came for my father just months after we lost Gran, and sometimes I can feel its breath against my neck like it's looking for any excuse to come for me, too. In a few minutes my mother might provide one. There's nowhere to hide, no way to avoid this. I can only hope of all the potential directions my life could take in this moment, she chooses one that will please me.

I bite my lip and push open the door. The Marrow is dimly lit and it takes my eyes a few moments to adjust. Flickering candlelight sends long shadows crawling up the stone walls, and thin tendrils of smoke curl toward the ceiling. In the center of the room, my mother sits on a large white rug. An empty stone basin rests near her knees, and a silver velvet-lined box is at her side.

She's dressed in red silk robes that bring out the blue in her eyes, and her pale hair is braided and looped on the top of her head like a crown. She looks like an older version of me.

"Saskia," she says. "Come. Sit."

I settle across from her. My heart is a hummingbird inside my chest.

"Are you nervous?"

I swallow. "Should I be?"

She opens the clasp of the silver box and tips its contents into the basin. Gran's finger bones clatter against the stone. The sight of them tugs at my grief. I've suffered far too much loss in the last few years. I pull my gaze away from the bones and find my mother studying me intently. "Do you trust me, Saskia?"

"Do I trust *you*? Or do I trust the bones?"

She presses her lips together. "It's the same thing."

But it's not. I know how the reading works—the blood and flame will combine, and my mother will see multiple possible futures for me. Branches that head off in opposite directions. Paths that diverge toward different destinies. But as a Bone Charmer, she's taken a sacred oath. She's duty-bound to pick the future that best uses my talents to meet the needs of the people of Kastelia. Even if it's not the path that would make me happiest.

"You have a choice," I tell her.

"Saskia—"

But I hold up a hand to stop her. "Don't. Just do the reading."

She opens her mouth, as if she's about to argue, but something about the look on my face must make her reconsider, because she snaps it closed again.

"Very well, then." She reaches for me and I wince as she pricks the pad of my middle finger with a sewing needle. She squeezes gently until a drop of blood wells at the surface. I hold my hand above the basin and let the blood spill onto the bones.

"It's not enough," my mother says. She pricks another finger, and then another, until Gran's bones are speckled in crimson. Once she's satisfied I've bled enough, she picks up a rock and a piece of flint and, with practiced hands, sets the bones alight.

My head swims, and I'm not sure if it's the nauseating combination of the smoke and incense, or the loss of blood, or the prospect of these particular bones being used against me. My mother's eyes flutter closed. She breathes deeply and the smoke seems to rush to her, as if it's ready to do her bidding. Several minutes pass and my eyes grow heavy. My limbs go slack. I forget what I was so worried about.

But then the clatter of an iron lid lowering onto the basin pulls me from my reverie. My eyes snap open just in time to see my mother spill the blackened bones across the white carpet. As she studies them, a crease appears between her brows. Her eyes are shimmering when she lifts her head.

"You'll be apprenticed at Ivory Hall," she tells me, her voice flat and emotionless. "You'll train as a Bone Charmer with the Second Sight." She swallows and her gaze slides away from me. "Bram will be your mate."

For a moment I'm too stunned to react. And then rage wells in my chest.

"Why would you do this?"

She doesn't answer. I can hear my pulse roaring in my ears.

"Which one of Gran's bones told you to ruin my life?" I ask, scooping a handful of them into my palm.

"Saskia." Her voice is low and threatening. "Don't."

But what could she possibly do to me that is worse than this? I'll be sent far from home to be trained to read bones—a fate I couldn't be less suited for. And she's paired me with a boy whose tattoos have made the whole town fear him, a boy who might have been my very last choice—if *choice* were actually a luxury that belonged to me. I'll not only live a miserable life, but I'll live it alone.

"Was it this one?" I ask, holding up a slender bone. When she doesn't answer, I throw it aside and pick up another. "Or maybe this?"

My mother's hand shoots out, her fingers roughly brushing mine as they close around the bone. Two bright splotches stain her cheeks and she has fire in her eyes. "Give it to me." She tugs. But I tug harder.

And the bone snaps in two.

All the blood drains from my mother's face. She sucks in a sharp breath and snatches the other half from me.

Broken bones are bad luck.

"What have you done?" Her voice is shrill, terrified.

But it should be me asking that question. She's destroyed any chance I have of happiness. And these bones are worthless now anyway—they can only be used once. I climb to my feet and stalk toward the door.

"The answer to your question is no," I say. "I don't trust you." But she doesn't respond. And when I cast a final glance in her direction, she's still staring at the fractured bone, one hand pressed against her mouth in silent horror.

I squint into the sunlight as I step outside the Marrow. The next girl in line is bouncing lightly on her toes. "So?" she asks brightly. "How did it go?"

I shake my head and brush past her. Suddenly the chatter in the square dies away and I feel the weight of a thousand stares fall on me. The townsfolk are watching me with expressions ranging from open curiosity to outright glee, as if scandal has a scent and they've just caught a whiff. But I refuse to give them the satisfaction of becoming a topic for their gossip, so I force a smile onto my face. I walk confidently toward the other side of the Marrow, where the boys are waiting.

Declan gives me a sheepish grin as I approach, and my heart twists in my chest as I pass him.

I stop in front of Bram. I don't know if I can find the courage to do this. But what choice do I have? No one ever rejects a bone match on the kenning day. I take a deep breath and hold out my hand. My fingers tremble. Bram's dark eyes widen and he retreats a step or two behind the other boys.

He actually backs away from me.

Heat climbs up my neck, floods my cheeks. I stand there with my hand outstretched for a beat.

Two.

Three.

Finally he rakes his fingers through his hair, leaving it sticking up in all directions. He gives his head a little shake of resignation and slides his hand in mine. Each of his knuckles is tattooed with a small black triangle. His palms are rough. It's been years since I've been this close to Bram. Touching him stirs up memories I've fought long and hard to suppress, and I force myself not to pull away.

We walk toward the bonfire, and slowly the low hum of conversation starts up again. We sit on a large, flat rock and a small girl thrusts a fluffy white blanket into my arms. "Congratulations on your pairing," she says. From the corner of my eye, I see Bram flinch. I want to tell her thank you, but the words feel stuck in my throat. Instead I just nod, which seems to satisfy her, because she smiles and scampers away.

I unfurl the blanket and settle it over both of our laps. As soon as our hands are hidden, Bram lets go of me.

I feel as if I've been slapped. After the sting fades, an older ache surfaces like a bruise I thought had healed long ago but is still tender when probed.

"You weren't my first choice either," I tell him.

His eyebrows pull together. "What?"

"I obviously wasn't your first choice," I say. "And I just want you to know that you weren't mine either."

He doesn't say anything for several long seconds, but when he speaks, his voice is dry, almost bored. "Duly noted."

We sit together in tense silence and I wonder what my father would think of this pairing. He and my mother were bone-matched, but he claimed he already loved her by the time she held out her hand to him on the kenning day.

"You most certainly did not." My mother scoffed when he

told me the story.

Father's palm covered his heart. "Della, my darling, I'm wounded. Just because you didn't love *me* yet doesn't mean I didn't love *you*."

"I don't remember seeing a red tattoo around your wrist," she said lightly. "We'd hardly spoken before the kenning day. When exactly did you have time to fall for me?"

A grin spilled over his face then. "The day Kyle Dennis challenged you to race him to the top of the Poulsens' huge oak tree, and you beat him by five minutes."

She shook her head, but her eyes were dancing. "How did that make you love me?"

"How could it not? If your gumption didn't win me over, your tiny little legs dangling from the branches as you hummed all three verses of 'Meet Me in the Treetops' would have."

The story earned a laugh from me and an amused gasp from Gran. "Della, you didn't!" The song is about two young lovers who have to keep their relationship a secret because they haven't had their kenning yet. Each night the boy climbs a tree to reach the bedroom window of the girl he adores to give her a midnight kiss. My mother humming that song was a taunt to the boy who challenged her. Not only did he lose, she announced to the gathered crowd that he was fond of her.

"To be fair," my father said, "half the town was head over heels for your mother. I was just lucky the bones chose to smile on me."

But I guess I didn't get my father's luck.

Gran's bones have paired me with someone who couldn't

be more opposite from my father. Someone who is marked with tattoos that hint of a dark past. Someone who has been matched as a soldier in the Ivory Guard.

And my apprenticeship . . . for the first time since I stormed out of the Marrow, it sinks in that I was matched with Second Sight. I always assumed, if I became a Bone Charmer, I would have First Sight like Gran or Third Sight like my mother. But the ability to see things in the present never occurred to me. It certainly sounds safer than the other Sights—finding misplaced objects, helping people make decisions, assisting Healers in diagnosing pain for patients who can't speak for themselves. But then I remember that Second Sight Bone Charmers are sometimes used to question accused criminals, and I feel queasy.

I turn my face toward the bonfire, let myself be mesmerized by the way the flames consume everything in their reach, at the wooden logs in the center that started out enormous and strong but will soon be reduced to ash. That's how I feel inside—on fire. Like no matter how strong I am, soon there won't be anything left.

Except bones.

When everything else is destroyed, the bones always manage to survive.

Saskia
The Second Kenning

My mother is holding two halves of a broken bone.

Smoke clouds my vision, and I fight the urge to let my eyelids slide closed again. I'm sleepier than I should be. The Marrow is too warm, and sandalwood incense snakes through my nostrils, making me light-headed. I rub my eyes and study Gran's blackened finger bones scattered across the white carpet among bits of ash. My head throbs lightly, and I wonder if it's normal for the kenning to be so much more draining than a typical reading. But it's not until I focus on my mother's face that the disoriented feeling turns to alarm. She's staring at the fractured bone as if it's her own broken heart she's cradling in her palm.

"What's wrong?" I ask.

Her head snaps up as if she's surprised to see me here.

"Oh, Saskia." There's a reprimand in her tone that I can't make sense of. Is she still upset that I wouldn't say I trust her? Did the bones tell her something terrible about my future? I wait for her to say more, but she doesn't. She turns her attention back to the bone, her lips pressed together in a thin, pale line.

"Mama," I say, suddenly feeling small. "You're scaring me."

"We've done this before," she says.

A chill inches down my spine. "Of course we have." She's given me readings dozens of times—they're as familiar as the berry-filled tarts she makes each year on my life-celebration day.

She shakes her head. "We must have argued," she says. "You must have broken this." She sets the two parts of the bone down carefully beside the others.

"What are you talking about?" I say. "No, I didn't."

She's not making any sense. But then again, that bone wasn't broken a moment ago. I'm sure of it. And tipping it onto the carpet couldn't have caused a fracture like that.

My mother sighs and covers her face with her hands. Her slender red tattoo—the one that etched itself over the contours of her wrist bone when she fell in love with my father—stands in sharp contrast against her skin, which has gone unnaturally pale.

"These bones were special," she says.

"Because they were Gran's."

"Yes, that too." Her hands tremble as they fall to her lap. "But there's more. I infused them with extra magic—the blood of three generations of Bone Charmers, each with a different Sight."

"I don't understand," I tell her. "We don't even know

someone who has the Second Sight."

Gran had the ability to see the past and my mother can read the future, but the present . . . and then it dawns on me. "My blood? I have the Second Sight?"

But how would she know? She hasn't finished my reading yet.

"The additional magic made them more powerful—they were supposed to allow me the ability to see your future much more clearly. The bones were from a close family member. They were woven with context from the past and the present—but it also made them more dangerous."

"Dangerous how?"

She swallows. "I'm worried . . . Saskia, I don't see the path for you that I was expecting to see."

The band of tension that's been tightening around my heart suddenly snaps and I feel lighter.

"Oh, well, maybe the bones just surprised you. Maybe my path is different from what you thought it would be."

"You don't understand . . . Look at the bone. Do you see how one side is blackened around the edges and the other looks like it's never been touched by flame? Something changed. The extra magic . . . It's possible that because this bone fractured, your future has *actually* split in two. Instead of possibilities, the path this bone represented may have become realities. That's why I'm not seeing what I thought I would. Because the path of one half of the bone is invisible to me."

I examine the broken bone. She's right—the two halves look different.

"But nothing terrible happened, right? We're still sitting here. Only one set of us and not two."

She gives me a look that makes my stomach squirm. *We've done this before.*

"You don't mean . . ."

"I think you're already living in an alternate reality based on the reading I gave you before."

All the breath leaves my lungs. "Which was *what*?"

"That's the thing," she says. "I don't know."

A tremor goes through me as if the earth has shifted. As if it's still moving. "How could you do this? Why would you make the bones *more* powerful?"

My entire life has been held captive by the iron fist of my mother's readings. I've had so many that my freedom has been peeled back layer by layer, like an onion, until I don't have any choices left. I can't imagine why she would need to increase the strength of the bones when they've already built an inescapable cage around me.

A piece of hair has loosened from one of her braids and blows across her face in time with her shallow breath. My mother is usually as unruffled as a lake on a windless day, but right now she looks more unhinged than I've ever seen her. She doesn't even seem to realize I've spoken.

"What do we do now?" I ask.

It takes her a long time to answer, but finally her eyes meet mine.

"My only option is to choose the best path from what is left. I can't read something I can't see." She takes a deep breath and studies the bones in front of her—not just the broken bone, but all of them. "I have to find a way to fix this. But I have no way of knowing what I selected for you before. Not for sure." The sadness in her voice sends a shock of guilt through me, even though I've done nothing but sit here.

She studies the bones for a long time, as if she's choosing between dozens of possibilities. Then, finally, she tucks the stray hair behind her ear and lifts her head. She sits up a little straighter. "You'll be apprenticed here in Midwood as a tutor," she says. The next words seem to take more effort, and she can't quite meet my gaze as she says them. "Declan will be your partner."

I step out of the Marrow in a daze and squeeze my eyes closed. The morning is aggressively bright and cold in contrast to the overheated darkness I just left behind.

The girl at the front of the line bounces on her toes. "So?" she asks. "How did it go?"

I open my mouth to answer, but then I find I have nothing to say. I got both the apprenticeship and the partner I wanted, and yet I've never been more worried for my future. My mother said we'd discuss it later, but I'm not sure this is something that talking can fix. The girl is watching me with an expectant expression, so finally I give her an answer. "Fine," I lie. "It went just fine."

A hush falls over the crowd as I make my way to the other side of the Marrow, where the boys wait. Declan is giving me an eager smile as if he knows exactly where I'm headed. And even though he's right, my gaze still wanders to the other boys in line. My mother said she would try to choose an alternate path for me. That my two futures will probably be quite different. Does that mean she suspects the bones don't think I belong with Declan? But then again, how could the bones show paths toward a different partner if it's truly a fated match?

A lump forms in my throat as I step forward and hold out my hand.

Declan flashes me a set of perfectly straight white teeth. His eyes are the bright green of a tart apple.

"I knew it," he says as we make our way to the bonfire. He grabs a blanket from one of the children and we sit on a large flat stone close to the flames. He traces small circles on my palm with his thumb.

"Are you happy?" he asks.

"It's what I hoped for," I tell him. And it's true. Relief cascades over me—I wasn't matched as a Bone Charmer and I won't have a binding ceremony; any potential for magic that I had will slowly ebb away. But my relief is tempered by unease. In another reality, am I sitting in this very spot with someone else? Is Declan?

Which version of me is better off?

For the first time in years, I long for the assurance of the bones, for a path I know is sanctioned by fate. Now that I don't have it, I feel like I'm walking along a rickety bridge toward an uncertain future.

My mother always tells me that bone readings are a privilege, something to be cherished. But I always thought choice was the greater luxury.

Maybe I was wrong.

Saskia
The Bone Charmer

The ship that will take us to Ivory Hall is nearly ready to launch and Bram still isn't here. Maybe the prospect of being paired with me was so objectionable that he decided to leave Kastelia—it wouldn't be the first time someone had gone missing after kenning day.

A breeze blows in from the harbor and sends a ripple of goose bumps racing across my skin. I rub my palms up and down my arms, trying to coax warmth back into my body.

"You forgot something." A heavy cloak settles around my shoulders, providing instant relief. I turn to see my mother, a tangle of different emotions playing over her face. She gives a rueful smile as she studies me. "Don't worry, love," she says. "He'll be here."

I finger the crimson fabric of my mother's favorite cloak. I've always loved how it flatters her complexion. And mine, too. Of all the things she could have given me—the future I wanted, a voice about my own life, a path different from hers and Gran's—she chose to give me this. I move away from her. "I'm not worried," I say with enough bite that she flinches. And then her expression shutters.

I let my eyes slide away from her, to the clusters of families gathered at the harbor. Everyone who was assigned an apprenticeship outside Midwood will board the ship today and travel up the Shard River to Ivory Hall. It's one of the reasons the kenning tax is so high—the sheer cost of moving so many people all over the country must be astronomical. The same scene will repeat in every town and village across Kastelia. The wind will push the departing ships upriver toward the capital—Kastelia City—which is nestled in the upper delta. From there, the apprentices will board new ships, and the current will carry them back downriver to the different villages and towns where they've been assigned. Except those of us apprenticed at Ivory Hall, of course—Bram and I will set sail only once.

He still isn't here.

"Saskia," my mother says, "there's something you should know."

She takes my hands in hers, her fingers brushing the tiny purple tattoo at the base of my thumb. It was my first. It appeared when I was five years old, on the day I started school, the moment I let go of my mother's hand and walked into the small stone building where my tutor was waiting. Tattoos always materialize as a result of intense emotional experiences—red for joyous ones, blue when the experience is sad, a hundred different colors for an array of feelings. When I got home that afternoon, I showed my mother the tattoo, a small, rounded shape that looked a little like the petal of a flower. It was at the exact spot on my skin where her thumb circled mine when we were hand in hand. "Why is it purple, Mama?" I asked. "Does it mean leaving you made me happy or sad?"

She pressed a kiss on my temple. "Purple is usually for bittersweet, my love," she said. "It means you were a little of both."

Her expression now is the same one she wore that day. It tugs at my edges, pulls me toward her like a shell in the tide. But I'm still too angry to give in. We've been dancing around each other since the kenning. For three days I've known there are things she wants to tell me. And for three days she's known she has nothing to say that I'm ready to hear.

But now I'm leaving for an entire year. The reality of it drops into my stomach like a stone. "What is it?" I ask.

She opens her mouth, but it's not her voice that comes out.

"Saskia!" Ami races down the path toward the harbor, her hair blowing wildly around her face. She catches me in her arms and pulls me tightly against her. "Thank the bones I caught you. I ran all the way here."

I hug her fiercely. "I'm going to miss you so much." As the words leave my mouth, I realize they're meant for my mother, too, even if I couldn't look her in the eyes as I said them.

"Promise to write?" Ami says.

"I promise."

We pull apart just as the bugle sounds. The crowd starts surging toward the waiting ship, and my mother's face falls. Whatever she wanted to tell me, it's too late now.

Instead she settles for a kiss on my cheek. "I love you, Saskia," she says. "I want the best for you. Please believe that."

It was the wrong thing to say, and I feel the walls around my heart grow taller. "If you wanted the best for me, you wouldn't have done this," I tell her. "Why would the bones pair me with Bram? He's not even here. How could I ever care about a person who is too much of a coward to show up and deal with his fate?"

Ami and my mother both freeze, identical expressions of horror on their faces. I bite my lip and slowly turn to look behind me. Bram stands a few feet away, a bag slung over his shoulder, his expression stony.

"Oh," I say. "Hello."

His gaze meets mine only for a moment before he stalks toward the dock without a word.

Later that night I stand on the deck of the ship and look toward home. The inky sky is full of constellations that remind me of small bones scattered against a velvet cloth. As if the future of the whole world could be read with just a glance heavenward.

Dozens of other apprentices mill around the ship—laughing, jostling, peppering one another with questions about what village they're from or where they're going to begin their training. But I'm not in the mood for small talk.

"Are you a leftover, too?" I startle at the voice. A girl leans against the railing, her face turned toward me. It's too dark to make out her features clearly.

The question takes me by surprise and it takes me a moment to answer. A leftover. It's a derogatory term used for those who can't afford the kenning or whose kenning was too murky to be useful. Those who are assigned an apprenticeship from whatever is left once everyone else has been bone-matched.

"No," I tell her. "I've been apprenticed as a Bone Charmer."

"Oh." I can hear the note of disappointment in her voice. "I just thought . . ." She turns her face toward the water. "You just didn't seem as happy as the rest."

An awkward silence stretches between us. How can I confess that she's right—that I'm not pleased with my match—when she has it so much worse? My parents could afford to have bones prepared for any reading they wanted, and my risk of being a leftover was practically nonexistent. My whole life has been sanctioned by fate.

I clear my throat. "Where will you be training?"

"Leiden," she says. "I'm apprenticing as a glassblower."

"I visited there as a child and I still remember how beautiful it was. The stained-glass windows, especially." I shove my hands into the pockets of my cloak. "I hope you'll find success." But my words ring hollow, even to my own ears. Because it doesn't matter how talented she is—no one quite trusts the skills of someone who isn't bone-matched.

"Yes," she says, pushing off the railing, "I hope so, too." And before I can say anything else, she fades into the night, as if she's already practiced at being invisible.

Bram is already asleep when I descend the ladder into the sleeping quarters. All the apprentices sleep in one giant room in the belly of the boat. But the others must still be in the mood for celebrating. Apparently, Bram and I are the only two miserable enough to want to turn in early. Not even the leftover girl is here yet.

Bram lies stretched out on one of the dozens of hammocks slung from the ceiling, his hands behind his head, bare feet crossed at the ankles, his face lit from the flickering light of the oil lamp that hangs from a hook on the wall. It's as if I've never seen him before. As if he's been transformed in repose, a different person when he thinks no one is watching.

The sight pins me in place.

And then I notice the tattoo—a slender green vine with leaves shaped like teardrops—that curls over the top of his foot and disappears under the hem of his pants. I've never seen one like it, can't even imagine what kind of experience would produce such a lovely, intricate design. It's so at odds with the violent black triangles on each of his knuckles. A sharp pang of both guilt and fear twists my heart as I stare at his hands.

Why would the bones pair me with a soldier? What if my mother made a mistake?

But it doesn't matter if she did or if she didn't. At the end of our year of training, we can each either choose to accept or reject the match. If we both accept it, we'll set a date for our joining ceremony. If either of us rejects it, we'll go our separate ways and spend our lives alone. No one wants a partner who was meant for someone else.

I select a hammock in the opposite corner from Bram, as far away as I can get. I feel uneasy about sleeping this close to him, even though I know the room will soon fill and there will be so many people between us that he won't even know I'm here. I watch his chest as it rises and falls.

Suddenly his eyes snap open. He turns his head and his gaze finds mine across the room. I freeze. He stares at me for several long seconds, as if he's not sure if he's dreaming or awake. And then his expression hardens and slowly, deliberately, he looks away.

It's going to be a long journey to Ivory Hall.

Saskia
The Tutor

$\mathcal{I}$ come downstairs the morning after the ship leaves Midwood to find my mother sitting in her favorite chair with an open spell book perched on her lap.

She leans forward, studying the pages, a crease between her brows. The delicate skin under her eyes is blue with exhaustion and she's wearing the same rumpled clothes as yesterday. Bone charming is an ability that takes more than it gives, but the last few days have exacted a higher price than usual. My mother seems lost in her own thoughts in a way I've rarely seen before.

As a child, I made a game of trying to catch a glimpse of the bone spells—creeping down the stairs hours after my mother had kissed me good night to peer around the corner where she worked at a small wooden table. But she would always turn her back at the last moment, positioning herself so that the spell book remained hidden.

"Your bed is calling, Saskia," she said each time, without turning around. I used to wonder if she could see my future without the bones. If she'd done so many readings on me that she could predict my every move without magic or ceremony.

But seeing her like this—unraveled, holding the spell book in plain sight, completely unaware of my presence—is like traveling along a swiftly moving river and noticing a hole in the bottom of the boat.

She's been searching for a way to heal the bone for three days now with no success. We've barely talked about what happened at the kenning.

"Did you find what you were looking for?" I ask.

Her head snaps up and she presses a hand to her chest. "Saskia," she says, her eyes wide. "I didn't see you there." The expression on her face tells me she feels it, too—the water seeping up through our weak spots, ready to swallow us if we don't act quickly.

"I didn't mean to startle you." My gaze falls to the open pages in her lap—to the diagrams of bone patterns and neatly written notes in the margins.

She notices me looking and closes the book. She nestles it inside a wooden box, which she locks with a key suspended from the ribbon around her neck. "I'm getting closer."

"What if . . . ?" I try to find a way to ask the question that's been itching at the back of my mind since the kenning. "What if we do nothing? What if I just move on with my life and we don't worry about trying to heal the bone? Would it be so bad living two alternate lives at once?"

My mother pushes open the window and a cool breeze blows into the room, carrying the delicate scent of lilac blossoms. "You won't be whole until the bone is," she says. "Doing nothing is not an option."

I glance at the bone resting on a shelf across the room. It split unevenly, leaving one half bigger than the other. What does she mean I won't be whole?

A gust of wind slams the window shut and I startle. But my mother doesn't react. She's staring into the distance, worrying her lower lip with her teeth. "I need you to go to the bone house for supplies," she says finally.

I feel guilty for the relief that floods through me at the thought of escaping for a few hours.

"Of course," I tell her. She scribbles a list on a scrap of paper and presses it into my palm.

"Be vague if anyone asks questions," she says. "And tell Ami I said hello."

Before I even have a chance to make it to the door, she's already unlocked the box and pulled out the spell book again. I'm not sure why she even bothered to put it away.

The bone house is on the edge of town adjacent to the Forest of the Dead. The smell reaches me long before it comes into view. I cover my nose and mouth with the back of my hand as I climb the hill, but the stench of death still curls up my nostrils and makes me light-headed.

The forest is filled with trees, the trunks carved with names, birth and death dates, and carefully whittled memories. In a few of the trees hang burlap bags filled with the bodies of the recently deceased in various stages of decomposition. It's the first step in bone preparation—to let the flesh rot away so the bones can be prepared for the family. Flowers, trinkets, and notes sit beneath the occupied trees, fresh symbols of grief.

Our family tree is bare at the base. My father's body hung here not long ago, and before him, Gran. But now the buttercups and bluebells have been swept away and the branches are unburdened. I run my palm across the rough bark, trace the smooth grooves that spell out the names of the people I loved. I rest my forehead against the tree.

What would Gran make of the kenning? She always thought I would be a Bone Charmer, and when I was a little girl, I hoped she was right. But then everything changed and magic was the last thing I wanted. I wish I could talk to her just one more time. I think of her last few months—when old age had taken its toll, and she started seeing things that weren't there, having nightmares, losing her grip on reality. At the end . . . I shake my head to clear away the thoughts. I don't have time for grieving. Not today.

The bone house is situated at the far end of the forest in a small stone building with ivy climbing up the sides. I push open the door to find Ami sitting behind a long counter, bones spread out in front of her along with a collection of tools—small brushes, tiny spoons, flat blades. Her ebony hair falls across her face as she works. At the kenning she was apprenticed as a bone handler. It's not technically one of the bone magics, but it's revered as if it were.

Ami looks up and a smile spills across her face. "What a nice surprise." She comes around the counter and folds me in an embrace.

"How's the new apprenticeship going?" I ask.

Her eyes flick to Master Oskar, who raises one hand in the air without looking up from the bone he's brushing. It seems that's as close to permission to take a break as Ami's going to get.

"It's going well," she tells me. "But there's so much to learn—thousands of ways to prepare bones depending on who needs them and what they're being used for. I'm afraid I'll never remember it all."

"Of course you will," I tell her. We sit on a long wooden bench on the far side of the room. Bones are everywhere—spread across the counters, soaking in jars filled with clear liquid, drying on shelves after they've been freshly painted to replicate the tattoos their owners wore. The center of the room is filled with tables in various shapes and sizes, all of them laden with open books and stacks of paper. Being here reminds me of why bones are so expensive. So much goes into getting them ready for use—from the caretaker of the Forest of the Dead, to the handlers who clean and prepare them, to the traders who bring rare supplies from the far reaches of the country and beyond.

"Have you started tutoring yet?" Ami asks.

I shake my head. "No, but soon. Audra and her son are

vacationing in the islands. I'll start when they get back." I hand Ami the scrap of paper, not quite meeting her eyes. "My mother needs supplies for some work she's doing."

Guilt worms through my stomach. Ami is the one person who knows my every secret, the origin of my every tattoo. Like the pink crescent-shaped mark that emerged on my left hip after a gust of wind blew my skirt above my head during a game of Dead Man's Prisoner; the other children joked about my "blushing cheeks" for weeks afterward. And the tattoo behind my right knee—a flame, tinged with hues of red and orange that blazed onto my skin after the most frightening experience of my life.

Ami has always been the person who listened to my worries and laughed at my jokes. When Gran died, and later Father, Ami was there to help shoulder my grief. Even my mother couldn't reach me then—her heart was too full of her own suffering to bear mine as well.

It hurts not to tell Ami what happened at the kenning, but I promised I would stay silent. If the town council found out about how my mother had Gran's bones infused with extra magic, she'd face a tribunal. Still, the secret lodges behind my ribs, an uncomfortable pressure that reminds me that we can't share everything anymore. The loss stings.

Ami studies the list I gave her. She grabs a basket and mumbles to herself as she collects tiny glass jars and pouches of powder from the drawers behind the counter. She pulls out a tool with a smooth wooden handle and a sharp, pointed end and drops it in the basket.

"What is that?" I ask.

She answers without looking up. "It's called a pinner. It makes tiny holes in the bones so the preparation solutions can penetrate more easily."

And then she comes upon an item that makes her pause.

"Master Oskar," she says, "where do we keep essence of horse hoof?"

For the first time since I got here, the man lifts his head. "Who's asking?"

Ami's glance skips from me to him and back again. "They're for Della Holte . . .," she says. "The Bone Charmer."

He grunts. "I know full well who Della Holte is. What I want to know is what business she has with essence of horse hoof?"

The question hangs in the air. My pulse rushes in my ears.

"I don't know," I say finally. "I'm afraid she didn't say."

He narrows his eyes, and for a moment I think he'll refuse me. Then he shoves back from the table, his chair scraping loudly against the wood floor. He fumbles behind the counter, opening and closing a half dozen of the hundreds of small drawers that line the back wall before finally finding what he's searching for. He deposits a small brown pouch into the basket, along with my other items.

I count out several coins and drop them into his outstretched hand.

He frowns. "I can't think of what a Bone Charmer would need with that."

"I wish I knew," I tell him. And it's the truth.

"We need to trick the bone into thinking it's inside a body," my mother says when I return with the supplies.

I give her a blank stare.

"A *living* body," she clarifies, as if that were the source of my confusion.

"And how do you plan to do that?" I fall into the chair beside her.

Bottles and pouches are spread out across the kitchen table. My mother picks up each of them, one by one, and examines the contents.

"I considered implanting the bone in my own abdomen," she says, "but then we'd have no way to know if it's healing—the bone, I mean, not my abdomen."

I gasp. "Mother! You can't be serious."

She shrugs as if she finds my squeamishness immature. "Bones have special properties. Inside a living body, they will mend themselves."

"Well, sure, if someone falls from a tree. But this seems"—I grapple for a way to express myself—"not the same as that."

She tucks a strand of pale hair behind her ear. "We're going to make the bone believe it's the same."

"So, what is all this for?" I pick up one of the bottles, and the liquid inside sloshes around. "Since we've ruled out *slicing you open*."

"We're going to make a nutrient solution," she says triumphantly.

I raise my eyebrows.

"Don't just sit there. Help me."

She goes to one of the cabinets in the kitchen and starts removing things—a bowl, a spoon, a mortar and pestle, a clear container made of glass.

"Fill this and put it over the heat," she says, handing me a pot.

Once the water comes to a boil, we add sugar, salt, and the ingredients I brought from the bone house—a bit of bone dust, the essence of horse hoof, a small vial of tears. And then my mother pulls a sewing needle from her pocket.

"Give me your hand," she says.

I sigh. "Why do you always need my blood?"

"Your blood is powerful," she says, pricking both of our fingers.

"No, *your* blood is powerful. Mine is only ordinary."

She freezes, one hand cradled in the other, a single drop of blood bright against her ivory skin. I wait for her to correct me. To repeat what she said at the kenning when she implied that I might have Second Sight. Or at least that's what I think she implied. I've been itching to ask her about it ever since, but she's been so focused on finding a way to heal the bone, I haven't dared. But she doesn't correct me.

"All blood is powerful," she says, finally.

We hold our hands above the pot and let a few drops fall, turning the liquid light red. While I stir the solution, my mother uses the pinner to poke several tiny holes in each half of the bone.

"Is that thickening?" she asks.

"I think so?" I lift the spoon from the pot. The liquid has congealed to something resembling jelly.

"Perfect," she says, taking the pot from me and pouring the contents into the glass container. She fits the two halves of the broken bone together and pushes them into the slightly gelatinous substance.

"What now?" I ask.

My mother wipes sweat from her brow. "We wait."

I press a palm to my sternum and think of the tattoo there—a curve like the string of a tightly pulled bow, a line running through it like an arrow. It appeared right after my gran died as a deep midnight blue. When my father died, it turned black.

"Can I tell you something?" I ask.

My mother's expression of surprise sends a jolt of guilt through me. I used to tell her everything, but as the kenning got closer, I pushed her away. The possibility of being matched as a Bone Charmer when I knew magic wasn't safe with me—when I would dishonor both her legacy and Gran's—weighed on me like a cloak of iron.

"Of course," my mother says, her voice a little too deliberately nonchalant. "You can tell me anything."

"I'm afraid of what will happen if the bone heals."

"You mean if it *doesn't* heal?"

I shake my head. The thought of two different versions of myself wandering around Midwood is frightening, but imagining a version of myself suddenly winking out of existence terrifies me. "No," I say, biting my lip. "I don't want this version of myself to disappear."

"Oh, Saskia." My mother folds me in an embrace. She smells of vanilla, and it's so reminiscent of my childhood that I can't help but sink against her. "I don't think I've been entirely clear, love. If the bone doesn't heal, *all* of your futures will disappear."

I pull away from her. "How is that possible?"

She presses her lips together. "I did something I shouldn't have," she says. "I used a magic that—it's expressly forbidden, and if the council finds out about it . . ."

"What?" I ask. "What did you do?"

"Bone reading is subjective. I wanted your kenning to be flawless." She sighs. "I infused the kenning bones with your essence."

"I don't understand. You *always* infuse the bones with my essence." I think of the hundreds of times my fingers have been pierced in service of one reading or another.

"No," she says. "I had the bones prepared with your blood. And mine and Gran's as well." I remember now what she said at the kenning, that she infused them with extra magic so she could see my future more clearly.

"What were my other paths? What were you choosing between?"

Her eyes slide away from me as she answers. "I'm sure your first kenning had many possibilities, but you know I couldn't see the other half of the bone once it broke."

"But still you saw more than one future, didn't you?"

She sighs. "You know I can't tell you that."

"Why not? It doesn't seem like you've been sticking strictly to the rules here."

She shakes her head. "It's not healthy to know too much about your own future."

My jaw falls open. "Are you serious? Do you have any idea how that sounds coming from you?" My whole life has been built around knowing everything about my future.

"It's not the same," she says. "There's a reason Bone Charmers can't do readings on themselves. Knowing too much changes your decision-making, alters your path. I can't tell you what I saw, Saskia. I'm sorry."

"You said . . ." I swallow. "At the kenning you said something about three generations of Bone Charmers?"

"I matched you as a tutor," she says softly.

"But—"

"I believe it was one of your possible paths, yes," she says. "I can't tell you more than that. Your kenning is final. You can't go through the binding ceremony now, and you'll never be a Bone Charmer. Not in this life."

A spasm of relief goes through me, knowing that without the binding, my potential for magic will slowly fade.

"So the bones weren't infused with the blood from three generations of Bone Charmers?"

She twists her hands in her lap. "Not in this reality," she says. "They're infused with the magic of two Bone Charmers and a tutor. Which makes them much more fragile than I wish they were."

"And if it doesn't heal . . ."

"Your fate is now intertwined with the bone. I'm so sorry, Saskia. After the kenning, I planned to lock the bones away. They would have lasted for generations. I never anticipated that one would break."

I feel as if the floor has shifted beneath my feet. I find the courage for one more question: "What about the bone in my other reality?"

"Now, *that* bone might be infused with the blood of three generations of Bone Charmers," she says, "which would make your two paths very different. Every alteration has the potential to change the future in both big and small ways. Perhaps, in that reality, I've thought of a different solution to make things right." She strokes my cheek with the backs of her fingers. "I can only hope I'm wise enough to fix it in one of them."

Saskia
The Bone Charmer

*I*vory Hall sits high on a hill just below the first fork in the Shard. It's a massive structure—white and gleaming, with hundreds of windows and dozens of square towers that stretch toward the sky. Four broad lanes spill down the hill, the closest of which runs parallel to the port where our ship is docked.

All the apprentices crowd on the deck, elbowing for a better view of both Ivory Hall and the pier. I press against the railing, as eager for a glimpse as the others. Rows of ships identical to this one are docked all along the shore.

Seagulls circle overhead in patterns that look too structured to be accidental. Onshore, I see several people in green cloaks, delicate bone flutes pressed to their lips, playing while they look skyward. A white stripe on each sleeve designates them as members of the Ivory Guard, but I can't think why musicians would be needed for protection. I study them for several minutes before I realize they must be Watchers—some of the select members of the Ivory Guard who also have bone magic. My father told me about them when I was small.

"Papa, if you could have any magic, what would you choose?" I asked him once. It was my bedtime, and the question was more of a stall tactic than actual curiosity. But he played along, as he often did.

"I'd be a Watcher," he said.

I'd scrunched up my forehead then. "No such thing." I knew all the magics had "bone" in the title. Bone Charmers, like Mama and Gran, Bone Masons, Bone Breakers, Bone Healers.

"Ah, but you're wrong, bluebird. The official title is Bone Singer," he said. "But that's not a very serious name for someone tasked with defending a country, now is it? They like to be called Watchers instead. Much more impressive." And then he told me about people who could control animals through song.

The Watchers are guiding the birds, seeing through their eyes to get a better view of the activities below. Huge white dogs pace along the shoreline and up and down the pier. Their owners stand at a distance, clothed in the same green cloaks but playing larger instruments. The flutes must be made from the bones of the same type of animal being controlled. I think of Ami back in Midwood, apprenticing at the bone house, and a pang goes through me. I wonder if she'll learn to prepare bones so Masons can carve them into flutes.

Someone squeezes in beside me and I glance over to see

Bram. He's been avoiding me for our entire journey, but maybe looking out across the capital, he feels it too—how everything is different here, how home suddenly seems so far away.

"Hello," I say.

He lifts his chin slightly, without answering, as if we're strangers exchanging pleasantries, instead of two people from the same town. As if we're not bone-matched.

I sigh and search for my patience. "Are you nervous?"

His dark eyes roam over my face. "Why? Because I'm too much of a coward to show up and deal with my fate?" He grips the railing so tightly that it turns his knuckles white. His black tattoos stand in such sharp relief that they practically leap off his skin.

My cheeks burn. "I didn't mean—" But he doesn't let me finish.

"Yes, you did."

One of the crew members lowers the ramp and announces that it's time to disembark. Bram turns his back on me and soon he's lost in the throng.

The pier is a riot of color and noise. Vendors selling food—long skewers threaded with tender chunks of meat and crisp vegetables, delicate bowls made from spun sugar and filled with ripe berries, bite-sized morsels of sweet bread.

Merchants walk along the pier, boxes slung across their chests, peddling their wares. They sell little toy flutes made of wood and painted white, sets of pretend bones so children can playact the kenning, and even bits of shell and teeth that are mostly worthless except for mundane readings like choosing fish bait.

Kastelia City is a trading hub, and snatches of conversation from beyond our borders float past me in languages I don't understand—the melodic long vowels of Cistonian, the guttural, harsh tones of the people of Novenium, and other tongues so unfamiliar that I can't place them.

Each of the ships in the harbor seem to have unloaded their passengers at the same time, and soon a horde of apprentices are all pressing forward, climbing toward Ivory Hall. I'm caught in a swiftly moving wave of people, and I can only trust that someone at the front of the crowd knows where we're headed.

The lane is steeper than it looks, and it's not long before the muscles in my legs are on fire. By the time we make it to the top, the afternoon has faded away. The sun dips toward the horizon, and soft pink light colors the sky.

A woman stands on a tall box, shouting directions and signaling for the group to gather around. Her silver hair is braided and rolled into a tight bun at the back of her head, and she has a yellow half-moon–shaped tattoo on the side of her neck. Both her voice and mannerisms suggest she's not someone to be trifled with. She reminds me a bit of Gran.

I crane my neck to get a better view of Ivory Hall, but we're too close now, and the structure is too massive. All I can see is a solid wall of white stone, broken only by a huge set of arched double doors made of iron and inlaid with branches that mimic the Shard River.

Once we're all assembled, the woman holds up her hands and the excited chatter dies away. "My name is Norah," she says. "I'm Steward of Ivory Hall, and I'll be making sure you get settled in today with a room assignment and your training schedule. If you're apprenticing in one of the bone magics, you'll also see plenty of me in your seminar classes."

She motions toward a younger man, standing off to the side. "If you are apprenticing in a standard specialty, please follow Jonas to the back entrance. Bone magic apprentices will follow me."

Norah steps off the box, scoops it under her arm, and walks purposefully toward the front door.

The group peels apart—the majority following Jonas, and the rest of us hurrying to catch up with Norah. Bram falls in step beside me and I turn to him, confused. Was he not listening?

I study him surreptitiously. His profile reveals wide cheekbones and a strong jaw with the barest hint of scruff. A battle rages inside me. Do I ask him if he's in the wrong place? I don't know if it will make things between us better or worse, if he'll see it as a challenge or a peace offering.

"Bram," I say carefully. "I think the Ivory Guard apprentices were supposed to go the other way."

A muscle jumps in his jaw. It's the only sign he heard because he doesn't look at me.

Then, finally: "I can follow instructions, Saskia."

"But . . . wait, are you training in *bone magic*?"

"It looks that way," he says mildly.

"Which specialty?"

"Bone breaking."

A ping of alarm goes through me.

"Why didn't you tell me?" I ask. "Why did you let me believe you were assigned as a regular part of the Ivory Guard?"

"You didn't ask."

"Should I have to?"

"I don't know. Should the great Saskia Holte have to ask for anything?"

I feel the words like a knife sliding between my ribs. It's a sentiment I've heard before—how lucky I am to lead a bone-charmed life, a life with nothing left to chance. As if not having ownership over my decisions isn't just another kind of prison.

"That's not fair," I tell him.

He shrugs. "Life is only fair for some of us."

I curl my hands into fists, my fingernails digging crescent-shaped impressions into the soft flesh of my palms.

My mother wasted her coin on having bones prepared for a matchmaking reading. Because it doesn't matter what she thinks my future holds—there's no way I'll ever fall in love with Bram Wilberg.

Norah leads us through Ivory Hall's enormous arched entrance. The moment I step inside, it's as if the pressure in the air changes. My stomach plunges and a buzz grows in my ears. The room seems to spin. I hold out a hand to steady myself, but the moment I touch the wall, the chatter of the other apprentices vanishes and

I'm engulfed in a silence so complete, it feels like sound.

And then a hum, a noise soft enough that I doubt I hear it at all, though I *feel* it there surrounding me. As if I've walked into a whisper.

Firm hands pull me away from the wall and the hum disappears. Norah guides me forward and helps me sink into a chair. "You must be a Bone Charmer," she says.

I can't manage more than a nod.

"Sit here a moment. It will pass."

I open my mouth to ask what's happening, but then another wave of dizziness washes over me and I can't get the question out. Norah pats my hand. "Ivory Hall is made entirely of bone, so you're going to be uncomfortable for a little while. It's always hardest on the Charmers, but you'll adjust. Until then, I suggest you touch as little as possible."

A tremble goes through me. I can't even fathom the number of bones it would take to build something this vast. And what happened when I touched the walls? Was that bone reading? Are these human bones? The hair on my arms stands on end.

When I was small, I used to have nightmares and wake up so frightened, I could scarcely breathe. My father would show up at my bedside, take my face in his hands, and gently press his forehead against mine. "Deep breath, bluebird," he would say, inhaling right along with me. "Now blow it out. In again. And out." We would sit like that, forehead to forehead, breathing in harmony until peace found me again, until it wrapped around me like sunlight.

His voice is in my mind now as I pull air into my lungs

and force it out again. Slowly, the dizziness subsides, and I can finally take in the grand foyer—the two staircases on opposite sides of the room that curve elegantly toward the upper floors, the chandeliers dripping with crystal, the gleaming white floors that look like marble but must be bone.

I turn my focus to Norah, who has launched into a speech about the rules we need to follow while living at Ivory Hall. I try to focus—something about two apprentices to a room, and meals in the dining hall, and a schedule of lessons, some of which will be one-on-one with our Masters and others taught together as a group—but I'm still not feeling like myself, and most of it escapes me.

Mercifully, she doesn't talk long before she announces that the staff will show us to our rooms. I make the mistake of touching one of the banisters on the way up the stairs and nearly lose my balance, but a hand reaches for my elbow to steady me.

Bram.

He lets go as soon as I regain my footing, and walks silently beside me. For a moment I think I can hear the sound of his blood sluicing through his veins. But then I realize it's only the whisper of the walls.

When we reach the point where the corridors split—the men's dormitory to the left, and the women's to the right—he walks away without looking back.

I wake the next morning to someone perched on the edge of

my bed. A girl my own age with large brown eyes and curly hair that reaches nearly to her waist. She's dressed in a white nightgown and she's studying me intently, as if she's been there for hours, watching me sleep.

I let out a startled yelp.

"Oh," she says, "sorry to scare you."

What did she think was going to happen when she sat on my bed? I scrub at my eyes with a fist. "Who are you?"

"I'm Tessa," she says.

I blink up at her.

She frowns. "Your roommate?"

"I'm sorry . . . I . . ."

"Are you feeling better? Because you were in really bad shape last night."

I search my memory for the events of the previous evening, but it's like trying to gather broken glass. Things come back only in bits and pieces. I vaguely remember walking toward the dormitories, a voice chattering in my ear, the sensation that the floor was disappearing beneath me, and then collapsing onto the bed. I look down. I'm still in the same clothes I wore yesterday.

And Tessa is still talking. "If we'd started our lessons already, I might have been able to do more to help you, but since we haven't even been bound to our magics yet, what could I do? I thought about finding a real Healer"—she laughs—"one with some actual training, but you didn't seem to want me to do that, so I hope you don't mind that I just left you alone."

"I don't mind," I say.

She lets out a relieved sigh. "Oh, good. I'd hate to get off on the wrong foot." A collection of white star-shaped tattoos curve around the back of her ear, and her right arm is covered in indigo whorls.

"I'm Saskia," I tell her, scooting into a sitting position. The room spins gently and my stomach rolls over.

"Yes," she says, "you told me last night. Right before you pushed me out of the way and fell face-first onto your bed."

"Sorry," I say. "I wasn't quite myself." I loosen my braids and run my fingers through my hair. My scalp is so tender, it makes me wince, and I wish I'd at least had the presence of mind to take out the pins before falling asleep.

Tessa gives me a sympathetic frown. "Is it the walls? I read they make Charmers feel especially unwell."

I attempt a nod that makes my head swim. "I didn't realize Ivory Hall was made from bone until I got here. It doesn't affect you?"

"It does," Tessa says. "Just nothing serious enough to make me ill."

"What *do* you feel?"

She tilts her head and stares at the ceiling as if trying to find the right words. "I feel . . . unsettled. I can sense the injuries in the bones—the ailments that killed their owners."

"So they *are* human?"

"Definitely," she says. "I think a lot of them were soldiers. Probably Kastelians who died in the Transdroimian Wars. Their bones are particularly potent. But other people must have died of natural causes and chosen this as their final resting place, because their bones feel . . . quieter to me."

I swallow. "You discerned all of that and you don't even have a headache?"

The tips of her ears turn pink. "What's it like for you? Other than being ill, I mean."

What's it like for me? For a moment I'm tempted to tell her the truth—that I'm terrified of bone magic. Since the kenning I've felt like I'm standing at the summit of a steep mountain, about to be pushed from behind. I'm in danger of careening downward, out of control. Destroying everything in my path. I hoped once I arrived at Ivory Hall, I might feel more empowered, more connected to the magic. Instead I was rendered incapacitated the moment I set foot inside the building.

But my secrets burn shamefully inside me, so I find a different way to explain: "It feels like the walls are whispering."

Tessa's eyes widen. "What are they saying?

The question takes me off guard. *Should* I know what they're saying? If I had more control over my magic, would I be able to hear something more than murmuring? A tight fist of fear closes around my heart. "I can't tell."

Tessa's expression melts into something like pity. "Oh, well, I'm sure it's just the nausea. Once you adjust, you'll probably have fascinating tales to share."

She sounds a lot more confident than I feel.

Maybe Tessa comes from a longer line of bone magic than I do. Maybe that's why she has more control of her magic already. Not because there's something wrong with me, but because she's exceptional.

My fingers worry at one of the hairpins I've been holding.

"Are you the first Healer in your family?"

"No," she says, and I breathe a little easier—until she continues. "My tenth great-grandmother was a Healer, so I guess it runs in the family but just skipped nine generations." Her laugh is easy. Carefree.

The hairpin in my hand snaps in two. I suddenly want to end this conversation. "Speaking of last night, I didn't really hear the instructions. Do you know where I'm supposed to be?"

Tessa gives me a bright smile. "That's why I was trying to wake you. We need to leave now if we're going to make it on time. Today is the binding ceremony."

My hurried steps echo in time with my heartbeat as Tessa and I rush down the long corridor toward the great hall, where the binding ceremony will be held. The kenning is only an invitation to study bone magic; it's the binding that seals the apprentice to their ability. Once the ceremony is over, there's no going back.

The great hall is a rectangular-shaped room three times as long as it is wide, with massive bone columns that support soaring ceilings. Sunlight pours through the windows that line the left side of the hall, bathing the room in a brilliant white glow. Rows of narrow wooden tables, each holding six stone basins, fill the entire center of the room. Next to the basins are neatly folded cloaks in a variety of colors.

Tessa's astonished sigh perfectly expresses my awe.

Norah stands on a dais at the far side of the hall. "Welcome, apprentices," she says. "Before we get started, please have a look around. Notice the ten windows—they represent the members of Kastelia's Grand Council. Five men and five women—one member from each of the bone magics and four members who have no magic at all. Perhaps some of you might sit on the council one day. Many of our current council members had their binding ceremonies in this very room."

She goes on to discuss how the trees carved into the walls mimic the many branches of the Shard River, how the circular window behind the dais should remind us of fate, while the stained glass inside symbolizes the three essential tattoos.

My knees feel weak, and I don't know if it's the bone walls getting to me again or if it's a side effect of being mesmerized.

"It's time," Norah says finally, pressing her palms together in front of her. "Please find your name and stand beside your basin."

Tessa turns to me. "Good luck." Her voice is just above a whisper, as if she doesn't want to spoil the moment with noise.

"Thank you," I tell her. "And to you, too."

I find my name on a table near the front of the room. My heart beats out a staccato rhythm. There was a time—when I was very young—that I dreamed of this day. Of becoming a Bone Charmer like my mother and Gran. Somewhere deep in the recesses of my memory, I can feel that little girl standing on her tiptoes, eager and excited along with all the other apprentices. But then more recent images rise in my mind—fire and flame, and the terrifying sensation of being trapped—and that ancient spark of anticipation vanishes. This isn't the future I would have chosen for myself.

Not anymore.

"You are all interconnected," Norah says solemnly. "Masons craft the bone flutes that Watchers use to control animals and the weapons that Breakers use to protect our country. Mixers blend bone potions that Healers use to treat patients. And, of course, Charmers perform readings on us all. You will get to know each other in your seminar classes as you learn the things that are crucial for all who practice bone magic—anatomy, history, ethics. I encourage you to help and support each other."

She lets her gaze sweep across the room and fall on each of us. "But your most important relationship at Ivory Hall will be formed as you receive individualized instruction."

A door opens near the front of the hall and dozens of men and women in colorful cloaks pour into the room.

Norah sweeps her hands in front of her, palms to the ceiling. "Masters," she says, "meet your apprentices." One by one the teachers find their pupils. My gaze sweeps across the room. A young man, no older than thirty, stands in front of Bram. An older woman, plump and friendly-looking, stands in front of Tessa.

And then, finally, someone stands in front of me. "Hello, Saskia," she says. "I'm Master Kyra." She's neither young nor old. Her skin is a warm brown, and her hair is pulled back from her face and gathered in an intricate twist at the nape of her neck. She wears a red cloak.

I open my mouth to reply, but Kyra gives a quick shake of her head. I press my lips together.

"Masters and apprentices," Norah says, "welcome to the binding. You may begin."

A low hum fills the room as the Masters begin talking all at once.

"Saskia Holte," Kyra says, "you have been chosen as a Bone Charmer with the Second Sight, and today you will bind yourself to this magic as it has bound itself to you."

She reaches for my hand and pricks my index finger with a needle. "In front of you lie the bones of Charmers who have come before. Do you witness with your blood that you will honor their legacy?"

"Yes," I say, tipping my finger until a single drop falls into the basin.

"Do you vow to use your gifts for the benefit of others and not for personal gain?"

"Yes." Another drop of blood.

"Do you vow to help your fellow citizens find happiness, while matching their talents to the needs of the country?"

"Yes." A third drop spills to the bones below.

"Do you promise to follow every tenet of your training, to uphold the values that you learn within these walls, and to use your magic for good?"

"Yes." I have to squeeze my finger to force another drop to fall.

Master Kyra picks up a stone and a bit of flint and sets the bones on fire. She pulls a pouch from her pocket and sprinkles it over the basin. The flames shoot higher and turn a bright, cool blue.

"Saskia Holte," Kyra says, "you have been bound to this magic and may now don your training cloak."

She nods toward the folded bundle at the side of the basin,

the same red shade that she wears. As I unfurl it, I notice that it's thicker than the silken robes the Masters wear. I glance around the room—each of the magics has its own color—black for Breakers, blue for Healers, green, purple, orange—but the apprentice cloaks are all a few inches shorter than the ones the Masters wear. And they're all made of wool.

I think of my mother placing her cloak around my shoulders before I boarded the ship, and a lump forms in my throat. It was identical to this one. I thought her favorite cloak was just a cold-weather version of the silk ones she usually wore, but now I see the gesture for what it was—she gave me her old training cloak. She was sending me on a journey with a little piece of herself.

And I barely spoke to her before I left.

I pull the cloak around my shoulders and finger the thick fabric. There's no going back now. I didn't want to be bound to magic, but like most things in my life, fate didn't care about my plans. And if I want to keep the people around me safe, I have to learn to control my abilities. No matter how impossible it might seem.

It's the only path I have left.

Saskia
The Tutor

*D*eclan is waiting on my front steps, a bouquet of purple blossoms clutched in one fist, bouncing nervously on the balls of his feet. For the entire year before the kenning, he'd done nothing but shamelessly flirt with me, but now that we're matched, he looks like a nervous schoolboy every time we're together.

I can't help but smile.

As I walk across the grass toward the house, I shift my basket under one arm to conceal the contents. I've just made my weekly trip to the bone house to get more crushed fragments for the nutrient solution, and even though there's nothing about the pouch that would incriminate me, I'd like to avoid questions.

"Hello there," I say.

Declan grins and thrusts the lilies toward me.

"They're beautiful." I take them and hold them under my nose. They give off a delicate fragrance reminiscent of honey. "Thank you."

"I was afraid I'd missed you," he says. "Where have you been hiding?" His tone is playful, but it still needles me. Maybe I wouldn't be so sensitive if I didn't have something to hide.

"Boring errands," I say lightly. And then, to change the subject: "How is the training going?" The topic is like sand poured into a jar of shells. It flows through every conversation in the weeks after the kenning, filling the gaps and squeezing into the pauses.

"As well as can be expected," he says. "Though I'd underestimated how much wealthy people will pay for rare items they don't need." Declan is apprenticed as a trader, and he's training with a man who deals in rare artifacts. He's been traveling from village to village, procuring items for collectors. "Present company aside, of course."

I frown. "We're not wealthy."

"You're not spoiled," he says. "There's a difference."

I make a noncommittal noise. Another topic I'd rather not discuss.

"What do you have there?" Declan makes a grab for the basket, and I move it out of his reach. He gets a mischievous glint in his eye and lunges toward me, trying to pry it from my fingers.

"Stop," I say.

He doesn't.

I yank the basket away and put a hand on his chest. "Declan! Stop it now!"

He freezes and his face falls. I drop my hand to my side. My breathing is ragged.

"I'm so sorry," he says. "I was just playing around. I didn't mean to be intrusive."

My flowers fell on the ground during the scuffle and now they're scattered at our feet, trampled. We both bend to gather them at the same moment.

"I overreacted," I say finally. I'm crouched on the ground next to him, our faces so close that I can feel his breath against my cheek. I tip the basket toward him so he can see inside. "It's just something from the bone house," I say. "For my mother."

He barely glances at the basket. "I'm just trying to be part of your life," he says. "But I'm not doing it very well."

His crestfallen expression tugs at a tendril of sympathy inside me. I long to confide in him, to let him pull me into his arms like he has done so many times before, and assure me that everything will turn out perfectly for both of us. But I'm afraid telling him the truth would only make things worse. How can I possibly explain the seed of doubt the kenning has planted in my heart? I don't know what the bones showed about my future. Did my mother match me with Declan in both realities? And if not Declan, then who?

The naked vulnerability in his eyes thaws what remains of my anger. I touch the back of his hand. "I know. I want to be part of your life, too."

He threads his fingers through mine. "Next time you go to the bone house, can I come along?"

I want to say no. I nearly do. But we're bone-matched—at

some point I'm going to have to stop second-guessing myself, and act like it.

I take a deep breath. "Yes, of course."

He tucks a flower behind my ear. "I can't wait."

Ami and I sit on the bank of the Shard, our feet dangling in the water. It's the first truly warm day of spring and my last day of freedom before I begin my tutoring duties.

Since we were children, it's been our favorite warm-weather tradition—packing a basket full of food and eating it on the grassy riverbank, throwing bits of bread to the ducks, depositing tiny boats made from hastily folded scraps of paper in the river and then placing bets about where they'll end up.

The sun on the back of my neck is decadent. It's nice to get a respite from home, where my mother's gaze is perpetually fixed on the broken bone, as if she can force it to mend with her will alone.

"So," Ami says, raising her eyebrow suggestively. "How are things going with you and Declan?"

"It's fine," I tell her.

"It's *fine*? That's not very romantic for a match sanctioned by fate."

The secret feels like a bubble in my chest on the verge of bursting. But I can't tell her that I'm not sure if the match was sanctioned by fate or not.

I twirl one of Ami's glossy black braids between my fingers

and then tuck it behind her ear. "You're the romantic, not me."

She smiles. "My parents couldn't afford a matchmaking reading and, apparently, whoever my soul mate is, he isn't rich enough to afford one either. Humor me."

"I don't know," I say. "Sometimes he's great and then sometimes . . ." I tell her about him trying to steal the basket from me a few days ago.

Her mouth twists into a disapproving frown. "You need to have an honest conversation with him, Sas. Do you remember when we were children and his parents asked him to gather wood for the fire? And he thought it would be funny to lie down and play dead next to the ax. When his mother found him, she screamed so loud that the whole town came running. She was ready to kill him—for real—but Declan had actually thought she'd be impressed with his joke. He always tried to make a game out of everything, but sometimes he goes overboard."

Ami is right. Declan was always the one challenging friends to impromptu races. Planning practical jokes. Making everyone laugh with his easygoing approach. It's one of the reasons I've always been drawn to him. Because the only risks he ever takes are playful ones. He only likes danger that ends in laughter.

She drags a toe slowly through the water. "Is it possible you're finding flaws because you're scared?"

My skin prickles. Ami knows me a little too well.

"Maybe," I tell her. "But haven't you ever doubted a reading?"

She's quiet for a moment. "What's gotten into you lately? There's something you're not telling me."

Guilt pools inside me. I reach for her hand. I may not be able to tell her everything, but she still feels like a lifeline.

"I'm just confused," I say. "Before the kenning, I knew Declan was perfect for me, and now . . ."

"And now that you're matched, you're avoiding him by spending all your time with me at the bone house." Her gaze cuts to me. "Not that it stops him from following you there like a lost puppy." She squeezes my fingers. "But the fact that you're keeping him at arm's length can't make him feel good. Maybe that's why he took it too far the other day? He was trying to draw you out. Though he still should have stopped once you asked him to. Now that you're matched, you have to be willing to talk to him when something bothers you. It's the only way to have a good relationship."

Even without knowing the whole truth, Ami's advice still hits the mark.

I kick a bit of water onto her calf. "Why do you always make so much sense?"

She grins at me. "Because I'm brilliant."

"But don't you ever wonder if the bones are wrong?"

Her answer is soft. "I never had enough access to readings to wonder."

My shoulders stiffen. Ami's parents aren't poor, but they're not wealthy, either, and bone readings have always been a rare luxury in her family.

"I'm sorry," I say. "That was insensitive."

She shrugs. "I just don't think you'd doubt the bones if they hadn't always been available, you know?"

Ami's words rattle around my mind for the rest of the day. When I walked into the Marrow, I *wanted* to be matched with Declan. I *wanted* to be a tutor. And now that I have everything I wished for, I'm not happy. What if that's only because I'm scared? What if I've let my mother cast doubt on everything because of the broken bone? If she chose Declan for me, it's because that was one of my possible paths, so why am I feeling doubts now?

It's not Declan's fault that my mother used extra magic on the bones. It's not his fault that the bone broke. In my head, I believe it. Now if I could only convince my heart.

Tutoring is not the fulfilling experience I imagined when I told my mother it was my dream.

Audra Ingersson paces across the length of the sitting room—it's one of at least ten inside her enormous mansion. She's continually building new spaces or tweaking existing ones, and now the rooms flow together without any rhyme or reason—bedrooms off the kitchen, hallways that lead to dead ends, windows between interior rooms.

"She's a bit eccentric," my mother warned me before I left this morning. But nothing could have prepared me for this.

Audra's boots click against the hardwood floor as she travels the length of the room. She seems oblivious to the fact that her son, Willem, is climbing up the banister.

"It's such a difficult decision," she says. "I don't know whether to have you teach grammar before penmanship or penmanship followed by grammar." She stops walking and runs a palm over the mantel above the fireplace. The white paint is chipped in spots, revealing a red color underneath. "Or maybe we could start Will's day with history?"

I grip the arms of my chair. It's upholstered in a silky material far too slippery for furniture, and I fear the moment I relax, I'll slither to the floor. "I'm not sure the order of the lessons matters very much."

Audra turns to me, her mouth an open circle of shock. "Of *course* it matters. I just forgot to ask the particular order of the lessons at my last reading."

The housekeeper glances up from her dusting to shoot me a sympathetic look. Willem slides down the banister and lands with a thump at the bottom of the stairs.

"I don't suppose you'd be willing to ask your mother?" Audra's voice is bright, eager.

"I really don't—"

But just then a bell sounds from somewhere on the grounds outside. Audra's hand flies to her mouth. "Is it that late? Oh no, I really must go. My last reading instructed me to be at the market at precisely noon." Even though it's a warm day outside, she grabs a shawl from a hook on the wall and slings it over her shoulders. "I'll be back soon." She points a finger in my direction. "Don't teach Willem anything until we've sorted this out."

Audra closes the door and I turn to the housekeeper with a helpless look. How am I supposed to keep Willem occupied all morning if I can't teach him anything? I assumed Audra wanted a private tutor for her son to have the added benefit of one-on-one instruction, but he'd be better off at the village school than lazing around here all day.

"Nothing to be done," the housekeeper says. "Audra won't make any decision until she's consulted the bones. And I mean not a single decision."

"But she hasn't been to visit my mother in years," I say. "At least, not that I'm aware of." I shift in my seat and slide to one corner.

The housekeeper tosses me a rough blanket. "For traction," she says with a wink. I tuck the blanket beneath me, and the chair finally stops trying to toss me overboard. "Audra doesn't get bone readings in Midwood anymore." The housekeeper glances at Willem to make sure he's out of earshot, and he is. He's nearly made it back to the top of the banister. "Your mother stopped putting up with her nonsense years ago. Said it was immoral to consult the bones for every little decision when others couldn't even afford the kenning. But Audra wants what she wants, so now she travels to towns where Bone Charmers are happy to take her coin"—she raises her eyebrows—"and happy to give her plenty of ways to spend it. Build this, redecorate that, buy new jewels during the new moon for extra protection."

I can't even imagine someone using their gift in such a corrupt way. I think of Audra running off to the marketplace because she thinks her fate relies on being there at a certain time. My mother has told me enough over the years that I know that's not how bone charming works.

And where does she even get bones for so many readings?

Willem flies off the end of the banister and crashes into a table.

"Maybe it's time to play a different game," I tell him. "Your mother isn't going to be very happy if you break something."

He shrugs. "She won't care if the bones don't."

And how can I argue with that when I know he's right?

"Audra Ingersson is *horrible*," I tell my mother later that evening.

We're sitting over a simple supper of bread and stew, though my mother just pokes at her vegetables with the back of her spoon without taking a bite. She's staring into the distance. I follow her gaze to the glass container on the shelf.

"Maybe it's best if the bone doesn't heal and I cease to exist," I say. "That might be preferable to trying to work with that woman."

My mother fixes me with a steely glare. "That's not funny."

"It's a little funny," I say under my breath.

"Audra isn't horrible," my mother says. "She's misguided. She believes that if she's careful enough, she can avoid tragedy. But none of us can."

"But why is she like that?" I ask. "And how did she get so wealthy, anyway?"

My mother gives me a disapproving look. "You know I don't like gossip."

"It's not gossip if it's true," I say. She purses her lips, but I cut her off before she can correct me. "Fine, it's not gossip if it's not malicious. And I'm not just asking to satisfy my curiosity. If I'm going to have to work with her, it would be nice to know what I'm dealing with."

She tilts her head, considering. When her shoulders drop and she sits back in her chair, I know I've won the argument.

"Audra's grandparents emigrated from Cistonia, where bone magic is uncommon," my mother says. "And so her family didn't believe in readings. They didn't even plan a kenning for her, or any of their other children." She traces a single finger around the rim of her mug as if lost in thought.

"So, what changed?" I ask.

"When Audra was fourteen, her family went on vacation—a week of hiking through the Droimian Mountains. On the first day, Audra fell and twisted her ankle. The local Healer recommended she keep pressure off her foot for the rest of the trip, so Audra stayed behind at the cottage they'd rented. On the last day of their vacation, there was a landslide in the mountains and her entire family was killed. Wiped out in a single tragic accident."

I suck in a sharp breath. "That's terrible."

"It was," my mother says. "Afterward, Audra became obsessed with bone readings. Maybe she thought if her family had sought out a Charmer, their lives would have been spared. She married one wealthy elderly man after another—Mr. Ingersson was only the latest in a long line—and grew her fortune by investing the money they left her. Once Willem was born, she became even more fanatical about consulting the bones." My mother sighs sadly. "Not that it makes it any easier to cope with her behavior—the bones know I've tried—but hopefully knowing her story gives you a bit of compassion."

A knock sounds at the door and we exchange a glance. Neither of us wants to get up.

"It's unlocked!" my mother shouts.

Ami walks in, her eyes red and swollen, her cheeks damp. I push my chair away from the table. "What's wrong?"

She takes a shuddering breath. "Something terrible has happened," she says, her voice high and reedy. "Someone robbed the bone house."

My mother covers her mouth with her hand. "Oh, love," she says, "I'm so sorry."

Ami shakes her head and squeezes her eyes shut. Fresh tears course down her face. "You don't understand," she says, looking back and forth between my mother and me. "The bones that were stolen . . . Saskia, they belonged to your father."

Saskia
The Bone Charmer

My training is not going well so far.

Master Kyra and I sit across from each other at a circular table in one of the tutoring rooms. A handful of small animal bones are scattered on a cloth in front of me. The air is choked with incense.

"You're not concentrating," Master Kyra says. I'm supposed to be doing a reading to divine what's currently hidden in her left pocket. It seems like a simple task, especially in comparison to what I've seen my mother do. But no matter how much I try, the only thing I see when I close my eyes is red-tinged emptiness.

"Is it a ring?"

She sighs. "No. Don't guess. See it in your mind."

A bead of sweat slips from the nape of my neck and creeps

down my spine. I think of my mother's face during readings—how it seemed as if she'd left her body behind, but her mind was somewhere wondrous and faraway.

"You're working too hard," Kyra says.

I open my eyes. "You just said I wasn't working hard *enough*."

"No, I said you weren't concentrating. Bone reading requires both total focus and the ability to let go."

"Oh, is that all?" I say under my breath.

Her jaw tightens. "Try again. Focus and relax."

I try to direct my thoughts toward the bones. I stare at them and will them to tell me something, but they just lie there, motionless and mute. My eyes start to water and I let them flutter closed. Maybe if I can at least feign concentration, Master Kyra will take it easy on me. I relax my forehead and shoulders. I take a deep breath, and the smell of the incense seems to grow more pronounced as if Kyra has moved the burner closer. Behind my lids, I see a twitch, a barely perceptible movement, and the shadow of something slowly starts to take shape.

And then an explosion trembles through the room.

The image dissipates and my eyes fly open. "What was that?"

But Master Kyra doesn't look alarmed, only irritated.

"Mixers," she says, dipping her head in the direction of the rooms across the hall. "They nearly bring down the entire training wing at least once a month. You'll have to learn to ignore them."

Thick black smoke curls under the door and Kyra sighs. "Now that is going to be hard to ignore." She throws open the window and cool air rushes in, bright and sharp. "Let's take a break," she says. "Get some food. Try to come back refreshed and ready to work."

She doesn't wait for a response before she opens the door and leaves. The training room fills with smoke that stings my eyes and burns my lungs. I stick my head out the window and take deep, cleansing breaths. Master Kyra's hacking cough grows more and more faint as she makes her way down the corridor.

Far below are the rushing waters of the Shard. On this end of the building, it's one long turquoise river with swells of whitecaps where the water slams into boulders. Ivory Hall—or rather the hill that it's perched on—is what first divides the river, lessening its power at the same time as it expands its reach.

"Everything all right in here?"

I turn to see a tall man in a red cloak held closed at the neck with a bone clasp shaped like a bear claw. His dark hair is shot through with silver at the temples and he wears it pulled back and tied with a slender leather cord.

"I'm fine," I tell him.

He chuckles. "You look like you're trying to escape. Was your first lesson that terrible?"

"Just trying to escape the smoke," I tell him, "not the building."

He pulls a small pouch from the pocket of his cloak and dumps the contents—a fine white powder—into his palm. Then he leans forward and blows gently, like a child scattering dandelion seeds. The substance hovers in the air like a small cloud before breaking apart into delicate tendrils that gather the smoke and absorb it. Suddenly the air in the room is as crisp and fresh as the breeze wafting through the window.

Delight bubbles in my chest and I laugh.

"Better?" he asks.

"Much," I say. "Are you a Bone Mixer?" I assumed from the red cloak that he was a Charmer, but maybe I was wrong. My mother has never performed magic like that.

"No," he says. "I just have very gifted friends. I'm Latham. The Third Sight mentor."

"I'm Saskia Holte," I say, taking his extended hand, "the Second Sight apprentice."

"Ah, I thought so. You're an exact replica of your mother." He lets go of my hand and leans back against the table, his arms folded across his chest.

"You know her?"

"We trained together," he says. "It was a rarity to have two Third Sight apprentices at the same time, so we grew close. How is she? It's been too long since we've seen one another."

"She's . . ." An unexpected wave of homesickness washes over me, and it takes me a moment to find my voice. "She's well."

"Glad to hear it," he says. "And how are you?"

Maybe it's the reminder of home, or maybe I've just been worn down by my failures this morning, but before I can stop myself, I'm sinking into one of the chairs with a sigh. "I've been better."

He leans forward and lowers his voice. "My first day at Ivory Hall, I got sick all over the entrance floor. In front of every single apprentice, no less. It was humiliating."

"Really?"

Latham had an even rougher start than I did, and he was able to become a Bone Charming Master. Maybe that means there's still hope for me to gain control of my magic? The assurance alone feels as if he's taken a pair of sharp scissors and snipped the string that tethers my worry. I feel lighter as it floats away.

"The first time within these walls . . . it's something else, isn't it?"

"Yes," I say. Though I've mostly adjusted, I can still feel the effects faintly—the gentle roll of my stomach as if I'm on a boat in the middle of the sea. The unsettled way my blood rushes through my ears. "Why don't they warn us first? I might have handled it better if I'd been prepared."

He shrugs. "I think they like to keep the mystery alive." His glance sweeps over the bones on the table. "Kyra isn't making you train with those, is she?"

"Yes . . . ?" I say uncertainly.

He shakes his head. "And let me guess: You couldn't read them any more than you could have read a handful of coins."

"I might have done better with the coins."

He goes to the back of the room and riffles through one of the cupboards along the wall until he finds a silver box with a fancy clasp. "Let's try with these."

Latham unfurls a square of navy-blue velvet on the table and then tips the box on its side. Eight small bones roll onto the cloth. They're black around the edges, as if they've already been used in a reading, but I can still make out the slender red lines that have been painted across each to mimic the tattoo that would have rested over them in life. Carpals from the left wrist, then.

"Whose are they?" I ask. Bones from human hands are extremely valuable. I can't imagine he really means for me to use these in a training reading.

"They're practice bones," he tells me.

"Practice bones? They're not real?"

"Oh, they're very real," he says. "They were prepared so that they could be read again and again. Without blood and with a bit more clarity than is typical."

I run a fingertip along the edge of the cloth, leaving a crooked path in the thick velvet. "I didn't know that was possible."

"We don't do it often," he says. "It requires the bones to be prepared with the blood of a Charmer, so it's not practical to do it with every set—there are only so many of us, and we don't fancy being used as pincushions. But it's very useful for training. It helps you get the feel of a reading without needing quite so much concentration."

"What were these used for?"

"A kenning," he says.

My hope deflates. "Oh. I have Second Sight, not Third," I tell him.

He waves a hand in the air as if clearing my words away. "Doesn't matter," he says. "You can still read them."

I start to ask how, but he's already lighting the incense. "Close your eyes," he says, and I obey. "When you're ready, touch the bones."

I take a few deep breaths and then inch my fingers forward

and scoop the bones into my fist. This time it's not a shadowy image I see behind my eyelids but a vision that unfurls before me in dazzling color and sharp sound as if I'm watching a life from the vantage point of a bird that hovers overhead. I'm in the future of a man—I'm not sure how I know, except that I can feel him there, as if I'm in his mind.

A multitude of paths stretch out before me—an endless array of possibilities, like the branches of huge tree. But two paths are wider than the others, and they seem to glow with a faint light.

I walk along one path and see the man as a carpenter. He loves his work—the clean smell of the wood, the roughness of it on his palm before he sands and then the satiny texture afterward, the warm satisfaction of making something useful with his own hands. One day a girl comes into his workshop to buy a birdhouse. She has emerald eyes and hair like flame. She makes him laugh. He asks her if he can make her dinner. A few weeks later he asks her to dance. And they do—barefoot in his shop, the soles of their feet coated in the feather-soft pine shavings that cover the floor like carpet. A few years and several dozen dances later, he asks if she'll agree to a joining ceremony because he can't imagine living without her.

I watch the two of them build a life together. A house in a pretty meadow with wildflowers in the yard. An orchard full of peach trees, which frequently results in fragrant pies cooling in the window. Moonlit nights sitting on the porch, her feet in his lap, talking until dawn.

They have three children—boys with dimpled knees and cheeks like small ripe apples.

I watch them celebrate and I watch them suffer. The man's mother dies—too young, he thinks, weeping, while he carves her name into the family tree. But then a few years later one of his sons dies, too—a drowning accident in the river—and he realizes what too young really feels like.

Breathless happiness and unspeakable sorrow weave together into a rich tapestry of life. By the time I'm at the end of the path, I know it's a good choice. A life that would bring him joy. I turn around and follow the path back to the beginning, watch his children grow younger and younger, watch the deep lines on his partner's forehead smooth away, see each scene in reverse.

Once I'm at the fork in the road, I turn left instead of right and make my way down the other path. This time the man lives in the capital. He can see Ivory Hall gleaming in the distance from the window of his workshop. He has bone magic—a Mason—and his hands move swiftly over various bones—shaping them into flutes for Watchers, weapons for Breakers, smooth boxes that are impervious to theft, and containers to hold memories. His work is deeply rewarding in an entirely different way than his other path. It's the same satisfaction of creation with the addition of feeling that he's part of something bigger. The man is different, too—a little bolder in this life, a little more confident.

His partner is a Healer—a quiet woman with a stillness that seems to envelope the people around her, to calm them with her presence. She's not as pretty as the girl on his other path, and not as lively, either, but she's a deep thinker and she makes him a better man. Their life is filled with joys both big and small.

A daughter—just one, though they wished for more—with raven hair and a knack for numbers. A spacious house halfway between his workshop and her clinic. Nights spent walking hand in hand along the cobbled streets near the river, bathed in the warm glow of the streetlamps. The man's mother still dies. He still weeps as he carves her name into the tree, still thinks *too young*, still grieves.

Some things are the same. And some things couldn't be more different. He grows old more slowly in this life, more comfortably. His partner's healing abilities are well used on his creaky joints and arthritic fingers. Another portrait of joy and sorrow. Another rich and happy life. But it's so different from the first.

I open my eyes and the room slowly comes back into focus. I feel hollowed out. Empty.

"Which would you choose?" Latham asks.

The question is like a weight on my chest. I had never fully appreciated my mother's burden—how selecting one path so thoroughly eliminates the other. The vision was so real, so vivid, that choosing feels like destruction. If I choose the path where the man is a Mason, those three apple-cheeked boys will never exist, will simply cease to be, even though I know the timbres of their voices, and where the gaps in their smiles will be when they lose their first teeth. But if they are born, the man's daughter won't be and the world will be robbed of her easy laugh and sharp mind.

But I don't have to choose. These are only practice bones.

"I don't know," I tell him. "One doesn't seem better than the other."

"That's the coward's way out," he says. "Choose."

I swallow. "The second path," I say, deciding that perhaps losing a child is a grief that should be spared.

"The Bone Charmer chose the first," he says. "Though the man never did fall in love with the redheaded woman."

At once I register both the sharp grief that pierces me and the surprise that it should be there at all. Grief for a man I never met, whom I wouldn't recognize if I passed him on the street.

"But why?" I ask. "How?"

Latham shrugs. "Fate is predictable, but choice isn't. I suppose, after his kenning, he made decisions that didn't lead to meeting her after all. Or perhaps he did meet her, but said something thoughtless and ruined his chances. We'd need a First Sight Charmer to do a reading of his past to know for sure."

My fingers curl around a fistful of my cloak. "Then what's the point of bone charming? Why bother if nothing is guaranteed?"

"Because information is power," he says, "but unfortunately, the Third Sight is limited—it only tells us possibilities, not realities."

"Then I'm glad I have the Second Sight," I say.

He laughs. "Well, then I am, too. Though I do wish I had an apprentice this year. But since no one was matched to the Third Sight, I'll have to settle for helping the other mentors where I can." He scoops up the wrist bones and puts them back in the silver box.

"Where is he now?" I ask, inclining my head toward the bones.

"Ah," says Latham, "he passed away a few years ago. We

never use training bones until the subject of the kenning is dead. Too dangerous." He closes the latch on the box and puts it back where he found it.

"Thank you," I tell him.

"Of course," he says. "But now that I think about it, we should probably keep this bit of extra help to ourselves." He nods toward the animal bones I was training with earlier. "Kyra prefers to teach the hard way before she uses practice bones, and I'd hate to get on her bad side. Especially since I didn't ask her permission first."

A prickle of unease goes through me at the thought of lying to Master Kyra, but I brush it aside. I won't lie to her. I just won't volunteer the information.

The bones know I need all the help I can get.

Saskia
The Tutor

*I*t's as if my father has died all over again.

A tight knot of grief wedges beneath my breastbone—a sensation that's at once heavy and hollow.

My mother and I stand in a huge room at the back of the bone house. Deep shelves filled with containers in all shapes and sizes stretch from floor to ceiling on three of the four walls. In the center of the room is a large, beautifully crafted box made from the crushed fragments of a whale's rib cage and inlaid with diagonal stripes of lapis lazuli. After my father's death, my mother had it commissioned by Hilde Bystrom. Even though she's the only Bone Mason in Midwood, there's no one more gifted within ten towns. The box is a work of art—ivory and blue, pearl-smooth, and now utterly empty.

Gone is the right humerus, which Oskar prepared with the same jewel-tone waves that graced my father's painting arm in life. The beautiful, swelling design seemed to grow more intricate each time my father completed a project he loved. And by the end of his life, the tattoo extended from shoulder to elbow, like a sleeve made of treasure.

His bare left humerus is gone, too. And his skull, and his sternum, and both patellas that were each marked with the three gray slashes that appeared when he was robbed as a boy and fell to his knees to plead for his life.

Everything is gone. All the evidence of his hopes and dreams, and loves and fears.

Master Oskar stands off to the side. His green apron is coated in bone dust. His face is haggard, and violet-blue half-moons curve beneath his bloodshot eyes. "I don't know how this could have happened," he says. His arms hang at his sides and his fists open and close repeatedly as if there's something invisible he keeps trying—and failing—to grasp.

"Why did they leave this here?" my mother says. Her voice is raw and gruff. She trails her fingers gently across the side of the box as if it's my father's cheek she's caressing.

"I . . ." Master Oskar pauses to dab at the sheen of sweat beading on his upper lip. "I'd imagine the box itself was too heavy to carry."

My mother cuts him with a sharp look. "No, why did they leave it here? In the middle of the floor where it would be obvious what they'd done? They could have put the box back on the shelf and let us discover the missing bones weeks or months or *years* from now."

He pales as if this thought hadn't occurred to him. His gaze sweeps over the shelves—over the hundreds of boxes that house the remains he's charged with protecting. I can see that he's wondering the same thing I am: *Are any of the others empty?*

"Perhaps they were in a hurry?" he says. "Surely they knew what was at stake if they'd been caught." Stealing bones is a crime punishable by death. Only a fool would take the risk. That, or someone very desperate.

"Or maybe they wanted to make sure we knew that the bones were missing," my mother says. "Maybe they wanted *me* to know." Her expression is a tangle of emotions—grief, fear, resignation. But oddly, not shock. Not the icy blow that *I* felt when Ami burst into our kitchen with the news, a chill that slowly enveloped me in unbearable pain until it finally gave way to numbness, leaving me feeling nothing at all.

My mother meets my gaze and a look passes between us. "Did you know this would happen?" I ask softly.

"Of course not," she says. But her eyes bore into me and they say something different—something akin to, *Don't ask questions like that. Not here.*

Master Oskar crouches down to study the thumb-sized indentation that serves as the box's lock—a lock that was sealed by bone magic and shouldn't have allowed entry to anyone but me or my mother. And yet the box is both open and empty. "Why would the thieves want to announce themselves," he says, "especially to you?"

She leaves his question unanswered. "We need to find who did this. Soon."

"I won't rest until the bones are located and the culprits are punished," he says. "You have my word."

But it's a promise he's in no position to keep. It might be impossible to find the bones—because what reason would anyone have for stealing them except to use them? The thought of my father's bones being wasted in a reading for a stranger makes my blood spike with fury and dread.

My mother shakes her head. "I'm sorry, Oskar, but your word isn't enough. Not for this."

"If people find out . . ." He trails off, but his meaning is clear. If the townsfolk don't believe he can keep the bones of their dead safe, he'll be ruined.

I think of the Healer who practiced in Midwood when I was a child. Three of her patients died within a week of one another, and even though there were explanations in each case—a small boy who choked on a bit of fruit and was already blue when the Healer arrived, an elderly man whose failing heart finally stopped beating, and then, a day later, his wife, who died of a broken heart—three deaths in such a short time was enough to cause whispers, and worries. Soon parents were taking ships upriver to Brisby or Colm to see the Healer there. Midwood's Healer quietly left town, and we were without that particular bone magic until a new apprentice was matched at the next kenning.

"I'm sorry," my mother tells Oskar. "I have no choice."

Before we leave, I place a palm flat against the box and close my eyes. It's the last resting place of my father, and I don't know if we'll ever find him again.

For the first time in my life, I long for bone magic. Not the Charmer gifts of my mother and Gran, but the powers of a Bone Breaker. The ability to mete out justice. To punish with pain.

To exact revenge.

The next morning—after a restless night—I finally give up on sleep and get out of bed just after dawn. My mother obviously slept poorly too, because she's already at the door when I come downstairs, fastening the button at the collar of her red silk cloak. Her hair is braided and twisted into a figure eight at the back of her head.

"I'm coming with you," I tell her.

"You most certainly are not." She says it without even glancing at me, as if I'm a puppy who will stay on command. She pulls a pair of long black gloves over her pale fingers. "I shouldn't be long."

My mother sits on the town council along with our Mason, our Healer, our Mixer, and two others—one man and one woman—who don't have bone magic. Midwood's council is modeled after the Grand Council in Kastelia City, and reports directly to them on anything that can't be solved locally. My mother called an emergency meeting last night after we returned from the bone house.

And I have every intention of attending that meeting.

I shove my hands into the pockets of my pearl-gray cloak and follow her out the door. She startles when she sees me there, and then presses her lips together into a thin line. "I said no."

The door remains ajar while she stares me down, waiting for me to go back inside.

I don't.

"Saskia," she says, exasperated. "I don't have time for this."

"I know my rights," I tell her. "If the council is meeting on a matter concerning a family member, I'm allowed to be there."

She presses a gloved hand to her forehead. "There is no reason for you to come," she says. "I promise to fill you in later."

"Like you filled me in on having Gran's bones specially prepared? Like you filled me in on what my other paths showed? No, thanks. I'd rather see for myself."

That flicker of non-surprise on her face yesterday when she saw the empty box shook something loose inside me—like a dropped spool of ribbon that has been slowly unfurling, and now my trust in her lies in a tangled jumble at my feet.

She opens her mouth to argue, but she must see the resolve in my expression, because she doesn't speak. Instead she reaches around me and pulls the door closed.

We walk silently toward Midwood Hall. Our breath curls from our lips in delicate billows, but the trees above us are alive with birdsong, as if the world still has one foot in winter and another in spring.

As we get closer to the town square, the pressure between us builds, grows into a tangible thing, as if I could put a palm against it and push it away. My mother has something she's trying to find the words to say. I'm not sure how I can tell— if it's the subtle inhale that usually precedes speech, a quick, expectant breath that keeps fading into silence. Or is it the way she keeps leaning toward me slightly, only to lean away again? I tell myself that it's *not* a premonition, not bone magic that's taking too long to fade. It's simply that she's my mother, and I've learned to read her rhythms. Like the way Gran used to know a storm was coming when her knees started to ache.

"What is it?" I ask.

The question melts her expression—her eyes soften, her mouth curves into a tender smile. But then she turns toward me and I see nothing but worry. "If you come today, the council might interrogate you," she says.

"*Interrogate* me? For attending a meeting?"

"You are one of only two people who could have opened that box."

I stop walking. "But I didn't open it. That's the point of getting the council involved. Unless . . . did *you* open it?"

"Don't be ridiculous, Saskia. It wouldn't be a crime if I'd opened it. But this is a serious offense, and the council will start by questioning people who had access. They'll be thorough. They'll leave no stone unturned."

I tilt my head to one side and study her. I can't tell what she's getting at. "Well, I doubt my not showing up would prevent them from questioning me some other time."

Her teeth catch her lower lip. She sighs.

"Oh."

She was hoping for a chance to prepare me. The thought shivers across my skin. Prepare me for *what*?

"The council has . . . methods of assuring they get the truth," she says.

"And they will. I didn't touch Papa's box."

"Yes, but you've been spending a lot of time at the bone house lately."

And instantly I see it, like the moment a candle wick catches fire in a dark room. I've been at the bone house at least once a week since the kenning. And though it had nothing to do with the crime at hand, the reason for my visits is something my mother would rather the rest of the council didn't know. If they know she tampered with my kenning bones, she could be removed as Bone Charmer.

I start walking again and she falls in step beside me. "So prepare me now," I say. "We're nearly there."

She stiffens—she must have hoped I would turn back toward home. But I have no intention of doing that.

"Tell the truth," she says finally, "as cleverly as you can."

Midwood Hall is the largest structure in town, three stories high and built from cream-colored stone. Ivy climbs toward the gabled roof where half a dozen dormers look out over the square like all-seeing eyes. The council chamber is situated in the center of Midwood Hall, which is in the center of the town square, which is in the center of the town.

As we step inside, I'm overcome with the sensation that we are gathered in the beating heart of Midwood. Energy thrums in the air like a pulse.

The six council members are seated behind a long stone table on a dais at the far end of the room. They are arranged by seniority from left to right—first the Healer, Anders, who wears a blue cloak; then my mother in red; Rakel, the Mixer in purple; and Hilde, our town Mason, dressed in orange. At the far right end of the table are Valera and Erik, the two non-magical members of the council, who wear no cloaks at all.

The walls of the room are stone, but heavy dark-blue draperies hang from floor to ceiling on all sides, adding warmth and softness, and probably muffling sound—eliminating an echo that otherwise might carry to the rest of the hall and compromise privacy.

I sit on one of the long benches at the back of the room along with Ami, Declan, Master Oskar, and a handful of others that the council sent for upon hearing that my father's bones were missing. My mother and I shared a look as they were marched in one at a time by the runners who were sent to fetch them. *See?* I wanted to say. *You wouldn't have had time to prepare me if we'd done it your way.*

Declan's fingers close around mine. "Are you all right?" he whispers. "Ami told me what happened and I feel sick."

It's the question my mother has failed to ask me. *Are you all right? How are you coping with losing your father for a second time?* She just saw a problem and went about trying to solve it. "Puzzle-mode," my father affectionately called it. When I was younger, I thought it was charming—that faraway look she'd get as she mulled over her spell book. The way the world seemed to disappear, leaving nothing except her and the magic. But as I got older, I started to resent that I seemed to vanish right along with everything else.

I squeeze Declan's hand. "I'll be fine," I tell him, though I'm not sure it's the truth.

"The council will sort it out," he says. "Whoever did this won't get away with it."

I'm about to answer him—to tell him I hope he's right—when Healer Anders stands and the chatter in the room dies down.

"You've all been brought here as witnesses," he says, "for the theft of Filip Holte's bones."

There's a collective gasp from the few people who haven't already heard the news, followed by an ominous silence. It's as if all the air has left the room, taking sound along with it. And even though I knew what Anders would say, the words still land like a blow.

"I will ask you to come forward one by one for questioning," the Healer says. "Starting with Master Oskar."

Oskar doesn't stand. His head is down and his hands grip his knees so tightly that his knuckles are white. Several breathless seconds pass without so much as a whisper.

"Oskar," Anders says gently, "please come forward."

The master of the bone house rises from his seat and moves toward the front of the room like a storm cloud. His stride is purposeful. His hands are clenched into fists at his sides. He isn't nervous, I realize.

He's furious.

Oskar sits in the witness chair at the right side of the room, positioned so that the entire council can see him, and the other witnesses can too.

"This isn't a formal tribunal," Anders says. "No one is accused of anything. We're simply trying to gather evidence so we know how to move forward."

But it's clear by the tight set of Oskar's jaw that he feels like a suspect.

A knock at the back door of the chamber brings Rakel to her feet. A journeyman—a girl by the name of Bette, who finished her Mixer apprenticeship at Ivory Hall last spring and has been training with Rakel ever since—enters the chamber holding a *keras,* a drinking horn. Judging from its small size, I'm guessing it came from a goat.

"Thank you, Bette," Rakel says, taking the horn from her. "That will be all."

Rakel's purple cloak flutters behind her as she approaches Oskar and hands him the *keras.* "Drink, please."

He licks his lips. "Is this really necessary?"

"If you having nothing to hide, there's nothing to fear."

A memory prickles at the back of my mind. I was young—no older than six or seven—when some of the trees in the Forest of the Dead were vandalized. Someone had taken a knife to several of the names, carving deep lines through them until they were an unreadable mess of slash marks.

"What if they never find who did it?" I asked my mother one night at dinner.

"They will," my mother said. "Now finish your potatoes."

I poked at my food with my fingers, but I didn't eat. "What if they don't, though? What if someone ruins *our* tree?"

"Don't worry, Saskia," Gran said, patting my hand. "We'll find them." Gran sat on the council then, and her voice was warm and confident. But still, it wasn't enough to quiet my fears. Gramps had died a few years before, and though I didn't remember him well, it still made my stomach squirm to think of his name erased forever.

"How do you know for sure?" I asked.

Gran leaned close to me and put her hand over mine. "Because the council has a secret weapon."

My eyes went wide. "What is it?"

"The veracity seat," she said. "No one who sits there can tell a lie."

And just like that, my worries drifted away like leaves on the wind. It was a power singular to my grandmother. She always knew the right thing to say. When I grew older, I assumed the story was the stuff of fairy tales, one of the many yarns Gran spun to soothe whatever troubled me. Like the owl that perched on the tree outside my bedroom window each evening, the one Gran claimed had been fated just for me: *He has a solemn responsibility to protect you—to watch for your nightmares and swallow them before they ever reach you.*

But now the story takes on new meaning and ice slides down my spine.

The veracity seat. Truth serum.

Oskar's hands shake as he brings the horn to his lips and

swallows its contents in one gulp. He passes the *keras* back to Rakel. His face and neck are red and splotchy. He tugs at his collar.

"Let's start with a few easy questions," Anders says as Rakel slides back into her chair. "What's your name?"

"Oskar."

"Nicknames?"

He presses his lips together as if willing the answer not to escape. He's quiet for several moments. A fine sheen of sweat breaks out on his forehead. Finally it's too much to resist. "Osky," he says tersely. "It's what my mother called me."

A chorus of soft chuckles ripples through the room. Oskar's partner, Markus, sits in the back, scowling at anyone who dares to laugh. He throws a particularly menacing glare in our direction. Beside me, Declan covers his mouth to hide a grin.

But I'm not amused. I'm terrified.

"What is your specialty?" Anders asks.

"I'm a Bone Handler and caretaker of the bone house."

"Would you say you treat your responsibilities with the care they deserve?"

His jaw goes tight. "Of course I do."

"Did you steal the bones of Filip Holte?"

"No," Oskar says forcefully, "I did not."

"Did you arrange for someone else to steal them?"

"No."

"Did you sell them or arrange for someone else to sell them in your place?"

"Of course not."

"Do you know who might have been involved in this crime?"

A pause. Then silence that stretches like molasses dripping from a spoon.

"Please answer the question," Anders says.

"I don't know," Oskar says. He pulls a handkerchief from his pocket and dabs at his forehead. "Maybe. It's just a suspicion."

"Who do you suspect stole Filip Holte's bones?" Anders says.

Oskar's gaze slides to the right and lands on my mother. "Della," he says. At first I think he's addressing her, but then his gaze slides away, and I realize I'm wrong.

He's not speaking to her. He's accusing her.

Saskia
The Bone Charmer

he dining hall is already teeming with people by the time I arrive. Apprentices are seated at long tables that stretch from one end of the room to the other. The brightly colored cloaks make the scene look like a kaleidoscope, as if one twist would produce a different, yet equally beautiful design. Everyone is already deep in conversation. Excited chatter fills the room like a low hum.

I don't know where to sit.

I stand there awkwardly, weighing my desire to escape to the privacy of my room against the gnawing hunger in my stomach. I'm just about to turn and leave, when Tessa comes jogging toward me.

"We sat in the back," she says. "Follow me." I'm not sure

who is included in the "we," since Tessa is one of the only apprentices I've interacted with so far, but I'm grateful. She leads me between two tables to the far side of the room. "I saved you a seat," she says, sliding onto one of the benches and indicating the space beside her.

"Thanks, Tessa."

I sit down and find myself face-to-face with Bram.

My heart flips over in my chest.

"Hello again," I say as casually as I'm able.

The girl next to him nudges him. "Do you two know each other?" Her dark hair cascades over her shoulders in glossy waves. Her black cloak matches Bram's—another Breaker, then.

Bram clears his throat and inclines his head toward me. "Linnea, this is Saskia. Saskia, Linnea."

"Nice to meet you," I tell her.

"Same." She smiles and turns to Bram with an expectant look.

"Saskia and I are . . . We're . . ."

Oh. He doesn't want to admit that we've been matched.

"We're from the same town," I say.

Bram's eyes flick up to mine. His expressions are like hearing words in a foreign tongue. I know they're rich with meaning, but to me, they're unfathomable. I don't know if he's relieved or annoyed or something else entirely.

Linnea sighs, drawing his attention back to her. "I'm starving," she says.

"Well, it looks like we won't have to wait any longer."

A small army of servers spills into the dining hall, carrying platters of grilled meat releasing fragrant curls of steam, bowls of sugared berries, and braided loaves of butter-glazed bread.

Tessa gives a happy sigh. "I was ready to eat my own leg, but that looks so much better."

My stomach growls in agreement and she laughs.

"Using bone magic must increase appetite," she says. "I don't remember the last time I was this hungry."

And judging by the hush that has fallen over the dining hall, I think she's right. For several minutes there's nothing but the sound of plates scraping across tables and people licking fingers. Gradually conversation picks up again.

As we eat, Tessa introduces me to the others at the table, including Talon, a Watcher with a shock of auburn hair and a smattering of cinnamon freckles across his nose and cheeks. I'm astonished at how quickly Tessa managed to collect a group of friends—like it's as easy as gathering seashells on the beach and slipping them into her pocket.

"So how did your first day of training go?" Talon asks me.

I tear a bit of bread from the loaf on my plate. "Not so great at first," I tell him, "and then a little better toward the end of the morning." I don't mention Latham or the practice bones. "How about you?"

"One of the dogs bit me," he says. "So . . . not well at all."

"My morning was terrible, too," Tessa says. "I was supposed to be relieving a patient's headache, but I'm pretty sure I made it worse. She looked like she was ready to burst into tears by the time she left. What if I never get any better, and I can only use bone magic to hurt people instead of help them?"

Bram tenses, a berry suspended halfway between his plate and his lips.

Tessa must notice, because her cheeks turn crimson. "Oh no. I didn't mean . . ."

Bram pops the fruit into his mouth and chews slowly. His fingertips are stained red.

"That came out wrong," she says. "I just meant that healing is supposed to be about helping people, while breaking . . ."

We all know what she's thinking—breaking is about hurting people. About using magic to snap the bones in their arms or legs, their fingers or toes. I shiver as I think about how Bram's and Linnea's training must have gone this morning, what *their* failures must have looked like.

Linnea gives Tessa a glare that could slice through glass. "Breakers protect people. Which is helping them."

"I know," Tessa says. "I didn't mean to imply otherwise."

"Really? Because it sure seems like you think some specialties are better than others."

"Stop it," I say. Linnea's eyes go wide, as if she isn't used to someone speaking so harshly. She presses her lips together, her jaw so tight that I imagine her teeth are grinding together. But I keep going: "Tessa wasn't talking about you or Bram. She was talking about herself and how hard this is. We've all had a bumpy transition. Maybe we could cut each other some slack."

She turns to Bram as if to say, *Can you believe this?* But he's not looking at her. He's studying me with an expression that's maddeningly unreadable. "Saskia's right," he says, finally.

Linnea rears back as if slapped.

Bram turns toward Tessa. "Don't worry about it. Really."

Her shoulders relax and she lets out a breath. "Thank you. And I'm sorry."

Linnea's gaze skips from me to Bram and back again. There's something calculating in her expression, something almost frightening. I get a glimpse of how fierce she's going to be as a Breaker. And then, like clouds parting, she smiles and is suddenly radiant, as if her anger was never there at all. She laughs. "I can get a little intense sometimes," she says.

Talon, who has been silently observing us during the whole exchange, suddenly perks up. "I heard the Mixers accidentally started a fire," he says. "So it sounds like they had a worse day than all of us put together." The tension dissipates and we all laugh.

Even Bram.

The sound is rich and deep, like the lowest notes of a melody. My eyes flick to him and I catch the barest hint of a smile before it fades away. For a moment I forget that I have good reasons for avoiding Bram, and I feel a pull toward him, as if he's just one of the others. Just someone I'm getting to know. Someone I might want to spend more time with. But then he scratches his forehead and I see the tattoos on his knuckles. It's like a kick in the stomach.

Bram is dangerous. I'm dangerous. And the two of us together would be a disaster.

I can't let myself forget.

I was twelve years old the first time I saw a prison boat docked in Midwood.

The worst criminals in Kastelia are sent to Fang Island—a prison at the far reaches of the country, beyond the point where the waters of the delta melt into the sea. It gets its name from the giant bones that encircle the island's perimeter—bones that are pointed on one end, like enormous tusks, and seem to sprout from the ground and stretch higher than the treetops.

Prisoners are taken directly from their sentencing at Ivory Hall to make the long journey to Fang Island. Bone Breakers transport them down the branches of the Shard to their final destination. The boats stop along the way to replenish food and supplies, but one had never docked in Midwood before.

So, when it was spotted, whispers and rumors spread through town like wildfire, and soon a big group was gathered near the shore, gaping.

Compared to the trade ships that usually landed on our shores, this vessel was tiny. A boat only big enough for a small crew. But the most remarkable sight was the cage made of bone that sat on deck.

A cage with a man inside.

"What do you think he did?" asked one of the Poulsen brothers. They were twins and I could never tell them apart.

"He probably killed someone," said Ami.

The other Poulsen brother laughed. "He must have done worse than that. My gramps was a Breaker at Fang Island, and he said hearing the things the prisoners did would keep you awake at night for the rest of your life."

Both Ami and I shuddered.

"I dare someone to go on board and touch the cage," Peder said. He was two years younger than I was and prone to issuing dares, but not to accepting them.

"No way," said Ami. "I don't have a death wish."

"I'm out," said someone behind me.

"How about you, Saskia?" Peder said.

I started to shake my head, when one of the Poulsen brothers laughed. "Saskia? She'll only do it if she can get a bone reading from her mama first."

The others—all except Ami—laughed, too.

It was as if someone had lit a match inside me, and my shame was combustible. Hot tears prickled at the backs of my eyes, but I refused to let those boys see me cry. To them, I'd always be the girl whose mother knew the future. The girl who had fate on her side.

And then I felt a tickle at the back of my mind. I saw myself dashing away from the ship after touching the bones, a triumphant smile on my face. The others watched with expressions of grudging admiration. This had happened at least half a dozen times in the last year. Small premonitions—a feeling that Ami was about to come over just before her knock fell on the door, a thought that my father would prepare roast goose for supper as he walked in from the garden with a handful of onions and a parcel wrapped in brown butcher paper.

Blossoming magic, Gran called it when I told her what was happening. "Though it won't really be yours until it's bound to you," she said with a wink.

And now here was the feeling again, like a reassuring good

omen. I'd show them I wasn't a coward. I took off at a dead run toward the boat and leaped aboard. Someone onshore started shouting at me, but so much blood was pounding in my ears that the words faded into the background. The boat rocked beneath me, but I pressed forward and laid a palm on the side of the cage.

The bones were blazing hot.

I yelped and yanked my hand back. They must have been magicked for security. I turned to run again, but something caught me, pulled me backward.

The prisoner was holding a fistful of my skirt. Each of his knuckles was imprinted with a black triangular tattoo. "Where do you think you're going, pretty lady?"

My heart slammed against my rib cage. "Let go of me."

He laughed, and it sounded like the crunch of glass beneath a boot. "Does a spider let a fly go when one ventures too close to his web?"

I could feel the heat rolling off the bones of the cage as he tugged me closer. The skin on my palm was already beginning to blister. I grabbed his wrist and dug my fingernails into his flesh. "Leave me alone!"

The prisoner grunted as a few drops of blood welled at the cuts I'd made. He twisted away from my grip and used the momentum to pull my hand against the enclosure. Fiery heat burned through my fingers.

My vision tunneled and went dark.

Suddenly I was standing in a cavern far belowground. Rippled walls rose around me like cresting waves, snow white and starkly beautiful.

116

A salt mine.

My lips were dry, thirst begging at the back of my throat. My muscles ached as if I'd been working all day, but a rage burning in my chest overshadowed it. I turned to the man next to me—a stranger, though somehow I felt as if I'd seen him before. And that's when I realized: It wasn't me who knew him. The prisoner did.

I was trapped inside his mind. It was *his* thirst. His sore muscles. His anger.

"No one crosses me and lives to talk about it," the prisoner said as his hands circled the man's neck. I could feel the contours of the stranger's throat against my skin—his rough stubble, the rise of his Adam's apple, the taut cords of muscle straining against death—as if it were my own fingers cutting off his breath.

It took all the strength I had, but I wrenched myself from the vision just as the stranger fell to the ground.

The prisoner sat in front of me, still trapped in the bone cage, a wicked sneer on his face, as if he were deliberately thinking of the worst thing he'd done and forcing me to bear witness.

"Please," I said, "let me go."

He didn't. He pressed my wrist against the side of the bone cage again and I was sucked into another vision. My mind flashed through a series of horrifying images that made my stomach turn: I watched him carve the still-beating heart out of a woman's chest, saw him bury another victim alive and then sit quietly by the grave until the sounds of struggle subsided. I could feel his emotions as if they were my own—his hunger to destroy, the way he fed on the fear of his victims, his sick satisfaction as the life drained out of them.

"Let go!" This time the words weren't mine, and they were accompanied by a hand reaching through the bars of the cage, followed by a hiss of pain from the prisoner. He released me, and his fist hit the bottom of the cage with a thud. His arm hung limply at his side, broken.

Relief flooded through me, and I turned to see Bram Wilberg.

"Thank you," I said, a bead of sweat slipping down the back of my neck.

Bram lightly touched my elbow. "Why did you do that? He could have killed you."

But I didn't have time to answer. The prisoner reached through the bars with his undamaged hand—a hand with the same four black tattoos as the first—and grabbed my ankle. Bram's eyes went wide at my sharp intake of breath. He pulled on my arm, but the prisoner was stronger. My whole body pressed against the bone cage, and a searing pain shot up my side.

I was plunged into another vision, but this time I wasn't in the prisoner's mind—I was in Bram's. He was maybe four years old, in front of a small, flame-blackened home, his face streaked with soot and tears. His mind was filled with rage, pulsing with the desire to destroy everything he saw. A man approached him and laid a hand on his shoulder. "It could be worse," he said. "You could have been in there, too."

Bram's eyes went wide. Unbelieving. "I wish I were with them. I'd rather be dead than out here with you."

The man frowned. "That's a terrible thing to say, young man."

Bram's expression darkened and the man yanked his hand away. He screamed. Cradled his broken fingers in the opposite palm.

"You're a monster." The man backed away.

"*You're* a monster," Bram said under his breath.

The vision shifted back to the prisoner. He walked through a barn with a torch in his hand, lighting bales of hay on fire. The air was filled with smoke and the panicked whine of animals.

A tug on my arm shifted the vision back to Bram. Flame and rage. And then back to the prisoner. Flame and rage. The two faces blended into one until I couldn't tell the difference. Fear climbed inside me and I felt as if I were on fire, too.

A crack split through the air, and I was thrust back into the present. Bram and I were lying on the ground. The bone cage was broken—several of the bars split cleanly through the middle—and the prisoner crawled through the opening.

Onshore, one of the Bone Breakers in charge of guarding the ship was screaming and running toward the boat. But he was too late. The prisoner had already run belowdecks.

Another Breaker came aboard, grabbed me by the shoulders, and shook me like a rag doll. "What were you thinking?"

"I— It was a dare," I said softly.

"What if I hadn't gotten to you in time?" The Breaker's voice was full of heat. My whole body trembled and I had to hold on to his arm to keep from toppling over. I wanted to tell him that he didn't get to me in time, that the prisoner took something from me I could never get back: Fate wasn't on my side. Magic had betrayed me entirely. I wouldn't leave the boat triumphant.

119

I would leave broken. But the words stuck in my throat.

"And you"—the Breaker turned to Bram—"were you taking a dare, too?"

"No." Bram pulled on the back of his neck. "Just trying to help."

"You should have left that to the adults." The Breaker leaned over to inspect the damaged cage. "This shouldn't be possible," he said more to himself than to us. He ran a palm just above the fractured bones. "Someone helped him escape."

A shiver of fear ran through me. "Who?" I asked. "Who helped him?"

The Breaker waved a dismissive hand in my direction. I was about to press him for an answer when a commotion on the other side of the boat drew our attention. The prisoner—chased by a man in the Ivory Guard—raced back up the stairs onto the main deck. He barreled straight for me, hands already outstretched, as if he planned to strangle me.

But before he could touch me, the Bone Breaker intervened. With one flick of his wrist, he snapped the prisoner's humerus. The man wailed and swore and pronounced a curse on my house for a thousand generations.

The guard who had been chasing the prisoner rounded the corner and wrestled him to the ground. "He killed three of the crew before I even made it belowdecks."

Time seemed to slow and stretch before dashing forward in a tumble. All the air left my lungs in a moment of swift, piercing horror. This was my fault. I trusted my premonition, and now three innocent people were dead.

eyes met for just a beat. He gave the rope an extra tug and the opposing team surged forward and toppled over.

The crowd broke out in rowdy applause.

But I turned and ran.

My next session with Master Kyra goes even worse than the first. It takes me most of the morning to see what's in her pocket, but finally a hazy shape forms behind my eyes.

"It's a key," I say, equal parts relieved and triumphant.

"Not even close." She pulls a feather from her cloak and shows me.

Icy fear trickles down my spine. Being wrong is worse than seeing nothing at all.

"There has to be an easier way," I say as Kyra scoops up the bones and slips them into the velvet pouch hanging from her waist. "Aren't there more powerful bones I could train with?" I'm itching to tell her about my progress with Latham, to beg her to let me use the training bones.

"You don't *need* more powerful bones for a task this simple," she says. "It's a crutch to use stronger bones than necessary. Not to mention unethical. Each bone you use for practice is a bone that can't be used for something else."

"But—"

"You'll catch on," she says, "and when you do, you'll be all the better for the struggle."

I don't see how failing is going to make me a better Bone

Charmer, and I open my mouth to tell her so, but she puts up a hand. "I'm the master and you're the apprentice for a reason. You do your part, and let me do mine. Now get to your next lesson." And with that she turns her back on me and walks away.

My gaze slides to the cupboard where the practice bones are stored. My fingers twitch at my sides.

But there's not time.

I step into the corridor and join the swarm of other apprentices who are spilling out of training rooms from all directions. Our next lesson is a seminar—one of a handful of classes we all have together, and it's supposed to take place in a room beneath Ivory Hall called the workshop.

We all inch along in the same direction, winding through the passageways like a giant colorful snake, until we reach the top of the stairwell—a wide, elegant set of steps that disappears belowground after the first graceful curve. I stand on my toes and search for a familiar face in the crowd—Tessa, Talon, or even Bram—but there are too many of us in too small an area, and I can't find anyone I know.

Everyone is eager to see the workshop, and so we pour down the stairs, descending shoulder to shoulder, filling every square inch. By the time we reach the bottom, I can hardly breathe.

I'm expecting a damp and musty room, but instead we step into a brightly lit, cavernous space that stretches farther than I can see. Dozens of fully assembled skeletons—humans and animals alike—hang around the perimeter of the room. Beside them are cases filled with identical bones that have been separated and neatly labeled, each with its name and what magics it's most useful for. In the center of the room are worktables where, presumably, we'll be tested on our knowledge.

"Keep moving forward, apprentices!" Norah shouts from somewhere in the distance. "Don't dawdle."

The workshop stretches on and on. We pass shelves lined with thick leather-bound books, tables spread with maps of Kastelia, and a large display on the wall, papered with diagrams of the body.

Norah finally comes into view. She's standing on a stage in the center of a small amphitheater. "Find a seat in the appropriate section," she says. "Hurry, now."

The benches are painted to match the cloaks we wear. Huge swaths of blue and green for the Healers and the Watchers, moderate sections colored black for Breakers, purple for Mixers, orange for Masons. And dead center is a tiny section in red, where no more than six apprentices could sit together at any one time.

This year there are only two of us.

A girl who I can only assume is the First Sight Bone Charmer sits at the edge of the red paint. Her sandy-brown hair is plaited to resemble the skeleton of a herring—small delicate strands interlaced to form a beautiful pattern. As soon as she sees me, her hazel eyes go wide and she grins. "I've been looking for you *everywhere*." She holds out her hand. "I'm Ingrid."

"Saskia," I say, sitting down beside her, "and I've been looking for you, too."

We chat while the rest of the apprentices fill in the seats around us. I discover she's from Nyburg—a town twice as big as Midwood; they had over two hundred candidates at their last kenning. She's the youngest of four siblings and the first Bone Charmer in her family.

"Did you get sick that first night?" she asks. "Because I was *miserable*."

I laugh. "Yes, my roommate was ready to go find a Healer."

"You did better than me," she says. "I collapsed the moment I came through the entrance."

Something bright and warm grows inside me, like I've stepped in from the cold to hold my hands above the fire. It's so nice to talk to someone without an undercurrent of resentment or suspicion. This must be what it feels like to belong.

Norah claps her hands three times and the room falls silent. Ingrid squeezes my hand before she turns to face forward. My gaze sweeps across the room and lands on Bram. He and several of the other Breakers are seated together, and I can tell from their body language that their conversation has just broken off. He looks relaxed, as if he's known the other apprentices his whole life. I press my lips together and turn away, angry at how my eyes always seem to find him no matter what I'm looking for.

When I was little, my mother used to give me false readings. She'd tell me about multiple paths and then lie about which one she chose, knowing it would nudge me the other way, which she actually preferred. It didn't take me long to catch on. I noticed the self-satisfied smile she wore when I chose the opposite path. I wasn't a fool.

But I hated how well my mother knew me. How easily she could manipulate me, even when I tried to resist.

Now I can't help but wonder what kind of mind game she played when she spoke Bram's name at the kenning. Who did she really see on my path? Where was she actually trying to guide me?

And am I resisting her plan or fulfilling it?

Norah's voice slices through my thoughts. "Welcome to your first day in the workshop, my friends. You'll be spending a lot of time here this year."

I let all thoughts of home, my mother, and Bram slip away and focus my full attention on Norah. I'm determined to learn everything I can at Ivory Hall so I can master bone charming once and for all.

Then everyone around me will be safe, and no one but me will ever control my fate again.

Saskia
The Tutor

Truth serum smells terrible.

I grimace as I bring the horn up to my lips. Partly because it turns my stomach and partly to buy myself a few more seconds while my thoughts are still safely locked away. *Tell the truth as cleverly as you can,* my mother said.

Like she did.

We've been in the council chamber for hours. Hours that feel like days.

Master Oskar laid out a convincing case against my mother—how I came to the bone house for essence of horse hoof, how I refused to tell him what she was using it for, how I've been spending an unusual amount of time with his new apprentice, how I often visited when he was away and he only found out later that I'd been there at all.

And of course, Ami's testimony confirmed everything he said. Yes, I did seem to purposely visit when Master Oskar wasn't there. *No*, I hadn't told her why my mother needed supplies. *Yes*, I had brought my intended along on one of my visits even though he had no business at the bone house.

The entire time, I watched my mother's face for any sign of worry, but her expression remained serene even as the other members of the council looked more and more concerned.

Declan's interrogation was the shortest, but the most painful. Anders asked him if he'd visited the bone house and for what purpose. Declan's answers were short and confident. He said he wanted to know where I was spending my time, wanted to get to know my best friend, wanted to be with me as much as possible.

"How well do you know Saskia?"

His gaze found mine and held it. "Very well," he said. "I've known her since we were children. And we've . . ." He abruptly stopped talking and his eyes went wide, like an animal who has just found itself caught in a trap.

"And you've what?"

Declan swallowed. "We've been seeing each other since before the kenning."

Anders's expression grew sharper. Inwardly, I flinched. Pairing up before the kenning has always been frowned upon. It creates problems when a candidate is bone-matched to a partner who is in love with someone else. Anders paused for a moment, seeming to consider probing further, but then seemed to decide to let the line of questioning drop. Still, it wasn't an ideal moment for me to be perceived as a rule breaker.

"Have you noticed any change in Saskia's behavior recently?

Declan bit the inside of his cheek. He didn't speak for several long moments.

Anders cleared his throat. "Well?"

"Yes," Declan said softly.

"In what way?"

"She's been less . . . herself since the kenning."

"Less honest?"

"I don't know that I'd put it that way."

"How would you put it?"

Declan shifted in his seat. "She's been more distant. Less open."

"Like she's keeping secrets?"

Declan's brow furrowed as if he was willing himself not to reply. But eventually the answer spilled from his lips like poison. "Yes."

The room went silent and still.

"Just one more question," Anders said. "Did you ever venture beyond the antechamber of the bone house?"

"No," Declan answered simply. "I was with Saskia and Ami the whole time."

"Thank you for your time," Anders said. "You're excused."

Anders turned to my mother then. "Della, I hate to do this . . ."

"Of course," she said breezily. "I don't have anything to hide."

She downed the truth serum in one swallow. Anders didn't

bother to open with easy questions as he had with every other witness: "Why did you need essence of horse hoof?"

My mother's voice was bell clear as she answered. "One of the kenning bones fractured. I wanted to repair it."

I stopped breathing. Blood roared in my ears, but the other council members didn't seem alarmed. It must have been the way she *prepared* the bones that was the problem. But Anders wouldn't know to ask about that, and her clever answer made it seem as if she were just repairing a small crack—not weaving two versions of the future back together.

"Why keep it from Saskia?" Anders asked. "Why couldn't she explain to Oskar what you were planning with the supplies?"

"I didn't tell her because I didn't want her to feel guilty."

"Why would she feel guilty?" My mother's gaze slid to me and it took her a moment to answer. "Because it was her fault. Saskia broke the bone."

The words sliced me to the core. Because she said them with accusation in her voice. She said them like she'd lost the ability to lie.

For the first time since the kenning, I realized that she resented me for something I didn't even remember doing. I stared at the ground in front of my feet for the rest of her testimony. I only looked up when Anders called my name.

Tell the truth as cleverly as you can. My mother told the council the truth—that the bone broke, that she wanted to repair it—but not the *entire* truth. Not that she'd infused the bones with extra magic. Not that the bone broke *during* the kenning instead of afterward. Not that she was trying to trick the bone into thinking it was inside a body.

She answered every question as if she had nothing to hide, even though she was hiding plenty. By the time she left the witness chair, even Master Oskar looked as if he felt bad for accusing her.

But I'm not my mother, and I can't be trusted with her secrets.

The horn trembles against my lips as I take a sip. Bitterness hits the back of my throat and I gag. I should have gulped it all in one shot. I drink the rest of the serum and pass the *keras* back to Rakel. Heat rises in my cheeks, and I try to cool them by pressing my palms to my face.

"Are you ready?" Anders asks. His voice sounds faraway, like he's shouting from the bottom of a pit.

I manage a nod.

"What's your name?" he asks.

"Saskia." The answer practically leaps from my mouth—like an unexpected sneeze.

"How old are you?"

This time, I'm more prepared. I avoid answering for a beat, but it's still irresistible. More like a cough that I can hold back for a little bit, but not forever. "I'm seventeen."

"And were you matched at your kenning?"

"Yes."

"To whom?"

"Declan."

"And are you keeping secrets from him?"

"Yes." As soon as the word leaves my mouth, I realize that I shouldn't have said it that way. I should have said, *I don't tell him* everything, *but I'm sure that will come in time.* From the corner of my eye, I see Declan flinch.

I don't have time to think about it though, because the questions keep coming: "When did you find out your father's bones were missing? Why do you visit the bone house so often? Did you know what your mother planned to do with the essence of horse hoof?"

And then a question I can't answer. "Why did you break one of the kenning bones?"

This time the words aren't waiting on the tip of my tongue. The absence is both a surprise and a relief. Like an itch that vanishes without being scratched. Maybe I have some control over the answer because there *isn't* an answer.

"I don't know," I say finally. And then after a beat: "It was an accident, and I feel terrible." My eyes cut to my mother and she gives me a sad smile. I'm not sure if it's genuine or if it's for show.

Anders expression softens. "I'm sure you do," he says. "First your gran's damaged bone, and now this."

A wave of grief washes over me and pulls me down to the same dark place I've visited so often since Gran and my father died. Anders words are the same ones that have echoed in my mind over and over for the past few years. *And now this. And now this. And now this.*

I'm not sure how many more fractures I can withstand until I crumble.

Declan, Ami, and I wander through town, all of us lost in

thought. The only sounds are the crickets chirping and the click of our boots against the cobblestones. We're vaguely aiming in the direction of Ami's house, but none of us seem in any hurry to get there.

The council excused all the witnesses, and is now meeting in private to discuss the next steps. Despite interviewing everyone who's even come within spitting distance of the bone house since my father's death, they're no closer to figuring out what happened.

The events of the day cling to us like moss to stone.

I wonder if the others are as afraid to speak as I am—if they worry that the serum hasn't worn off yet, if their secrets feel like unbridled horses inside them, snuffling and stomping and just waiting for an opportunity to break free.

"Are either of you hungry?" Ami asks.

We're passing the Tib & Fib—a tavern named for a patron who got so drunk that he took a tumble and broke both of those bones in his leg. I've always been surprised that the place could stay in business with such an unlucky name, but maybe people drowning their sorrows in strong drinks don't care. Maybe they feel like fortune has already abandoned them.

"Not hungry enough to eat there," Declan says. A customer opens the door as we pass, and raucous laughter spills out into the street along with the smell of grilled meat.

Ami smiles. "The Sweet Tooth was closer to what I had in mind." She turns to me. "What do you think?"

I nearly tell her no, but, on second thought, I have the overwhelming urge for something sweet, to let a bit of sugar melt on my tongue and drive away the taste of the last few hours—the bitter truth serum, and the even more bitter look in my mother's eyes when she blamed me for Gran's broken bone.

"Yes," both Declan and I say at the same moment. All three of us laugh, and a bit of my tension ebbs away.

We make our way to the end of the street—past the White Dragon Inn and the Healing House, with its hundreds of bottles of bone remedies lined up inside the windows. When we arrive at the bakery, Ami pushes open the door and the smell of sugar wafts toward us.

We order enough for ten people—tiny sweet buns filled with almond paste, bits of fried bread rolled in cinnamon and sugar, squares of velvety cheese topped with purple elderberries. The baker wraps our treats in cloth and layers them in a small wicker basket that he holds out to Ami.

"Enjoy," he says.

It takes Ami a moment to answer. Her expression is anxious, as if she senses danger in responding to something even so innocuous as common pleasantries. And then, finally: "Thank you. We will."

We eat as we walk, each of us snatching another dessert from the basket slung over Ami's elbow the moment we've finished chewing the first. Eating mouths can't be talking mouths.

Of the three of us, Ami lives closest to the town square, in one of the friendliest houses in Midwood. On warm days, the door is always open and the smell of baking bread floats on the breeze like an invitation. Flower boxes in the top windows spill out colorful blooms that trail down the facade so that it looks as if the house is weeping petals. When we were small, our homes seemed more alike to me. Both were bursting with love and noise, both were filled with family—parents and grandparents who adored us. But slowly, my home emptied—grief squeezing into the hollows death has left behind—while hers has stayed the same.

The juxtaposition is a constant ache.

By the time we make it to Ami's front door, the day is almost over. The sun melts into the horizon, leaving behind a shimmering puddle of orange light.

Ami turns to me before she goes inside, and folds me in an embrace. "I'm sorry." Her voice catches on the words.

"Ami, don't," I say. "It's not necessary."

But her eyes fill with tears. "I made you seem guilty," she says, "when I know you're not. But the answers just came and I couldn't . . . I had no control. It's like I couldn't clarify or put anything in context."

I squeeze her hand. "I know. It was the same for me." I glance over my shoulder at Declan, who has backed off to give us privacy and is studiously examining the plants in the vegetable garden at the side of Ami's house. "You did nothing wrong. But I understand the urge to apologize. I think I have some explaining of my own to do."

Ami gives me a sympathetic look. "You were just being honest."

"Yes," I say, "which makes it all the harder to explain away."

She cuts a glance toward Declan and then back to me. Her voice lowers, conspiratorially. "You'll have to fill me in later on what secrets you're keeping from him."

I try to laugh, but it comes out forced and stilted.

Ami bumps her hip lightly against mine. "Unless you're keeping secrets from me too." She sounds playful, but I know her well enough to hear the note of insecurity in her voice.

"Ami . . ." I want to explain, but I can't find the words. And what if the truth serum is still in effect? What if I start talking and accidentally say too much?

Her expression falters and a chill falls between us.

I've lost so much. I can't lose Ami, too.

"We'll talk tomorrow. I promise."

She nods once, but her expression is wary. She hands me the basket full of treats. "You need these more than I do."

My feelings are a tangle inside me as I walk back toward Declan. He stands up and brushes the dirt from his palms. "Is Ami all right?"

"Yes," I say, "just a little unsettled from the truth serum."

"I think we all are." Something shifts in his expression, and I suddenly understand that he's been acting for Ami's benefit. He's obviously more hurt than I realized.

"Declan—"

"If you don't want to be with me, why not just reject the match?"

"*Of course* I want to be with you."

He shakes his head. "I can't have a relationship with someone who keeps secrets from me, Saskia."

A coil slips around my heart and cinches tight.

This is all my mother's fault. She should have never given me a matchmaking reading. I had already fallen for Declan before she said his name at the kenning and filled me with doubt. But a bone-matched partnership that fails never bodes well for either party. I need to find a way to fix this.

I put my hand on his forearm. "Declan, you know how I feel about you. I'm sorry for how I've been acting lately."

"I just don't understand what I did."

"You didn't do anything. My mother . . ." I struggle for a way to tell him the truth without revealing too much. "She knew I didn't want a matchmaking reading, so when she said your name . . ."

He puts up a hand to stop me. "This story isn't making me feel better."

I laugh. "No, not because I didn't want us to be together, but because I wanted *you* to choose me."

"But, Saskia," he says gently, "I already did."

Everything inside me goes soft, like butter in a warm kitchen. I've been so unfair to him. I run a hand from his shoulder to his palm and link my fingers through his. "Can we start over?" I ask him. "Please?"

His expression is stony. "I just have one question."

A sliver of dread burrows into my heart. I swallow. "What is it?"

"How many of those desserts do you think I can fit in my mouth at one time?"

I smile, and my worry unwinds in one swift motion, like the string at the end of a kite reel. Declan never was good at keeping conversations serious for long. "Hmm. Four?"

He puts a hand to his chest. "Your utter lack of faith offends me, Saskia."

"Five?"

He shakes his head in pretend exasperation as he scoops up a handful of treats, unwraps them, and begins stuffing them into his mouth as we walk.

One. Three. Five. Eight.

"Stop," I say. "You won't be able to breathe."

He shrugs as if air—or lack of it—is inconsequential. Especially if a challenge is on the line.

Ten. Twelve. Fourteen.

He turns to me, his cheeks bulging like a feasting chipmunk.

I giggle—softly at first—and then it's as if a dam has burst, and soon I'm laughing so hard that tears are streaming down my cheeks. So hard that it's me, not Declan, who really is having trouble breathing.

"What's so funny?" Declan asks. Or at least I think that's what he's saying. It's hard to tell with his mouth so full. He tries again, but a bit of elderberry dribbles from his lips and lands on his chin.

"Charming," I say, wrinkling my nose. "Really. You've never looked more handsome."

The corner of his mouth ticks up. He works his jaw up and down, chewing for several minutes before he finally swallows and lets out a contented sigh.

"Very impressive," I tell him. "It's a wonder you weren't matched as a taste tester. You could get so much done in so little time."

He grins at me. His teeth are purple.

We're nearly to my house. It's so different from Ami's— sprawling where hers is tidy, formal where hers is welcoming. A full moon hangs low in the sky, making the white stone luminous, and etching the leaves of the oak trees in silver. An owl hoots softly in the distance, and I imagine the bird catching and swallowing a nightmare.

Declan walks me up the path to the front door.

"Thank you for making me laugh," I say.

"Thank you for laughing," he says. "It made me feel better." His eyes are soft now, and all the humor is gone from his expression.

"I'm sorry about today," I tell him. "I didn't mean . . ." I lace my fingers together and hold them in front of me. "I didn't mean for my answer to come out quite that way. It's not that I've been lying to you. I only—"

"Saskia," Declan says, "don't apologize for telling the truth."

"I just don't want you to think . . ."

He reaches up and tucks a stray hair behind my ear. "I can be patient," he says, "as long as you promise I have a chance to become the person you trust with your secrets." His thumb grazes my cheek. As he drops his hand back to his side, I notice the tiniest hint of pink that circles his wrist—a line so faint, it might just be a trick of the light.

The events of the day weigh on me—my father's bones going missing. The truth serum. The look on my mother's face as she accused me with her eyes. None of it exactly conducive to romance. But somehow Declan has managed to cut through all that and make me feel completely safe. He loves me. Even with all my flaws.

"I promise," I tell him. And I mean it. It's time for me to take control of my own destiny and trust my own heart. Declan chose me long before the bones spoke.

It's time I chose him, too.

Saskia
The Bone Charmer

I didn't walk into my lessons this morning intending to steal training bones.

But several weeks have passed and my progress is painfully slow. Tessa is already healing complicated injuries; Talon has mastered canine sight and has moved on to controlling birds; even Ami's letters suggest she's quickly mastering her duties at the bone house in Midwood. But I'm still struggling with the basics.

And Master Kyra doesn't seem the least bit concerned.

After our lesson today—one where it took me most of the morning to discern what she'd just eaten for breakfast (dry toast, tea with one lump of sugar, and a bowl of berries)—she patted me on the shoulder and told me I was making great progress.

Why then do I feel like I'm failing at every turn? Yesterday I saw Ingrid leaving one of the training rooms with a spell book tucked under her arm, her cheeks flushed with pleasure. Being issued my own spell book is yet another milestone Master Kyra doesn't think I'm ready for. I come from a long line of Bone Charmers. Shouldn't it come effortlessly to me—the way my eyes are the exact same shade as my mother's, or my laugh sounds just like Gran's?

When I was young, I could feel magic thrumming inside me like a pulse. That day on the prison boat it felt more like a tidal wave, so strong that it threatened to pull me under. So strong, it destroyed three lives. Afterward, I spent years pushing the magic away. But what if that made everything worse? Because now that I'm actually searching for my power, I can't seem to find more than a drop. What happens if it surges again and I haven't learned to control it? The stakes are so much higher now that I've been bound to bone magic. I'll start getting responsibilities soon.

What if someone gets hurt? What if I'm called on to determine the guilt or innocence of a prisoner and my vision is inaccurate? I could end up condemning someone to hang who doesn't deserve it; or someone guilty could walk free and their future crimes would be my fault.

Master Kyra might not be worried, but I am. I can't afford to move so slowly.

Now I stand in front of the cupboard at the back of the room, waging a war with myself.

Going behind Master Kyra's back feels like cheating. I'm sure she'll introduce the practice bones when she thinks I'm ready, but at this rate it won't be for months. Even though Latham thought I was ready the first day. My palms grow clammy and I wipe them on my cloak. Maybe Master Kyra's teaching style is just too rigid. The thought feels like a breeze through my mind. Like a justification.

I ease open the cupboard door and find shelves packed with plain brown boxes in various sizes. They're each labeled with small, neat handwriting. *Bones of a long-eared owl, full set, strength: 38. Bones of a spoon-billed sandpiper, cervical vertebrae only, strength: 52. Bones of a brown rat, tarsus and metatarsus only, strength: 5.*

An adjacent shelf holds a stack of small stone basins, lumps of flint, and bundles of incense wrapped with twine. And yet another shelf is lined with leather-bound books: *Bone Charming: A Complete History, Basics of Bone Charming, Human Anatomy, Zoology: Animal Skeletons in Bone Charming Applications.* But no spell books. Those are always stored under lock and key. My mother kept her own spell book carefully guarded even from me.

And no practice bones either. I open every cupboard in the room with the same result. There are a variety of ordinary bones, but nothing like what Latham showed me when I first arrived. Maybe he relocated them to remove temptation. I'm just about to give up, when a burst of sunlight floods through the window and, from the corner of my eye, I catch a glint of gold on the top shelf of one of the cupboards.

The box of practice bones Latham found was silver, but maybe . . . I drag a wooden bench to the back of the room. The extra height is just enough for my fingertips to graze the top shelf. I stand high on my toes and reach blindly, pushing aside the boxes that feel plain until my hand closes around a metal one—something fancy, from the feel of it. My pulse spikes. I climb down and examine the box. It's silver with clawed feet, and the top is adorned with a raised pattern of gilded vines and roses—it must have been the gold flowers that caught my eye in the light. It's not the same box that I used earlier with Latham, but Ivory Hall must be filled with hundreds of sets of practice bones. Carefully, I turn the box over and examine the bottom. A small label is affixed to the underside. *Bones of an adult female, phalanges only, preserved for study (First, Second, or Third Sight, general use), strength: 486.* I unlatch the silver clasp. The box is lined in plush blue velvet.

And the bones inside look just like Gran's.

I should have expected it, of course. One set of female finger bones is bound to look like another, but the sight still gives me a lump in my throat that I can't quite swallow. I wonder who this woman was, what would compel her to donate her remains to be used like this. The thought of Gran's bones tucked away in a cupboard somewhere, exploited over and over for strangers, makes me ill. I close the box and climb back onto the wooden stool. It's not as if I even know what I would do with the bones.

I open the cupboard and slide the box back inside. My fingers brush leather—what feels like the bumpy spine of a book. My breath catches. Why would someone put a book here, tucked behind boxes of bones, unless they were trying to hide it? I inch my fingers forward, nudging the book toward me until it's close enough to grasp. And then I pull it from the cupboard.

It's a spell book.

Maybe I'll take the training bones with me after all.

I try to stroll calmly back to the women's dormitory, but the closer I get, the faster I move—it's as if my legs are convinced I'm being followed even if my eyes are certain I'm not. The last few steps are practically a sprint. The stolen items feel like a lead weight at the bottom of my bag.

My hands shake as I fumble with the doorknob.

Tessa sits at her desk, a spell book open in front of her; she's so absorbed, she hasn't heard me enter the room. She rests her chin in her palm and her curly hair falls over her shoulder like a curtain.

The sight of her sends a jolt of alarm through me.

I clutch my bag more tightly to my side.

"You're back early," I say. It comes out more accusatory than I intended, and Tessa looks up, startled.

If she notices the bite in my voice, she doesn't show it. She gives me a tired smile. "Actually, I think you're back late."

I glance out the window. She's right. The sun is high in the sky, and warm yellow light floods into the room without casting much of a shadow. The morning is gone.

I sink down onto my bed and slide my bag off my shoulder, surreptitiously shoving it behind me. "I guess I lost track of time."

147

She tilts her head to one side. "Are you feeling all right?"

"I'm fine. Why?"

"You just look a little feverish," she says. "Want me to take a look?"

Sweat beads on my forehead, the heat suffusing my cheeks. The last thing I need is for Tessa to examine me and decide that I'm not ill but that I'm exhibiting classic signs of deception. "No," I say. "I think I'm just tired."

She bites her lip. "Is it that you don't trust me? Because I'm much more proficient than I was a few weeks ago." She motions toward the book on her desk. "I've been studying like mad, and even if I can't make you feel better, I can at least promise not to make you worse. Or I can get Master Dina, if you'd rather. She'll have you feeling like new in no time at all."

A wave of affection washes over me. Tessa's loquaciousness has grown on me, and now it's as comforting as listening to the ocean lap at the shore. Which makes me feel even more guilty for lying to her.

"Of course I trust you," I say. "It's just exhaustion. I'm sure of it."

"Maybe you should rest instead of coming down to the dining hall," she says. "I can bring something up for you if you'd like."

Hope leaps in my chest. It's the perfect solution—guaranteed time alone to study the spell book without having to explain away a conspicuous absence.

"Thank you," I say. "Maybe I will lie down for a bit."

Her expression is the same one my mother always wore right after she'd gotten me to swallow a spoonful of medicine as a child—a hint of exasperation just as it melts into relief.

Tessa stands up to stretch, and I admire—not for the first time—the swirling tattoos on her arms. They remind me a bit of my father's, but she hasn't mentioned being an artist. Even though it's considered rude to ask about the source of someone's tattoos—they almost always come from experiences too personal to casually share—I'm still curious enough that I'm tempted. Maybe later, when we know each other better.

Tessa shrugs her cloak over her shoulders. "I'll tell the others that you stayed behind to rest," she says. "I'm sure they'll miss you."

I recline a bit to show her that I'm anxious to fall asleep, but I forgot that my bag is behind me. The corner of the bone box digs into my lower back and before I can stop myself, I wince. Tessa hesitates in the doorway. Bites the inside of her cheek. Studies me like she's adding a series of large numbers in her head.

And then she opens her mouth, no doubt to pummel me with a barrage of questions. But I don't let her get that far.

"You're a good friend, Tessa," I say. And then I roll onto my side and close my eyes.

I lie frozen, feigning sleep, for what feels like an eternity. I'm half-expecting Tessa to burst back into the room at any moment to check on me one more time. It's not until I hear the low burble of chatter floating up from the dining hall that I dare sit up and pull out the spell book.

It's covered in a dark blue leather—a color so deep, it's nearly black—and accented at each corner with triangles of burgundy. On the front in gold swirling script is one word: Spells.

I open the book, and a torrent of emotions bloom inside me, like a deadly flower—it's the thrill of the forbidden, but the fear of it too.

The pages are filled with diagrams of bones in different configurations, long paragraphs of explanations, and notes scribbled in the margins. One inscription reads: *Heavy Heart Spell (First Sight): The sternum of any warm-blooded animal or human along with four ribs from the same source. Especially revealing for past deeds that have caused guilt or pain. Works as a bloodless spell, but blood and flame produce greater accuracy.*

I flip to the section on Second Sight. *Prison Spell (Second Sight): The ischium of a flightless bird placed parallel to a femur of any four-legged beast. Particularly useful for detecting reasons a subject may feel trapped.* In the margins is scrawled a note: *Ostrich bones far superior to penguin. Chicken bones produce fuzzy vision.*

I skim through page after page of spells, patterns, and tips for making visions more accurate. An entire section at the back discusses the kenning—how it's important to use the most powerful bones available, human if at all possible. And how the more closely related the bones are to the subject, the clearer the kenning will be. *Bones of direct family members produce readings with the most pure outcomes.* I run my fingertip over the words. It's why my mother wanted Gran's bones prepared in time for my kenning.

Who does this book belong to? And why does it have

information for all three Sights? Spell books are supposed to be highly individualized. They are the most valuable and closely guarded possessions of anyone who has bone magic. I search through the pages for a name, for any sign of the book's owner, but I find nothing.

Voices outside the door pull me from my thoughts. I shove the spell book under my pillow and close my eyes just in time. Noise spills into the room—chatting and laughter, along with Tessa's increasingly irritated shushing. "Saskia is trying to rest. Keep it down."

I roll over and open my eyes. Tessa holds a tray with bread and fruit. "You're in luck," she says. "Norah announced that we have the afternoon off, so you can keep resting." Talon, Bram, and Linnea stand behind her, bags in hand.

"Where are you all going?"

Tessa sets the tray on my lap. "We decided it would be a good time to explore Kastelia City," she says. "I wish you were feeling better."

Disappointment tumbles inside me. I would love nothing more than to get out of Ivory Hall for a few hours, but I can't very well stage a miraculous recovery after such a short time. "Me too," I say. "But I hope you have fun."

Bram is studying me with a dissecting expression. "What's wrong with you?"

"Nothing is *wrong* with me," I say. "I'm just tired."

His eyes hold mine. "We're all tired. There's something you're not telling us."

Linnea puts a hand on his elbow. "Come on now. No need to

interrogate her."

Bram ignores her. "Your skin is all splotchy."

The comment makes my cheeks flame. I can almost feel the ruddiness creeping down my neck and chest.

Talon laughs. "It's the fair skin," he says. "I get a bit spotty too when I'm ill."

"Saskia gets splotchy when she's nervous," Bram says. I press a palm to my neck. My skin is on fire.

"And also when I'm ill," I say defensively, which is true, though my voice trembles on the words. Bram's gaze makes me feel as if I've been turned inside out for inspection.

Tessa purses her lips and touches the inside of my wrist with her fingertips. "Your pulse is fast. Maybe I should stay here with you."

"No," I say. "I'm fine."

"I don't mind. I'll just—"

"I'm fine," I say more firmly. "Please go."

If I didn't feel like lying down before, I do now.

The group leaves, though Tessa throws one more worried glance over her shoulder before she goes. The soft click of the closing door produces a waterfall of relief. But it only lasts a moment before it's replaced with a sharp sense of loss. I'd rather be sightseeing with a gaggle of new friends than stuck in a stuffy room. Instead my inability to control my magic has stolen yet another bit of joy.

I'm suddenly homesick for Ami's laugh. For my mother's beef stew. For the owl that nests outside my bedroom window. I let myself indulge in a stretch of self-pity until I'm hollowed out. Then I shove all of my feelings behind a locked door in my mind.

And I reopen the spell book.

Saskia
The Tutor

ran's broken bone has started to heal.

A soft callous has formed around the edges of the break—a thick network of newly woven bone that my mother claims is a good sign that the solution is working.

"How long do we have?" I ask. We stand in front of the shelf, studying the glass container that houses the bone. Looking but not touching—it needs to stay as still as possible.

"In a living body, a bone will mend itself in only a month or two. But I expect this to take longer. . . ." She sighs and massages her temples. "Though I don't know for sure." The hollows under her eyes are more pronounced today. I can tell she isn't sleeping well, and I wish there were something I could do, something I could say. But I don't know how to scale the wall that has sprung up between us.

"What happens when the bone is completely healed?" I ask. "One of my realities just disappears? In an instant?"

It's a conversation we've had before, but I still can't wrap my mind around it. The fear in my heart is like a sleeping beast. Sometimes I forget it's even there—whole days go by where I don't think about the fact that I'm living in a fractured reality. Then something happens to make the fear stir, wake, stretch, and I remember just how big it is, how at any moment it could swallow me whole.

My mother's mouth turns up at the edges. A sad smile. She reaches for me and tucks a stray hair behind my ear. "It won't hurt, love. You won't even know it's happened."

Somehow that isn't comforting.

"What other paths did you see for me?" I ask. "I need you to tell me." She doesn't answer immediately, and so I rush on. "If this isn't the reality that survives, I'll never know we discussed it. And if it is, then the other paths don't matter, right? Fate will have spoken."

"Saskia—"

A sharp whistle pierces the air, followed by the screech of a bird. Watchers.

The town council petitioned Ivory Hall to send reinforcements after Oskar discovered three other sets of remains missing from the bone house. Several days ago—almost a month after they were requested—a cadre of Bone Singers arrived, and now birds circle overhead, dogs patrol the streets of Midwood, and a large prowler—a creature that looks like it's half-wolf, half-lion—guards the entrance to the bone house. Even though I know the animal won't attack without a specific order from the Watcher who controls him, it still makes my mouth go dry whenever I visit Ami. Our little town, which has always felt so safe, now feels like it's holding its breath, bracing for a blow that might land at any moment.

A week ago I'd never even seen a bone flute, and now I can distinguish the melody of a canine stay command from an avian return call. But the whistle we just heard is completely unfamiliar.

My mother and I both hurry to the window. Dozens of ravens fly in formation at the north end of town. The Watcher dogs are barking wildly off in the distance, though they're too far away to see.

"Do you think they found Papa's bones?"

Her expression trembles on the edge between hope and fear, and I'm not sure which way it will fall. Her gaze is fixed on the sky. For a moment I think she might not answer, that she's gone somewhere in her mind where I can't follow, but then, abruptly, she looks at me. Her face is smooth and unreadable.

"Let's go find out," she says.

It seems as if all of Midwood had the same idea.

We pass people standing on their porches with their faces tipped upward, children who scramble up trees for a better view, and still more of the townsfolk who spill into the streets and follow the birds like a beacon.

The ravens keep shifting positions, as if trying to get a better view of whatever is happening below. Each time I think I've pinpointed where they are, they shift, and my perspective along with them.

As we pass through the town square, Willem Ingersson races past me, and Audra trails behind, shouting at him to slow down. I've been to the Ingerssons' house at least two dozen times to tutor Willem, with mixed results. Sometimes Audra is calm, collected, and lets me instruct her son without interruption. Other times, she's agitated, claiming the bones need to be consulted before I can say a word. Those are the bad days. It's fortunate that Willem is bright and picks up concepts quickly, because it takes ten times longer to teach him than it should.

Audra notices us and stops. "What is happening, Della?"

My mother shrugs. "I'm afraid I don't know. Saskia and I are trying to figure it out along with everyone else."

Audra narrows her eyes. "You're lying," she says. "Why won't you tell me?"

"I don't know anything more than you do."

"I don't believe you." Audra's eyes are wide and she seems to have forgotten that Willem was running from her. I crane my neck and scan the crowd, relaxing a little when I finally spot him talking to a few of the other children near the Marrow.

"You may believe what you wish," my mother says. "It's of no concern to me." She tries to move away, but Audra grabs her arm.

"Della, please. I consulted the bones only this morning. Why wouldn't they reveal this?"

Instead of answering, my mother looks pointedly at Audra's hand. It takes several seconds, but Audra finally lets go. My mother levels her with a steely gaze. "Maybe they didn't reveal anything because whatever is happening has *nothing to do with you*. The bones don't serve you and you alone just because you're wealthy, Audra. Have you ever thought of the hundreds of children who could have avoided being leftovers if you had done something less foolish with your excess?"

Audra's startled expression matches my own. I rarely see my mother's temper run short, let alone see her lose her grip on it enough for a rant.

"Leftovers aren't my responsibility," Audra says between clenched teeth. "And if you cared about them so much, you should have continued to do readings for me. You would have made plenty of coin to save a few." With that she spins on her heel and storms away. In the opposite direction of Willem.

I watch her long enough to make sure that she turns back to find her son. It takes her a disturbingly long time, but finally she does.

"That was . . . interesting," I say.

My mother's face and neck are flushed and blotchy—her skin reacts to situations of high emotion exactly as mine does.

"That woman . . ." She glances at me and startles a little, as if she's forgotten I'm here. "I'm sorry, Saskia. I shouldn't have spoken to Audra that way."

She takes several deep breaths and her complexion returns

to normal. I've always envied her ability to slip on an aura of calm as easily as putting on a robe, but this time it makes something inside me deflate. It's such a rare occurrence to know exactly how my mother is feeling, and I hoped it wouldn't be so fleeting. She guards her thoughts as closely as her spell book, and now that she's caught me gawking, she's slammed herself closed again.

"Why not? If that's what you really think, why wouldn't you be honest?"

"We ought not give ourselves the luxury of saying something unkind just because it's true. Unless we actually think our opinion might make a difference for the better."

"And you don't?"

She shakes her head. "Audra Ingersson knows how I feel about her use of bone reading. She has for a long time."

"This might make my next tutoring session awkward," I say.

My mother waves a hand in front of her face as if swatting away a fly. "Audra will forget all about it by then. That's part of her problem—she only lives in the moment and never considers the long-term consequences. She wants to see her path far enough to know what's around the next bend, but she doesn't much care where the path is actually headed. Or how her choices affect her future."

Where is my path headed? Will this path survive? They're the questions I'm longing to shout at her. Questions that make me want to grab her by the shoulders and shake her until the answers spill from her lips like water over stones. But I know she won't discuss it. Especially not here, as the town square grows more and more crowded.

The ravens have shifted again, circling in a more typical pattern. They're even farther north than I first thought. We cross the town square and walk down a wide lane, finally ending up in a neighborhood with large homes and small yards—my father used to call this street busy but barren. The people who live here have plenty of coin but no time to care for flowers or trees.

A flurry of activity at the end of the street hurries our steps forward. At least a dozen Watchers are gathered around one of the houses, along with dogs, horses, and a crowd of townsfolk. Master Anders stands on the porch, talking to one of the Watchers—his arms wave wildly in the air, and it's clear he's yelling, though we're still too far away to hear anything more than the drone of a hundred people talking at once.

My mother's sharp intake of breath cuts through the noise.

"What is it?"

She's gone pale and she presses her palm to her chest.

"Mother, what? Who lives here?"

Her voice is filled with dread. "Rakel," she says softly.

Rakel. The Mixer who serves on the town council. A buzz grows in my ears.

"Do you think *she* stole the bones?"

"Of course not," my mother says. "She would never do that." But the apprehension in her voice tells a different story. She and Rakel have been close for years, and I can't imagine what that kind of betrayal would do to her. But what else would cause such a stir?

I spot Declan at the edge of the crowd and call out his name. He waves and jogs over.

"What's going on?" I ask. "Do you know?"

His brown hair flops across his forehead and he pushes it out of his eyes before lacing his fingers through mine. His wrist is circled in pale pink, a shade darker than the last time I saw him. My wrist is still bare, even though I check every morning to see if the love tattoo has begun to surface. "Something to do with Master Rakel," Declan says, "but that's all I've heard."

"Follow me," my mother says. She pushes through the crowd, nudging people out of the way. "Excuse me. Coming through. Step out of the way, please." Her voice is loud and authoritative, and everyone moves aside without argument. Declan and I trail behind her.

"I don't understand how this happened," Anders is saying. "Midwood is crawling with Watchers. Isn't that what you're here for? To prevent tragedies like this?"

The hair on the back of my neck stands on end.

The Watcher's expression is tight—like he's a cord stretched too far, about to break. "You asked us to focus our attention on the bone house, so that's what we did," he says. "Going forward, we need to surveil the entire town. Obviously."

My mother climbs the porch steps. "Anders"—she touches his elbow—"what's going on?"

The Healer turns to her. "Oh, Della." He says her name like a parent whose child has stumbled in the room during a vicious argument—startled and then full of regret that he can't turn

162

back time. That he can't make it unhappen. Grief is written all over his face.

"It's Rakel," he says finally. "She's been murdered."

Saskia
The Bone Charmer

"Bones are the source of all magic," Norah says, pacing along the stage in the amphitheater. "They are the most permanent part of us, enduring long after the flesh has rotted away. But even while our bones are still within our bodies, they are powerful. If broken, they can heal themselves. And the marrow within them fights off evil, wards off disease, and keeps you well. But eventually we all succumb to the grip of death; the magic in our bones is all that remains."

She turns to us and smiles. "And you are the lucky ones who are entrusted to wield that power. Use it wisely. Make us proud. You're dismissed."

I stand up and stretch. We have only a short break before we start bone races on the other side of the workshop.

Ingrid puts a hand over her mouth and stifles a yawn. "That was a good lecture," she says. "But a little redundant, since all the same information is on the first pages of our spell books."

A pang goes through me, but I try to make my voice light as I answer, "I guess a little review isn't the worst thing." I don't tell her that I've only just been issued my spell book this morning and have yet to crack it open to discover what is on the first pages. I don't say that I've been studying a stolen spell book that is full of mysteries but has no such lofty notions on any of its pages.

Ingrid gives me a warm smile. "You're right. Master Yaffa is always saying that repetition is the fastest way to learn." She gathers her things and touches my shoulder lightly. "I'm going to head down there before all the Breakers take the best tables. I've never seen people move so fast."

"Sure," I say. "I'll catch up with you later."

My days at Ivory Hall have fallen into a rhythm. Lessons with Master Kyra in the mornings, sessions in the workshop in the afternoons, meals in the dining hall with Tessa, Talon, Bram, and Linnea.

And every moment I have to myself, I study the stolen spell book. It's become an obsession, a yawning need inside me—to master bone charming, to control my magic instead of letting it control me.

I sling my bag over one shoulder and weave my way between the benches, down the steps, and across the length of the room to the opposite side of the workshop. Rows of small tables fill the center of the space, and apprentices are gathering around them, three or four to a table.

I search for Tessa in the crowd, but I can't find her. The tables are filling up fast, and I debate whether to grab a spot now or keep searching for a friend to pair up with. A hand on my elbow makes me spin around. I'm expecting to find Tessa or Talon, but it's Latham.

My heart stutters. I haven't seen him since the second day at Ivory Hall, when he showed me the training bones.

"Saskia," he says, his voice full of warmth. "I've been meaning to check on you. How are things?"

"Fine," I say, "I'm doing great." Inwardly, I cringe at the false brightness in my voice.

Latham's eyebrows pull together and he leans in a little closer. "How are you really?" The question reminds me forcibly of my mother, who could always hear the lies my voice told, even if my words were true. I suddenly feel as transparent as a pane of glass.

"I . . . well, I guess I wish I were making faster progress."

"Is Kyra still moving at the pace of a glacier?"

My eyes widen and I weigh an honest answer over speaking ill of Master Kyra to one of her colleagues.

He laughs as if he can see my thoughts. "No need to answer that. I'm rather surprised you haven't sought me out, though. I told you that I'm happy to help."

But I feel strange about training with him when I already have a tutor. It seems disloyal to Master Kyra somehow. "Thanks anyway," I say, "but I'll get it eventually. I probably just need more practice."

"Well, if you change your mind, feel free to come by my office," he says. "I'm usually around after the evening meal. We'll have you performing readings like a master in no time."

He doesn't wait for me to answer before he pats me on the shoulder and walks away, which makes it feel decided. Like fate has already determined my path.

My conversation with Latham slowed me down enough that now nearly all of the tables are occupied. I wander up and down the aisles, looking for an empty seat. I pass Tessa—sitting with Talon at a full table—and she gives me an apologetic smile. Finally I spot a table with only two other people. They face away from me, but I see a black cloak and a purple one. I circle the table. The Mixer is a boy I've seen around but don't know well.

And the Breaker is Bram.

"Mind if I sit here?"

Bram puts his foot on the seat across from him and slides it out for me. "You don't need my permission."

"I know." I sink into the chair and drop my bag onto the floor. "I was just being polite."

"Oh, my mistake. I didn't realize you did polite."

I glare at him, but the corners of his mouth turn up just a little. Is he teasing me? The possibility breaks apart my impression of him, and I struggle to rearrange the pieces into something familiar.

It doesn't work.

"Where is Linnea?" As soon as the question leaves my mouth, I regret it. It makes it sound as if I'm jealous of their friendship, and I don't want him to think I care. I *don't* care. I simply need a way to put him back in context. To find the person I know from Midwood—quiet, dangerous. Not this stranger I can't quite read.

His eyes flick to mine. "I haven't seen her today. I'm sure she's around here somewhere."

"Did the two of you have an argument?"

His expression goes dark—finally something I recognize. "No," he says tersely. "Why would you ask?"

"Just that you Breakers all seem inseparable." I try to keep my tone light.

"Ah, well, it seems I forgot my weekly payment to the Watcher who keeps tabs on her with his espionage cat."

This time it's the corners of my mouth that lift just a little.

The Mixer looks back and forth between us as if he can't make sense of the exchange. He's not the only one.

Norah claps her hands sharply several times and the room falls silent. Bone races are a favorite among the apprentices, and there's an air of anticipation in the room.

"Ready for the countdown?" Norah asks. She's rewarded with several hundred fists pounding in unison on the tables. "Very well then. Three. Two. One. Race!"

I rip the cloth from the center of the table and toss it onto the floor. A pile of bones lies in a disorganized heap—our task is to work as a team to assemble them into a proper skeleton and identify the animal they came from.

Bram's hand brushes mine as we both reach for the skull. His fingertips are soft. They twitch at my touch.

I pull away first. "Go ahead."

Bram picks up the skull, turning it over in his hands as he studies it from every angle.

I start assembling the other bones—ribs, femur, tibia, fibula—threading them together and hanging them from the training frame. The Mixer boy bites his lip, staring at the vertebrae without touching them. He looks out of his depth. I reach around him and scoop the thin, delicate bones into my palm, counting them before I put them in their proper places.

"It's a *Bradypus*," I whisper.

"How do you know?" Bram doesn't glance up from the bones he's working with. His fingers are deft and they move quickly, sorting and assembling.

"Nine cervical vertebrae. High-crowned, open-rooted teeth. No incisors."

Bram examines the ulna, radius, and digits. "I think you're right."

"What's a *Bradypus*?" the Mixer boy asks.

"Three-toed sloth," Bram and I say at the same time.

We slide the last few bones into place and leap to our feet. "Finished!" Bram shouts.

A chorus of disappointed groans fills the room, but no one stops working. We won't be declared the winners until our work is inspected for accuracy.

Norah comes to our table and studies our skeleton. "Nicely done," she says. "Have you identified the animal?"

"It's a *Bradypus*," I tell her.

Her eyebrows arch appreciatively. "Correct again. You make a good team."

She says it to all three of us, but the Mixer boy barely touched the bones. It was me and Bram. She thinks the two of us make a good team. I think of the prison boat—of the last time we combined forces—and feel suddenly uneasy.

"We just got lucky," I say.

Bram dims. His smile falters, then fades, and I'm struck with a sudden, swift loss.

A storm of confusion rages in my chest and I force myself to look at his hands splayed on the table. At his knuckles. Bram follows my gaze. His fists close and then disappear into his pockets.

"Bram—"

But he doesn't let me finish. "I have somewhere I need to be."

"Bram, wait—" I catch a bit of his cloak between my fingers, but he pulls away without looking back.

He's gone before he gets to hear us pronounced the winners of the bone race.

Bram doesn't show up in the dining hall for the evening meal.

I slide into my usual spot at the table between Tessa and Talon. Linnea sits across from me. Next to her, Bram's seat is conspicuously empty. Though I try not to react to his absence,

I must fail, because Tessa replies to my unasked question: "He has a headache."

Linnea nods as she dips her spoon into her soup and brings it to her mouth, blowing delicately before she takes a bite. She swallows. "He's resting in his room."

"Poor guy looked like the bones had just predicted his untimely demise," Talon says.

An uncomfortable feeling crackles inside me. Did Bram share his troubles with everyone except me? Did he tell them I offended him? The thought sits in my stomach like spoiled food.

I stir my soup absentmindedly, scoop up vegetables just to let them dribble off my spoon again. I've lost my appetite.

"So how is everyone's training going?" Tessa asks.

"My ear-training drills must be paying off," Talon says, "because I was finally able to identify the difference between the summoning tune for a spotted owl and the one for a gray wolf."

"Those seem like they'd be really different melodies," Linnea says playfully. "You must be a terrible singer."

Talon lobs a piece of bread at her head. "They have the exact same tune, just in a different key. And for your information, my voice makes both men and women swoon."

Linnea rests her chin in her palm. "Oh, now you've turned into a braggart? All right then, let's hear it. Sing something for us."

"I couldn't," Talon says. "Think about how it'd make the lesser apprentices feel. But if you don't mind boasting, I have a particular Watcher in mind who could use a few bones snapped."

She laughs. "If I wanted, I might actually be able to soon. The past few days, I've started breaking more by intention than by accident, which is a nice change of pace."

"This must be a lucky week," Tessa says. "I managed to completely close up a laceration in the clinic today. It's the first time I've healed a problem without causing another one." She turns to me and nudges my ribs with her elbow. "How about you, Saskia? Can you tell us what questions will be on our exams?"

I force a tight smile. "Only if Talon sings for us." But I feel like a noose has tightened around my lungs. They're all making such good progress and I'm failing at everything—bone reading, friendship, basic human interaction. Maybe I am foolish not to accept Master Latham's help.

I stand and scoop up my tray. There's no use sitting here and wasting time when I could be working with the practice bones.

"Not hungry?" Talon asks.

"Not really. And I have something I need to do."

"Can't it wait?" Linnea says. "You barely touched your food."

My hands clench around the tray. It trembles in my fingers. Why does she think she can talk to me like I'm a child? Several seconds pass as I try to regain my grip on my temper. No good will come from snapping at Linnea. I channel my mother's practiced calm, force my fingers to relax, my expression to go slack.

"I'm afraid not," I say. "I should have eaten faster, but it's too late now. I have an appointment with one of the Masters."

Latham's office is nearly as large as one of the practice rooms, though much more lavishly decorated. Thick red velvet drapes held back by golden cords hang on either side of the large picture windows, so long that they pool on the glossy white floors. White shelves filled with books, bones, and artifacts line the walls. Latham and I sit across from each other at a large table in the center of the room in plush, oversized chairs. A pile of practice bones lies on a black velvet cloth in front of me. Not finger bones this time, but human foot bones, the seven that make up the tarsus—calcaneus, talus, cuboid, navicular, and three cuneiforms.

Anticipation prickles over my skin.

"Has Kyra worked with you on bloodless readings?" Latham asks.

"No," I tell him. Several of the entries in the spell book mention bloodless readings, but not in enough detail that I've been able to figure out how to do them.

"It's an advanced skill," he says, "one that takes a tremendous amount of time to master, but the practice bones should allow you to have some success." He runs his hands across the bones, shifting them into a straight line.

"Bone Charming requires blood from the subject of the reading in order to bind the magic to the bones—otherwise, the past, present, or future is too vast to see at once. The magic must have direction and focus. The blood provides that—it serves as a kind of frame for what we wish to see. But very skilled Bone Charmers can direct the magic with their thoughts."

I think of all the times my mother has pricked the pads of my fingers and wonder why she didn't just perform a bloodless reading. Or maybe occasionally she did and just never told me.

"How does it work?"

"Place your hands on the bones," he says. "You need to be in contact with all of them."

I put my palms on the line of bones, making sure I'm touching each of them.

"Good," Latham says. "Now close your eyes and think of someone you know well. Someone you can imagine with perfect clarity." He pauses. "Your mother, perhaps."

My eyelids slide down, and I try to focus, but the first person who pops into my mind is Bram. I take a deep breath and try again. My mother flits into my mind—the fine lines that crinkle around her eyes when she smiles, the way she hums to herself when she's in a good mood, the sprinkle of freckles that dusts the bridge of her nose in the summertime. I miss her more than I thought I would. It will be nice to see her again.

I allow my memories to sweep me away, feel the familiar tug of the bones just before a vision.

But it's not my mother I see.

It's Bram.

He lies in his room on his bed. His hands are tucked beneath his head and he stares at the ceiling. Startled, I yank my hands from the bones and open my eyes.

Latham studies me with his head tilted to one side. "You're fighting it."

"I just . . . I didn't see what I was expecting."

"You saw what you wanted to see."

I flatten my palms against the table. "I'm distracted," I tell him. I refuse to believe that I wanted to see Bram.

My father gave me a puzzle once—two interlocking rings made of steel that he claimed could be separated if I was clever enough. I spent weeks fiddling with it—examining it from every angle, twisting it in different directions, putting it down in frustration before picking it up again a few minutes later. I was obsessed with the rings, until I discovered the solution. Once I finally freed them from each other, I never picked them up again.

Bram is just another puzzle I can't solve. The moment my mother said his name at the kenning, she turned him into an enigma. Since then, the prison boat has loomed large in my mind. The killer is the most terrifying person I've ever encountered, and I can't stop picturing his face merging with Bram's—both of them lit by flames, their hearts full of anger as they watched the world burn around them. The common thing I saw in each of their pasts is a sliver in my heart. Whenever I see the black triangles on Bram's knuckles, I'm taken right back to that horror. Spending time with Bram hasn't gotten me any closer to answers—he doesn't *seem* like the person I've imagined over the last five years. But why would he have the exact same tattoos as the prisoner unless they had something essential in common?

Once I figure out Bram's secrets, I won't need to think about him anymore.

I cover the bones with my palms and try again. This time the bones tug me even more swiftly into a vision.

A knock at Bram's door. He sits up and scrubs a hand over his face before he answers. Talon stands at the threshold, a paper bag in his hand. "Nothing cures a headache like stolen sweets." Talon shakes the bag gently before offering it to Bram. "I risked my life to pilfer those from the kitchen, so I hope you appreciate them."

Bram smiles wanly. "I promise to eat the evidence."

"Good man," Talon says. "Feeling any better?"

Bram pulls at the back of his neck. "Not really. I think I just need to sleep it off."

"Well, then, I'll leave you to your sweet rolls and your pillow."

"It was good of you to come by," Bram says. "And thanks for these."

"Don't mention it." Talon ducks out of the room and closes the door behind him.

Bram sets the bag on his bedside table. He pulls his bedcovers back and strips off his shirt.

My breath catches. I open my eyes. Fold my hands in my lap.

"What did you see?" Latham asks.

"Nothing," I tell him. "I couldn't see anything at all."

Saskia
The Tutor

Midwood is supposed to be safe. It's why I longed to stay here, far from the dangers of bone magic. But ever since Rakel's murder, my mind has been filled with vivid, horrible images—a slash across the throat, blood burbling at the wound, wide, dark eyes that slowly dim.

It makes it almost impossible to focus on tutoring Willem.

He's supposed to be labeling the map of Kastelia I gave him—landmarks, cities, towns, distributaries that flow from the Shard River. Instead he's drawing animals in the margins.

"Willem," I say, "you need to focus or we'll never finish."

"Do you think they'll come back?" he asks. He draws scales on a fish at the bottom of the map.

"Who?"

179

"The killers."

An ache fills my chest. This is not something a child should have to worry about. It's not something anyone should have to worry about. And yet the same questions have rustled in the heart of everyone in Midwood since the murder: Who did this? And why? Will they kill again?

"You know what?" I say. "I think we need to do something different today. How about a game?"

He perks up, pushes a tangle of curls out of his eyes. "What kind of game?"

"How about we go on a scavenger hunt for things that look like places on the map?"

He hops up from his chair. "That sounds fun!"

Audra's house is perfect for an activity like this—it's full of hidden passageways, nooks and crannies, and rooms filled with random treasures. Willem skips along as he points out landmarks—a bit of rope that is shaped like the slender town of Selvag, a miniature tree for holding jewelry that looks like the Shard with its many branches, a quilt with a pattern that reminds Willem of Midwood's town square: brightly colored blocks that decrease in size as they get closer to the center.

This is as engaged in learning as I've ever seen him. It's as if his feet need to feel like they are traveling far from the horrors of the last few weeks as much as his mind does.

The lesson turns from a game of learning to a game of hiding. On any other day I would try to pull Willem back, remind him that he needs to focus on the task at hand. But I don't have the heart to do that. Not today. So I cover my eyes and count, listening as his footsteps grow distant and then disappear.

Searching for Willem in this house is like walking through a dreamscape. I open doors that lead to nowhere, walk through a passageway that has a window in the floor with a view straight down to a sitting area on the bottom level, and find a room decorated with hundreds of different-colored crystal baubles that dangle from the ceiling.

"Willem," I call, "where are you?"

I open a closet door and find a row of ball gowns; all of them are floor-length and covered with various embellishments—sequins, feathers, pearls, flower petals. Not one of them looks as if it's ever been worn. I wonder if Audra's bone readings have nudged her toward clothing purchases, too.

This seems like the kind of place a little boy might choose to hide.

I push the dresses aside. But instead of a solid wall, I find a set of double doors, the kind that might normally grace the entry of a fine home. They appear to be made of walnut, and the top half is inset with frosted glass. I turn the handle.

"Willem? Are you in here?"

I push the door open the rest of the way and my breath catches. The room is filled with bones—hundreds of them, carefully labeled and displayed under glass. But these aren't ordinary bones. These have already been prepared by a Handler—they've been bleached bright by sunlight, and they are painted to match the colorful tattoos of their owners.

It's a bone museum.

I step up to one of the cases and lay my hand against the

glass. Inside is a femur painted with three purple slash marks, a skull with orange coils across the top, a clavicle with a row of flowers. Each bone is labeled with a name, a gender, an age at the time of death. None of these bones came from people in Midwood, and as far as I can tell, none of the people they belonged to are related to Audra.

So why does she have them?

Something in the corner of the room catches my eye. A case with the top off, as if the display is still in progress.

Inside is a bone with a tattoo I would know anywhere.

A drumbeat starts in my center and grows so loud, it's all I can hear, all I can feel. It's as if my heart is beating everywhere all at once—in my chest, my throat, my ears.

I go to the case and run my fingers along my father's humerus, trace the jewel-tone waves that Oskar so carefully painted to match his mastery tattoo.

A sudden, sharp tug in my stomach makes the room tilt. I squeeze my eyes closed and my father's face appears behind my lids. It feels exactly like falling into a premonition. My pulse spikes and I yank my hand away. This can't be happening. My tendencies for magic should be disappearing by now. I didn't have a binding ceremony, and I've never heard of an unmatched affinity lasting for this long beyond the kenning. I pull in slow, deliberate breaths and let my fear recede. When it does, I'm filled with an ache so strong, it brings tears to my eyes. This isn't a prisoner whose memories will haunt me. This is my father— and I'd do *anything* to see him again.

Even bone magic.

I scoop up the humerus and cradle it in my arms. Then I close my eyes and allow myself to be swept away. My father's face appears again, a paintbrush in his hand and a canvas in front of him. He smiles as a younger version of me enters the room.

"What do you think, bluebird?"

It's a painting of my mother. She's seated on a swing that hangs from a giant oak tree. Her bare toes point toward the sky and her head is thrown back in laughter, pale hair streaming behind her. I've never seen her look that carefree in real life.

"I love it," I tell him.

His smile is radiant. "The two of you look so much alike, don't you think?"

Too soon, the vision fades and bittersweet pain blazes through me, burning away every emotion until there's nothing left but rage. Audra has no right.

I storm out of the room and slam the door behind me. The sound brings Willem running.

"Did you get lost, Saskia? *Everyone* gets lost in our house." He notices the bone in my arms, and his eyes go wide. "You have to put that back. Mama won't like that you touched it."

I duck to avoid hitting my head on the crystal globes dangling from the ceiling. "I don't care what your mother likes," I snap.

He sucks his lower lip into his mouth. I sigh and remind myself that he's just a child. It's not my place to tell him that his mother is a thief and maybe even a murderer, though I long to shout the words at someone—*anyone*—if it will quiet the thoughts inside my head. My mind is like a hive of bees—noise and chaos and worries so frantic, they blend together into a low buzz. But Willem is no more responsible for his mother's actions than I am for mine.

"Everything will be fine," I tell him as we walk back to the front of the house. "Now, why don't you go to your room for a bit?"

Through the large window, I spot Audra walking across the lawn toward the door. My heart leaps into my throat. It's too late to leave without her seeing me. I can either put the bone back and report her to the town council later—let them recover the bone and mete out an appropriate punishment—or I can confront her now. If this were any other bone, I would avoid an altercation with Audra and run toward safety like I always do. But it's my *father*. I won't leave any part of him here one moment longer than necessary.

I imagine myself flying across the room when Audra opens the door, pinning her against the wall and pressing my father's bone to her throat until she tells me what I want to know.

But when I finally hear the key in the lock, something inside me goes very still. I sit down, my back as straight as the edge of a blade, and place my father's humerus across my lap. Audra saunters into the room with several bags slung over both arms. She startles when she sees me. And then her gaze drifts to the bone.

"What do you think you're doing with that?" Her voice is shrill. The bags slide to the floor.

"I think you're the one who needs to answer that question."

Audra narrows her eyes. Her lips twist cruelly. "How *dare* you?"

"This was stolen from the bone house a few weeks ago." My voice is calm and even. Fury has gathered inside me, focusing into a sharp, icy point that I'm ready to use as a weapon. "The town council has been searching for the culprit, so they can mete out the appropriate punishment."

Audra blanches. My words have found their mark.

"You know what they do to bone thieves, don't you?" I ask.

She fingers the jewels at her neck. "I didn't steal that bone, Saskia. I—"

"They hang them."

Audra presses a palm to her chest as if she's trying to hold her pounding heart in place. "I didn't steal *anything*. I bought that bone at a fair price—more than fair—and it belongs to me."

And just like that, my anger explodes inside me, breaks into a thousand jagged pieces that feel as if they've sliced into every part of me. "It belonged to my father!"

Audra pulls in a quick breath. "No, that can't be right. . . ."

I stand up so fast that my chair topples over. "Where are the rest of them?"

She backs away from me until her back is pressed against the window. "The rest of them? I don't know what you're talking about."

"All of my father's remains were taken from the bone house. I want them back."

Something in Audra's demeanor changes. She straightens. Her expression grows distant. "Well, I only bought the one bone."

"*Where* did you buy it?"

She gives me a tight smile. "I'm afraid that's none of your business."

"None of my business? It's my father's bone. It belongs to my family."

"How was I to know it was stolen? If a crime was committed, it wasn't by me."

Suddenly the pieces fall into place. If only this one bone had been stolen, who else could the town council blame? But the other missing bones give her cover. She must be telling the truth. She doesn't know where the rest of them are.

A weight settles in my stomach. I think of my father, who loved games. He always said the secret to winning was understanding not only your own greatest strength, but also your opponent's greatest weakness—and then finding a way to pit the two against each other.

My mind scrambles for a way to shift the power balance again. To loosen Audra's tongue. "I guess my mother was right. You won't be needing a tutor for Willem anymore."

Audra's expression freezes. She blinks.

"What do you mean? Of course he needs a tutor."

I gather my bag and head toward the door. "That's not what the bones say."

Audra grabs my arm and spins me around. Her eyes are wild. "Your mother did a reading?"

I throw her own words back in her face. "I'm afraid that's none of your business."

"Saskia, please." Audra's voice is all softness and honey now. "Did your mother really do a reading?"

I hesitate and pretend to consider her request. I think of Gran's warnings about liars, and then close my heart against her memory. If this is what I have to do to find my father's bones, then I will. Even if it costs me my honor.

"How do you think I knew where to find the bone?"

I should be ashamed at the stab of satisfaction I feel when fear creeps over her expression, but I'm not. "What else did the reading show?"

"I shouldn't say," I tell her, which I know will only make her more desperate.

Her gaze drops to the bone in my hand. "I didn't know it was your father's. I'm sorry."

She's not. It's a manipulation to get what she wants, but Audra isn't the only one who knows the rules of that game.

"My mother saw two paths. One where you help me find my father's bones. The other where you don't and something terrible happens to you." I pause. "And Willem."

Audra's face goes slack. "What is it? What happens?"

I shake my head. "I don't know. She thought it would distress me too much if she gave me the details. So, Audra, which path are you going to choose?"

"But how can I help you? I don't know who stole the bones or where they are now."

She's avoiding the question I've already posed. I ask again: "Where did you buy this? Who sold it to you?"

Audra swallows. A sheen of sweat glistens on her upper lip. "I can't tell you that."

I give her what I hope is a sad smile. "No, my mother didn't think you would. Will you tell Willem that I'll miss him?"

I don't wait for her answer before I leave. I'm halfway out the door when her footsteps rumble behind me.

"Wait." The word scratches from her throat. Feral. As if it cost her something to say it.

I turn. Raise my eyebrows.

"There's a merchant ship that sometimes docks nearby. They sell wares that are . . . unconventional."

"By unconventional, you mean stolen?"

She dries her palms on the hem of her shirt. "No . . . I mean"—she motions toward my father's humerus—"obviously some of them are. But others are . . . frowned upon."

"How do I find the ship?"

"It docks somewhere new each night. You can't find it without a contact."

"You can be my contact," I tell her.

She shakes her head. "No. That's not possible."

"Do you prefer the alternative path?"

We're interrupted by the thundering of small footsteps on the stairs. "Hi, Mama," Willem says. And then to me: "What's an alternative path?"

Audra's gaze skips between me and her son. Her fingers twist together.

"Your mother is taking me on an adventure this evening," I say brightly. "I'll tell you all about it the next time I come to tutor you."

Audra's shoulders slump. As with everything else in her life, her freedom has been snatched away by her fear of the bones.

She knows she has no choice. "We'll leave at nightfall," she says.

For the first time since this conversation began, I take a deep breath. *I'm coming for you, Papa.*

Saskia
The Bone Charmer

The next time I meet with Latham, he has an extra bone on the table.

"Since you couldn't see anything during our last attempt, I thought we'd try this." His hands are splayed in front of him, and I notice a faded red tattoo around his wrist, as if he loved someone once a very long time ago.

He tracks my gaze to the tattoo, and a flicker of pain crosses his expression. "She was . . ." He gives his head a little shake. "Never mind, it's ancient history."

"Did she die?" As soon as the question is out of my mouth, I wish I could take it back. It's far too personal, and I feel heat rushing to my cheeks.

"No, nothing like that. I loved her, but the rules of the Grand

Council didn't allow us to be together. Like I said, it was a long time ago. Now, should we get started?"

But the comment nags at me. What rules would prevent a couple in love from being together? Unless the girl he loved was matched to someone else—and she wanted to accept the pairing? Maybe he was in love with her, but she didn't return his affections?

Latham clears his throat and my attention snaps back to him.

I examine the bone between us. It's larger than any we've ever worked with before—a femur, probably from an adult man. "What does it do?" I ask. "Is it another practice bone?"

"Of a sort," he says. "It's called an intensifier. All of the practice bones we've been using are intensifiers, but this one is particularly potent. Using it during a reading should increase both your power and your range."

"My range?"

"Every Bone Charmer has a limit to how far they can see. One person with Third Sight might be able to see only a year or two into the future, while someone more gifted might be able to see several decades. The same goes for a Bone Charmer with First Sight—how far they can reach into the past is determined by their range. For you, the intensifier should stretch your ability to see a bit in both directions. If you usually have a range of only a few hours, it will let you see forward or backward a few days, or even a few months."

Another thing Master Kyra hasn't bothered to mention. A well of resentment bubbles up inside me. I can't help but wonder if she sees so little promise in me that she doesn't think I'm worth her best efforts.

I think about confessing that I actually *did* see a brief vision during my last attempt, but I don't want to risk Latham putting the intensifier away. I'm curious what will happen if I use it. My training with Master Kyra has been painfully boring over the past few weeks and I'm craving a challenge.

"Do I need to do anything special to use it?"

"No," he says. "It works just like any other bloodless reading. You'll need to be in contact with the training bones and the intensifier the entire time."

I take a deep breath. I'm determined to see Ami. I've been thinking about her all afternoon, letting memories of her tumble around my mind—her raven hair, her easy smile, the way she bounces on her toes when she's excited. I hope it will help me see her more clearly during the reading.

"Ready?" Latham asks.

I nod and I lay my palms across the bones, making sure I'm touching all of them. I close my eyes. The pull in my stomach is almost instant.

Ami. Long hair falling across her face. Green apron coated in a fine layer of white dust hanging around her neck. She leans against the counter at the bone house, her elbows propping up her chin. Her cheeks are flushed pink. She's smiling.

"You've been here every day this week," she says. "If you're not careful, I'm going to think you're just showing up to flirt with me."

"But what if I *am* just showing up to flirt with you?"

Declan. The sight startles me so much, I'm yanked out of the vision. I'm suddenly aware of the feel of the bones beneath my palms. Of the breeze blowing in from the open window. Of the swell of homesickness that pushes against my rib cage. Ami hasn't mentioned in any of her letters that Declan has been hanging around the bone house. Maybe she's worried about how I'd feel? Declan and I were seeing each other before the kenning. But I haven't thought about him since I arrived at Ivory Hall. Not once.

"You've lost your focus." Latham's voice pulls me back to the task at hand. He taps the bone clasp at his collar. "Don't allow your attention to wander."

"Sorry," I say. I clear my mind and concentrate on finding Ami again. But before I can conjure up a clear picture of her, I'm swept away in another vision.

A large room with long benches against each wall. Dirt floors covered in a layer of straw. Two boys facing off against each other in the center of a ring. One is tall and muscular with short-cropped hair and a fierce expression. A ragged tattoo that looks like the edge of a saw loops around his neck.

The other boy is Bram.

The vision slips and tilts as if my mind has stepped on a sheet of solid ice. I start to pull away. *Don't fight it.* Latham's words reach me like they're coming from a distant mountaintop—I can barely hear them, even as they echo with authority.

The boys circle each other as their mentors yell instructions from the sidelines. *Look for an opening. His weakness is your opportunity. Strike.*

Bram reaches into a small velvet pouch filled with tiny bones that hangs from a belt at his waist. He pinches a bone between his thumb and forefinger and bends it slightly. His opponent grimaces and cradles his elbow.

Bram's expression is sharp. He watches the other boy carefully, not pulling his gaze away for a moment, even as his fingers rummage through the pouch. He finds the bone he's looking for and squeezes it in the center.

His opponent snarls, reaches into the pouch at his waist, and snaps one of the bones in half.

Bram groans and crumples to the ground. His face has gone pale and his breaths are coming in jagged gasps. His left leg is bent at an unnatural angle.

"Unacceptable!" shouts Bram's mentor, storming into the ring. He turns to his colleague. "Darius, your apprentice is out of control."

Master Darius turns to the boy with the sawlike tattoo. "Ease off, understand? You can do plenty of damage without actually breaking the bone."

The boy shrugs. "But it's so much more fun to break things." His expression makes me want to slap him. My hands curl around the bones beneath my palms.

"Have a seat," Master Darius says. "You're sidelined for now." Then he turns to Bram's mentor. "You're being a little soft. We're teaching them to be warriors. Not diplomats."

"Yes, and your apprentice needs to learn that there's a difference between being a warrior and a brute. He'd do well to practice a little self-control."

I listen to the two men argue with a growing dismay. No one is helping Bram. His lips are pressed together as if he's trying to keep himself from crying out. His fingers curl around handfuls of straw. I try to surge forward, and then remember I'm not really here. That I can't call for a Healer, that I can't go to Bram and promise that he'll be all right.

The vision goes black around the edges as if I'm moving backward through a tunnel. The last thing I see is Bram's face go slack, his eyes slide closed.

I gasp as Latham's office materializes around me. Stark white walls, a gentle breeze rippling over my skin.

"It seems you've had success," Latham says.

I nod. But the sensation inside me is hollow—it feels far more like defeat than victory.

"Did you see something unpleasant?" Latham asks. "Tell me."

"Yes," I say. "One of the other apprentices. A boy from Midwood. He was hurt in his training."

It isn't until Latham's face falls that I recognize how hopeful he'd looked before. "Did I do something wrong?" I ask.

"No." He shakes his head. "No, of course not. I just assumed you'd see your mother, that's all."

My gaze flits to his wrist and the pale tattoo there.

"You remind me of her," he says, as if reading my thoughts.

"Only in appearance," I tell him. "We've never been very much alike otherwise."

"I suspect you and your mother have more in common than you might think."

But he's wrong. He doesn't know me well enough to compare me to my mother. And I might tell him so if not for the pit in my stomach, the gnawing need to find out what happened after Bram closed his eyes.

Lessons have been over for an hour, but the training corridors are still bustling with noise—apprentices standing in clusters, bragging about the successes of the day, Masters grumbling to one another about the failures, the rustle of dozens of cloaks as people shift and move.

But Bram isn't here.

I wander through the men's dormitory, the training wing, the dining hall, and even the infirmary, but I can't find him.

Panic flutters in my chest like a bird held too tightly.

I tell myself that my worry has nothing to do with Bram specifically, that I would be wandering these halls searching for any apprentice I saw injured. I don't even need to speak to Bram. I'll feel better if I can just get a glimpse of him, enough to know he's breathing, that his wounds have been healed.

The temptation to go back to Latham dances at the edge of my mind like a bit of meat held out to a puppy. I could ask to do another reading. I could actually try to see Bram this time instead of resisting. But the thought of opening up to Latham like that, trusting him with my worries—I can't do it. It's one thing to accept his help with training, but sharing something personal feels like crossing a line.

I think of the training bones in my room. I haven't attempted to use them on anyone but myself. Without another source of blood, it's been my only option, so I've focused more time on the stolen spell book. Now that I know about bloodless readings and have some experience with focusing the magic, the bones could prove far more useful.

My feet start moving before I've consciously made a decision—they carry me back to the women's dormitory. I pause outside the door and listen. If I'm not alone, I won't be able to do a reading.

Tessa isn't here. My breath sags from me.

I kneel down and search for where I've hidden the bones under my bed. I pull out the box, the spell book, a velvet cloth. My heart beats a staccato rhythm as I flip through page after page until I find the "well-being" spell I'm looking for. I arrange the bones just as they are on the pages—each bone touching at the center point and fanning out like the spokes of a wheel.

I place my hand over the bones and close my eyes, letting Bram's face fill my mind—strong jaw, dark eyes, a messy mop of chestnut hair. The magic starts to tow me under when an image of Bram's hands floats into my memory.

A sensation needles across my skin like ice. My fingers tremble, itch to move away from the bones and end the reading, but I force them to stay. I nudge my thoughts toward Bram's face. I think of the day of the bone race—the concentrated set of his mouth as he worked, lips slightly pursed, his triumphant expression when we were the first to finish, the sharp hurt in his eyes when I refused to acknowledge that we'd worked well together. I don't have time to process my regret before I'm swiftly pulled into a vision.

Bram walks on the grounds outside Ivory Hall. His hands are stuffed into the pockets of his black cloak, and he looks lost in thought. I study him for any sign of injury—a hint of favoring his right leg, a limp, a wince as he lands on his left. But I don't find anything. Physically, he looks to be in perfectly good health. I keep watching. He softly kicks a pebble and watches it roll down the hill. He sits on a low stone wall and puts his head in his hands.

The vision fades. I don't feel any of the pleasure I thought I might at completing my first bloodless reading. I'm not sure what I was expecting, but somehow witnessing such an unguarded, private moment makes me feel untethered instead of triumphant. I scoop the bones into my palm and deposit them in the box. Close the spell book. Put everything back in my hiding spot.

I sit on the edge of my bed and stare at the bone-white walls without really seeing them.

Bram isn't hurt—that's all that matters. Not the lack of color in this room. Not the sinking sense of disappointment over something I can't quite name.

Maybe my readings are inaccurate. Maybe Bram was never hurt at all. Maybe he's sitting in his room at this very moment.

There's only one way to find out. I slide my arms into my cloak and rush out the door.

Bram is exactly where the bones said he would be.

He sits with his back to me on a low stone wall overlooking the city. The sun is setting and the horizon is blood orange. With his chestnut hair and his black cloak, he looks like a smudge against the vibrant sky.

If I leave now, he'll never know I was here.

I don't.

I take a step toward him. The toe of my boot catches a stray rock, sending it skittering across the cobbles. Bram turns, and for a fraction of a moment, his expression is utterly blank, as if his mind hasn't caught up to his eyes. And then surprise washes over his features. "Saskia," he says, "what are you doing here?" He moves to make room for me and I sit beside him.

"I was worried about you," I say.

He cocks his head to one side. A question.

"Second Sight."

His expression changes. He looks at me warily. "You saw me?"

"I did," I say. "You were training. You got hurt."

"I get hurt every day. That shouldn't be a shock under the circumstances."

My cheeks heat. I look away and study the city that lies beneath us, at the lights that spill across the valley, and wonder how many people are laughing at this very moment. How many are mourning? How much of what's happening has a Bone Charmer already seen?

"Is your leg feeling better?"

"My leg?" He shifts on the wall. "I didn't hurt my leg."

"You didn't?" I turn toward him and he laughs at my surprise. The sound is deep, melodious. It makes my stomach rise and fall.

"Maybe you need more practice," he says, nudging my shoulder with his.

"Probably," I say. But then realization settles on me like a layer of frost. The intensifier. Latham said it would increase my range. Maybe what I saw hasn't happened yet. "Is there a Bone Breaker with a jagged tattoo on his neck? One that looks like a saw?"

"That would be Viktor," Bram says. "He's built like a mountain and has a temperament of a bear who's just been shot in the hindquarters with an arrow."

I smile. "Not a great disposition for a Breaker."

"Oh, you know us Breakers. We're all brutes." He says it lightly, but there's a note of bitterness in his voice.

The air between us chills. And it's all the more biting because of the warmth that came before.

I find a loose thread at the hem of my sleeve and wrap it around my finger. "Be careful of him," I say.

Bram's gaze finds mine. "I don't need your advice." His voice is soft in the way a snake moving through the grass is soft—quiet, but still dangerous. It stirs up memories of the same words coming from my own mouth. I resented it every time my mother gave me a warning based on a reading. Her admonitions always felt like ropes tying me down, binding me to one path or another. And now, as I look into Bram's defiant eyes, I wonder if she felt the same helpless sensation I do now.

My mother's advice always felt like her trying to impose her choices on me. But maybe she was only warning me to be careful of my own.

I stand up and brush invisible wrinkles from my cloak. "Viktor doesn't fight fair," I say. "Just be careful."

He makes a soft noise that indicates he heard but promises nothing.

"And, Bram?" I touch his shoulder. "I don't think you're a brute."

As I say it, I realize it's true. My perception of him has gradually shifted over the last few weeks. Like the way darkness moves toward dawn in hundreds of small moments—each one looking identical to the one before—until suddenly you open your eyes and find the world transformed.

I'm still not sure who Bram is, but I know he's not who I thought he was on the day of the kenning.

My fingers fold over the top of his scapula. "I'm sorry that I misjudged you." I swallow. The next words are harder to say. "And I'm especially sorry if I let other people misjudge you too."

He lifts his hand, and for just a moment I think he intends to touch me. That he will place his hand over mine, and we'll be able to start over. But he rakes his fingers through his hair instead. Chooses a different path. Drops his hand to his lap.

I let my fingers slip from his shoulder. And I walk away without saying goodbye.

Saskia
The Tutor

Audra's small boat glides silently through the still black waters of the Shard. The two of us sit facing each other, though we don't speak, don't meet each other's eyes. The only sound is the gentle splash of the oars as two of Audra's servants row us toward a town I've never visited.

In the distance I can see the ship, nothing more than a dark shape against the night sky. I've been running from danger for years, and now here I am sailing toward it. But if there's even a chance to find out what happened to the rest of my father's bones, I have to take the risk. I adjust the hood of my gray cloak to make sure that my face is in shadow.

"You won't get close enough to see anything if you're recognizable," Audra said before we left. "And if we get caught once we're on board, they won't let us leave alive."

My braids are pinned at the back of my head, and a dark scarf covers my bright hair. I wear a pair of Audra's satin elbow-length gloves to hide the petal-shaped tattoo on my thumb.

Audra is often surrounded by servants, so her showing up to the shadow market with a maid to help her carry her purchases won't be unusual. But it's still risky. Even though we're unlikely to see anyone from Midwood, it's not impossible. Someone stole those bones, which required at least one visit to our town.

Maybe I should have gone to my mother and the rest of the council instead of chasing down a ship full of criminals. But it's hard enough to get scraps of information from my mother about my own life. She'd shut me off from this completely.

I think of all the things that might go wrong—my hood could fall and expose my face. Someone might recognize me even in disguise. Audra could slip and give us away—she's far from the steadiest person I've ever met.

Her thoughts must be dancing with my own, because she leans forward. "This is a terrible idea. It's not too late to turn back."

She can't lose her nerve now. She holds my life in her palms.

"If we turn back, your fate is sealed." The reminder fastens her lips together as surely as if I had smeared them with hot wax. She straightens and looks away.

We pull alongside the dock, and the two oarsmen hold the boat steady while we disembark. Audra leans toward me and hisses in my ear. "Keep your head down and don't speak. Not a word."

The pier is populated with a half dozen men. If I didn't know that the ship in port housed an illegal shadow market, I would think nothing of the scene before me—one man out for a bit of late-night fishing, two others deep in conversation, a fourth gazing out over the water lost in thought, as if he's nursing a broken heart or worrying about how to pay off a debt.

Instead I see the men for what they are—sentries, strategically placed to guard the ship from every direction.

Audra makes eye contact with one of the men and touches a finger to her temple. He acknowledges her with a subtle dip of his chin. We've been granted access.

I follow Audra up the gangplank, my heart thundering so loudly in my chest that I'm sure the first person I encounter will hear it, suspect me, stop me, and rip the hood from my head. But when we make it to the top, the deck is vacant and as ominously quiet as a graveyard. I'm about to ask Audra what's going on when she cuts me a sharp, silencing look.

As we round the corner, I see the reason for her glare. The main deck isn't completely empty after all. A man sitting in a wooden chair guards the ladder that leads belowdecks. His fingers are interlaced behind his head and he's leaning back—balancing the chair on only two legs. When he sees us, he stands and the chair lands on the deck with a thud.

"Lady Ingersson," he says, "back so soon?"

She gives a light laugh as if she doesn't have a care in the world. "What can I say? I have an insatiable appetite for fine merchandise."

"And excellent taste, too." He peers around her to get a

glimpse of me. "Who's your friend?"

Audra waves a dismissive hand in front of her face. "Not a friend. A maid. I can't really be expected to carry all my own bags, can I?"

"I'm supposed to clear any new patrons with the boss. She better wait up here with me until you've finished your business."

"She's not a *patron*, Max." Audra's voice drips with disdain. "She's a servant. Now, if you'll please let us pass. I don't have all night."

Max shifts on the balls of his feet. He runs a hand across his brow.

"I spend more than your next ten customers combined," Audra says. "I'd think twice before you turn me away."

Max sighs and steps aside. "Fine. But next time—"

Audra pushes past him without waiting for the end of the sentence, and I scurry behind her, positive I look exactly like a timid maid would.

We descend the ladder and step into another world—one bustling with people talking in hushed voices, stalls overflowing with merchandise, men and women sitting at tables, eating, drinking, silently laughing at whispered jokes. It's the kind of setting that should be bursting with noise. But instead it's a vision of chaos with the sounds of a sober garden party. The juxtaposition is unsettling.

Lanterns hang from hooks on the walls, casting the market in flickering light that only adds to the eeriness.

I keep my face in the shadow of my hood as I examine the stalls we pass. One has trays full of rare gems—probably stolen, since each is one of a kind, and some are set in jewelry with initials already carved into the gold. Another stall has potions made from bone powder—some that promise to cure illness, others that guarantee beauty, potions that claim to deepen feelings, and potions that claim to make you stop feeling at all.

We pass a vender selling artifacts made of bone—plates and spoons, sculptures and wreaths. Bile rises in the back of my throat. Now I truly understand my mother's frustration with the way Audra spends her coin. Before I started working with Audra, I never gave much thought to the way bones were used, but now, thinking of how some are drinking from teacups made of bone while others are too poor to afford a proper kenning makes me feel ill. The shelves are brimming with merchandise. How many bones were sacrificed so that the wealthy can flaunt their riches? How many children grew up without the benefit of seeing where their paths might lead so these bones could be molded into something useless?

I shove my hands into the pockets of my cloak to keep them still. I have a nearly irresistible urge to take a swing at the display, to send all these profane trinkets tumbling to the ground and watch them smash into a thousand pieces.

The next stalls are worse.

Kenning bones priced by how powerful their owners were—metacarpals that claim to be from a Bone Healer, phalanges that promise they belonged to a Bone Mason. They're obviously stolen, since those without deceased family of their own can buy kenning bones from the market in the town square. Honest people don't need to sneak like a thief in the night to get them.

Another vendor sells stolen memories. A sign in his stall reads: EXPERIENCE THE DANGER, WITHOUT THE RISK! The memories are trapped inside small bones that are housed in colorful glass containers of various shapes and sizes. They are labeled by event: GO OVER A WATERFALL IN A WOODEN BARREL! CLIMB TO THE TOP OF MOUNT OSTA! SWIM WITH A WHALE! MAKE LOVE TO A BEAUTIFUL WOMAN!

My fingernails curl into my palms, cut half-moon shapes into my flesh. These memories were extracted from real people.

Audra reaches for my elbow. "Hurry along now," she says in a singsong voice. But then she pinches me. Hard. My horrified gawking must be drawing attention. She leads me through row after row of stalls until finally she stops.

I lift my eyes and my ribs collapse around my heart. My father's bones are displayed as unceremoniously as apples at a fruit stand—his ribs, his skull, baskets full of the bones from his fingers and toes. A sign on the wall proclaims: EXPERTLY PREPARED BONES! MULTIPLE USES!

Anger fractures my vision. I suddenly understand the desire that drives someone to violence.

Audra looks at me over her shoulder as if to say, *You've seen them. Now let's go.*

"Buy them," I say.

Panic sparks in her eyes. "Pardon me?" Her voice is indignant.

"Buy them all."

Audra grabs my elbow and drags me out of hearing range of the vendor. "That wasn't part of our bargain," she says.

I fix her with an icy glare. "Either you buy every single one of those bones or I will make a scene so big that this whole ship will know you're a traitor."

She swallows. Her eyes are filled with both hatred and fear, but we both know which emotion will win. She pulls out her coin purse and makes her way back to the vendor.

"I'll take the entire set," she says.

The vendor gives a low whistle. "I can't sell you all of them, lady. We'll be out of stock."

"My coin is as good as anyone else's," Audra says haughtily. "What does it matter?"

He leans forward and rests his elbows on the counter. "It matters because if other patrons come by and I have nothing to show, they might not come back again, understand?"

I'm about to yank my cloak off and cause a scene when another voice comes from the back of the stall.

"Go ahead and sell them. We have more coming in soon."

There's something familiar about the voice, but I can't quite place it over the low murmur that buzzes through the rest of the market. I sidle closer to Audra and try to get a better look, but the back of the stall is too dark to see more than a shadow.

The vendor turns toward the voice. "You're sure about that?"

"I'm sure," he says. "Another full collection arrives tomorrow, and then in a few weeks we'll score big. We just took down a Mixer in Midwood."

My blood runs cold and my knees go weak. They're talking about Rakel, about murdering her for her bones. And that voice—

It belongs to Declan.

209

Audra buys the bones. The vendor puts them in a burlap sack—the kind used for holding the dead. He gives the bag to me, as if I really am Audra's maid, as if he isn't handing me my own stolen heart. I clench my jaw, grind my teeth together to prevent myself from spitting in his face. I keep my head ducked inside my hood, and I don't let my gaze wander to the back of the stall, where Declan lingers in the dark.

Silently, I carry the bag out of the shadow market and wrest it into Audra's small boat. Her servants row us away. When the ship is out of sight, I lean over the side of the boat and vomit.

I tell myself that it wasn't cowardice that prevented me from launching over the counter and fixing my arms around Declan's neck. I tell myself that I have vital information to bring to the town council. Information that I can't share if I'm dead. I tell myself a lot of things. But the trouble is, I can't tell the truth from the lies.

I think of Declan's hand sliding into mine. Of his breath against my neck as he told me he'd fallen for me. Of the hopeful way I've examined my wrist each day for any sign of a love tattoo.

Nausea threatens again. My thoughts chase one another around until I'm dizzy with them. How could I have been so stupid? Am I such a bad judge of character? And then a terrible thought—one that slices through me like a blade—what price would my bones garner on the shadow market? Especially if someone thought—months ago—that there was a chance I would be matched as Bone Charmer at the kenning. How valuable would my mother's bones be?

It must be so much easier to kill someone who trusts you.

Audra doesn't speak all the way back to Midwood, which is probably for the best. Something dark and ugly is growing inside me. I can feel the rustle of its wings.

The boat slides alongside the dock, and I don't wait for Audra's servants to steady the craft before I scramble to my feet and lug my father's bones to shore. I heft the sack over my shoulder and start for home.

"Wait," Audra says. Against my better judgment, I turn. Her gaze darts to the bag. "You'll need to provide payment for those."

My blood turns to fire in my veins. "Fate will pay you back, Audra. I'm counting on it."

My mother sits in a chair by the fire, an oil lamp burning low on a nearby table. Her spell book rests on her lap, but her palm is pressed firmly on top of the leather cover, as if her instinct is to protect it even in sleep.

I clear my throat and she stirs. Her eyes flutter open and then go wide with fear. She flies to her feet. The spell book tumbles to the ground. She grabs a poker from where it hangs near the hearth.

Suddenly I realize how I must look—hooded, gloved, a bag slung over my shoulder—as if I'm here to rob her, or worse.

"It's only me," I say.

"Saskia?" Her voice is still hazy with sleep and confusion. "You frightened me. Where have you been?"

I lower the burlap sack to the floor. "It's a long story."

"I tried to read the bones to find you," she says. "But I needed someone with Second Sight. You were too close to the present for me to see."

"I'm sorry." I take off the cloak, pull the scarf and the pins from my hair.

"You're crying," she says.

"No."

But when I touch my fingers to my cheek, the black satin comes away damp. I can't stand the feel of Audra's fancy gloves on my skin for a second longer. I strip them off one by one and throw them into the hearth. I watch as their fingers curl and melt. A bitter odor chokes the air.

My hands are sweaty and one of my knuckles is smudged with dye—how fitting that Audra would loan me a fabric that bleeds when it weeps.

I rub at the stain with my thumb, but it won't budge.

I bring my hand closer to my face and examine the mark. It's not dye. It's a small black tattoo. And it's shaped like a triangle.

Saskia
The Bone Charmer

I sit beneath the shade of an aspen tree, leaning back and resting my elbows in the cool grass. Tessa lies on her stomach next to me, quizzing me about the bones of feathered vertebrates. The gentle warmth of spring has given way to the heat of summer, which makes studying on the slopes surrounding Ivory Hall far more pleasant than being inside the stiflingly hot dormitory or in one of the training rooms. Talon and Linnea sit nearby, working with replicas of animal bones. They're practicing identifying them only by feel—an important skill for all of us, but especially for Linnea and the other Breakers. Which is why it's unfortunate that Bram isn't here. I try not to imagine where he might be, try not to think of him at all. He's obviously not interested in mending the rift between us. He made that perfectly clear the other night when I tried to apologize.

"Saskia?"

My head snaps up. I can tell by the impatient tone in Tessa's voice that it's not the first time she's said my name.

"Sorry," I say, "what was that?"

"You're so distracted today. Is everything all right?"

"I'm fine. My mind just wandered for a moment. Can you repeat the question?"

Tessa looks down at her book. "Name three birds whose serrated bills are often mistaken for teeth, and the primary magical uses for them."

I bite the inside of my cheek while I think. "The greylag goose, the toucan, and . . . the tooth-billed bowerbird?"

"Good," Tessa says. "Magical uses?"

I tap my fingers in the grass. "Mixers use them for potions that dissolve metal. . . . Are there more uses?"

"Masons use them to make knives," Talon calls out. His eyes are closed and he's feeling the contours of an alligator ulna.

"They do?"

"Yep," he says. "They're not the most powerful tools Masons make, but they're good for cutting through soft things. Like tomatoes."

Linnea laughs. "Only you would think to use magic for cutting food."

Talon gives her a goofy grin, his eyes still tightly closed. Linnea is studying him with open affection. It's an expression I've never seen on her before. Her cheeks are flushed pink and her eyes are particularly brilliant today. Emerald and arresting.

"I take my food very seriously." Talon's fingers close around one end of the bone. "Is this a forearm of some kind?"

"Be more specific," Linnea says.

"Radius?"

Linnea's mouth curves. "Nope."

Talon opens one eye and peeks at the bone. "I meant ulna."

"Cheater," Linnea says, swatting at his arm.

"Saskia is the one who cheated. She got her answer from me."

I start to protest, when Tessa glances over my shoulder and brightens. "Oh, good. Bram is coming."

I lift my elbows off the grass and sit up. Talon's easy banter created a delicate bubble of contentment around me, but the moment I spot Bram trekking down the hill, it pops like it's been jabbed with the swift prick of a pin. It's not just the way he holds himself—stepping stiffly and precisely like he's avoiding any nonessential movement—that makes me go still, but it's the raw expression on his face. The vulnerability.

He's hurt.

I'm on my feet before I remember deciding to stand.

"What happened?" I ask.

Bram's eyes meet mine. He gives me an odd look. "Viktor."

I think of the angle of his leg when I saw him in the vision. "Then how are you walking?"

I can sense the rest of the group watching us. Can practically feel the weight of their questions at my back.

Tessa breaks first. "What's going on?"

"Bram got hurt in training today," Linnea says. Her gaze

215

flicks to me. "But I'm not sure how Saskia knows about it."

"I saw it during a bone reading." I don't mention that I saw it days ago—so far back that it shouldn't have been possible for someone with Second Sight—and neither does Bram. Luckily, the others seem too concerned about him to ask more questions.

I turn to Bram. "In my vision your leg was broken."

He winces as he lowers himself to the grass. "Healers," he says, "good ones."

"So why are you still in pain?" Tessa asks.

"My mentor doesn't believe in pain control. He thinks learning to manage discomfort is an important part of my training."

"Oh, for goodness' sake. That's ridiculous." Tessa kneels in the grass next to him. "Saskia, I brought some bones with me. Would you grab them for me please?"

I find her satchel leaning against the tree trunk. "Do you need your spell book, too?"

"No," she says, "I have the pattern memorized. I just need the bones and a needle."

As I search through Tessa's bag, I can hear her asking Bram questions about his pain—where it hurts the most, how long he's been injured, what the other healer did to help him. Her voice is soft and soothing.

I find a needle and the small container of bones and hand them to her. Tessa places them in a pattern next to Bram and then pricks his finger and lets a few drops fall onto the bones. She touches his leg, running her palm from his hip to his ankle, softly at first and then more firmly.

Bram's expression looks like a man dying of thirst who's just been given a jug of water. Relief washes over him. And then so much bliss that it makes color rise in my cheeks.

Tessa sits back on her heals. "Is that better?"

He reaches up and catches her fingers in his. "Yes," he says. "Thank you."

I think of my hand on Bram's shoulder the other night and wish I hadn't put it there.

"Your improvement is remarkable, Saskia," Master Kyra says. I've just identified the total number of Masons in the training room next door and managed to eavesdrop on the Mixers' lesson across the hall.

In the last few weeks we've moved on to more and more challenging tasks, and between my sessions with Latham and my regular lessons, I finally feel like I'm making progress.

"At this rate, it won't be long until you get your mastery tattoo," Kyra says.

The comment feels like standing near the fire on a chilly day.

Our history books say there are three essential tattoos that indicate a life well lived: a love tattoo, which can be acquired from any especially strong bond, not necessarily just the romantic kind; a loss tattoo, which usually appears after the death of a loved one; and a mastery tattoo, which is the most unique and comes from high achievement in one's specialty. Those who die without all three are mourned especially intensely. Mastery tattoos are commonly the first to appear—many people achieve expertise in their discipline before finding a great love or losing someone close to them—but only the top apprentices achieve a mastery tattoo before they finish training.

I think of the jewel-tone swells on my father's right arm—a work of art that perfectly captured not only his skill as a painter but his joy as well. And my mother's mastery tattoo—a vertical oval inside a larger horizontal one, both framed by thick, arching lines on the top and the bottom. Like a cat's eye. It sits just below her shoulder, smaller and more reserved than my father's, but it suits her just as well.

"A mastery tattoo? Do you really think so?" I ask.

She gives me a rare smile. "I do. Shall we try another task?"

"Yes," I say. "Give me something challenging."

She taps her finger against her lips while she thinks. "Choose someone specific—someone here at Ivory Hall—and see if you can locate them." I start to close my eyes. "This is going to be more difficult," she warns. "Directing magic toward a specific person without the benefit of their blood is an advanced skill."

But Master Kyra doesn't know I've been practicing bloodless readings with Latham for weeks.

"How about Norah?" I ask.

Kyra laughs. "You never choose the easy path, do you? Norah will be wearing a shield. She'll be impossible to see."

"A shield?"

"A talisman crafted by a Mason that blocks magic. Most of the Masters wear them to protect against disgruntled apprentices. Imagine the damage an angry young Breaker could do. Or a Mixer who whips up a poison." She raises her eyebrows playfully. "Or a Bone Charmer who can spy on every private moment."

I wrinkle my nose. I have no desire to see Norah's private moments. "How about my roommate?"

"Very well. Give it a try."

I lay my palms flat on top of the bones. I picture Tessa as clearly as I can—her wide brown eyes, the curls that frame her face and cascade in a tumble down her back, the star-shaped tattoos on her neck, the comforting melody of her voice. The tug in my stomach tells me I'm close. Shadowy figures move in and out of my vision, but they don't solidify into anything recognizable.

Frustration invades my mind and the image breaks apart.

My hands twitch over the bones, but I leave them there. I can do this. I pay attention to my breath moving in and out of my body, to my lungs filling with air, and then deflating.

I try again.

A pull toward the bones. A silhouette—the contours of Tessa's curls falling across her face as she leans over something. But I can't go further. Trying to hold the image is like trying to hold water in my cupped palms. I can only manage for a few moments before it starts to seep away.

Sharp pain carves through my head. I bite my lip and try to hang on, but it's no use. The vision is already fading.

I lift my hands and lean back in my chair. My temples throb, and when I open my eyes, the room looks red-tinged and blurry.

"You did well for a first try," Master Kyra says. "What do you think went wrong?"

The pounding in my skull is relentless. It makes it difficult to think clearly. "I don't know," I say. "I just couldn't get a clear image. Maybe I could have done it with an intensifier."

Kyra's breath is a hiss. "What did you say?"

"I just . . ." The expression on her face makes the words die in my throat. Her palms flatten against the table, and her eyes are wild. I should have told her about Latham's extra lessons. I don't know why I didn't. At first, each time I was tempted to bring it up, I stopped myself, worried she would put an end to my sessions with him. And then later, when I actually started making progress, I wanted Master Kyra to be impressed with me, to think I'd gotten better all on my own. Now I can see that was a mistake.

"Have you been using an intensifier in your practice?"

"I didn't mean any harm," I say. "I was just trying to get better."

"Dark magic should never be a shortcut to getting better." Her voice is only barely controlled. Like a rabid animal on the end of a taut leash.

Dread seeps into me. "I didn't know it was dark magic." My voice sounds small to my own ears.

Master Kyra's fist comes down on the table. "Intensifiers are the darkest kind of magic. You must know how they're made if you've been able to get your hands on one."

It's as if her anger is pulsing in my head. I feel it throbbing at the base of my skull.

"No," I say, "I don't."

Her gaze bores into me. "They can only be made from

the bones of a person who was murdered." She swallows. "Violently."

The words fall like blades. Nausea threatens at the back of my throat.

"No," I say. "That can't be true. Maybe I got the name of the bone wrong?"

"Where did you get an intensifier, Saskia?"

"I don't have one," I say. "Master Latham let me borrow his. He's been helping me with extra practice."

Kyra's mouth flattens to a thin, harsh line. I can feel her disbelief like a weight against my chest. "Please don't lie to me. The punishment for using dark magic is severe. Your honesty would go a long way toward lessening your sentence."

"My sentence? But I didn't know it was dark magic. Latham said—"

She holds up a hand. "I'm incredibly disappointed. This will have to be reported to Norah. She'll decide whether to bring the case to the Grand Council."

"Please," I say, "this is all a misunderstanding. Ask Latham. He'll corroborate everything I told you."

Sunlight pours through the window. Earlier I thought it seemed cheery, how it sent the dust motes dancing through the air suspended in golden warmth. But now it's harsh. Glaring. My clothes are pasted to my skin.

Master Kyra's gaze is steely. She doesn't believe me.

But she will. As soon as she talks to Latham, she will.

Two members of the Ivory Guard escort me to an assembly room. A long table fills the center of the space. Seated along one side are Norah and all three Bone Charming Masters. My breath sags out of me at the sight of Latham. He can explain and end all of this.

An empty chair waits for me on the other side of the table. I try to catch Latham's gaze as I take my seat, but he won't meet my eyes.

"Saskia," Norah says, not unkindly, "I'm sure you realize why you're here."

"Actually, I don't," I say. "Not entirely." My gaze settles on Latham. I wait for him to intercede, to offer a few words of explanation or apology.

He doesn't.

Certainty drains from me in one swift motion, like water from a tipped glass.

Norah gives me a searching look. "Is it true that you've been using intensifiers in your bone-reading practice?"

I sit straighter in my chair. I won't let them convict me of something I didn't do. "Master Latham approached me shortly after I arrived at Ivory Hall and offered me additional tutoring. He's the one who introduced the intensifier. I wasn't aware it was forbidden magic until Master Kyra told me earlier today."

Norah's glance slides to Latham, who shrugs. "Like I told you before, I have no idea what she's talking about."

I feel as if I've missed a step. As if the ground beneath my feet has abruptly disappeared and now there's nothing but air. His denial makes no sense. "Why are you lying?" I search Latham's face, try to find some hint of the mentor I've come to know, but he looks like a different man. The crinkles at the corners of his eyes have smoothed over, and his mouth—usually slightly upturned as if only moments away from a smile—is now a flat, hard line.

He leans forward and rests his arms on the table. "Whatever your plan is, it won't work. We have ways to find out the truth."

His words send a chill through me. We both know it's not the truth he's after, but I can't figure out what he gains by his dishonesty. Is helping another master's apprentice such a great offense?

Latham turns to Norah. "Have you searched her room?"

The blood drains from my face. Norah notices. I see her notice. See the shift in her expression. Watch as her sympathy fades away.

Understanding unfolds inside me. Latham isn't trying to protect himself. He's trying to implicate me.

"Search her room," Norah tells one of the guards, "and bring us anything relevant."

My throat closes off. I see the outcome as clearly as if I had Third Sight. When the guard searches my room, he'll find the stolen spell book and the stolen practice bones—two items that have nothing to do with Latham. Yet somehow I'm certain he knows they're there.

I'll look like a liar.

Latham's help was a shiny object I never should have touched. I didn't realize it was a weapon until it sliced into me and left me bleeding. Until it was too late.

The guard returns with the spell book and the box of bones and sets them in the middle of the table.

"Explain this," Norah says.

The silver box glitters. I resist the urge to reach for it, to trace my fingers along the raised pattern of the vines and roses one final time.

I swallow and thread my fingers tightly together. "I found them in the training room and took them for practice."

Master Kyra slides the box toward her and lifts the lid. Her eyebrows arch. "These didn't come from my training room."

I lift my gaze to hers. "They did."

A flicker passes over her expression, and for just a moment I think she might believe me. And then she sighs. "You had so much promise, Saskia. You didn't need to resort to this."

"I'm sorry I took the practice bones," I say. "It was a mistake. But you have to believe—"

"Practice bones? The bones we use in the workshop for study are practice bones. These"—her mouth thins as she looks at the box—"these are something else altogether. We never train with intensifiers."

"Latham told me they were practice bones. He said they'd help me progress faster." My gaze skips from Master Kyra to Norah to Master Yaffa, desperate for one of them to believe me. "How would I have known how to use these on my own? How would I have known about any of this if he hadn't told me?"

Latham clears his throat. "Perhaps you learned about it at home. Your mother is a Bone Charmer as well, is she not?"

Fury snakes through my veins. "You know she is. You trained with her."

Latham goes very still. "Oh," he says softly, "I think I understand what this is all about." He turns to the others. "Della Holte and I had somewhat of a rivalry during our days as apprentices. I considered it friendly competition, but I'm afraid Della didn't always see it that way. Perhaps she's aired her grievances to her daughter? Perhaps that's why my name was the first one to come to Saskia's lips when she was feeling cornered."

I fly to my feet. "How dare you? How dare you pin this on my mother when you've done nothing but scheme and connive since I got here?"

"Scheme and connive? I only realized who you were a few moments ago. Though I should have known as soon as you stepped into the room. You're an exact replica of your mother."

He said the same thing the day I met him. Yet he looks entirely innocent; his expression is as smooth as a pebble plucked from the bottom of the Shard.

"Someone must have seen us together," I say. "There has to be a way to find out that he's lying."

"There is a way," Norah says. "Yaffa?"

Master Yaffa pulls out a velvet cloth, a sewing needle, and a set of bones. "Let's have a look through your past, my dear." Relief floods through me. I've never been more eager to offer up my blood. I watch Master Yaffa's face as she does the reading, try to interpret every movement, every twitch. Is she seeing Latham offer to tutor me? Is she watching as he finds me in the workshop and asks me to come to his office? Tension coils inside me.

When Yaffa finally opens her eyes, her expression is blank for several long breaths. And then she turns to Norah and gives a subtle, sad shake of her head. How could she not have seen him in my past? How could he possibly have managed to trick a First Sight Bone Charmer?

The last of my hope trembles and tips. And like a goblet of spilled wine, it bleeds away drop by drop until there's nothing left.

Norah sighs and massages her temples. "I'm sorry, Saskia. We have no choice but to ask you to leave Ivory Hall. Your apprenticeship is terminated."

Saskia
The Tutor

I've heard my mother cry three times in my entire life. Once on the day Gran died. She held it together until I went to bed that night, until she dried my tears and listened to my memories. Later, when she thought I was asleep, I heard the muffled sobs from her bedroom—uncontrolled and forsaken.

She sounded exactly like a child who has lost her mother. The realization sunk in and rippled through me like a stone thrown into a tranquil lake—my mother was someone's child. She must feel like an orphan now.

Twice, I heard her cry over my father. The day he died, and again on the day we had his death ceremony and hung his body on the family tree. It was the day she pressed her last kiss on his temple, gazed on his face for the final time.

But I have never—until this moment—*seen* my mother cry.

It's as if her grief couldn't find full expression until it eased into relief. Silent tears creep down her cheeks as she empties the bag I laid at her feet. As she counts my father's bones to make sure they're all here. And they are, including the one I took from Audra's house.

The bones lie spread out on the floor between us, and so does the memory of my father. The ghost of his laugh. The faint smell of paint that always clung to him.

"You shouldn't have done this alone," she says, dabbing at her face with the hem of her sleeve. "You could have been hurt. Or killed."

"But I wasn't. So what do we do now?"

"We'll inform the town council and let them handle it."

Her gaze falls to my hands and I see her register the new tattoo that has appeared on my knuckle. "Oh, Saskia," she says sadly.

Shame shudders through me and I move my hand beneath me so the tattoo is covered. "I didn't hurt anyone," I say. "I only wanted to."

A crease forms between my mother's eyebrows. "Why would I think you hurt someone?"

The question takes me off guard. My thoughts slow. "The tattoo . . . I guess I always assumed it was for violence of some kind."

"No," she says softly, "it's a rare tattoo, so we don't talk about it much, but it usually means the owner has been betrayed. Saskia, what happened tonight?"

I think of the handful of times I've seen this tattoo before, and in a single wave, facts rearrange themselves in my mind. Like the tide pulling out seaweed and leaving shells behind.

"We can't inform the town council," I say. "Declan was there." Saying it out loud is a fresh shock. I assumed the tattoo appeared as a result of me picturing my hands around his throat, but it must have come from his betrayal.

"Declan was *where*?"

"At the shadow market." I swallow. "Not buying. Selling."

Her mouth tenses. I can see the cords in her neck. "Your father's bones?"

Guilt rises in my throat. For being the bearer of bad news. For not seeing Declan for who he is. For failing to be the daughter my mother wanted. "Yes."

Her gaze drops. She traces a slender finger along my father's shoulder blade the way she might have done when he was alive.

"You're not surprised," I say.

"No," she says. "I guess I'm not."

"Yet you matched me with him anyway." It's what I wanted at the time, but she is my mother. She is a Bone Charmer. She should have known better.

"It's complicated."

"How, Mother?" I ask. "*How* is it complicated?"

She doesn't answer, and her silence is thunderous inside my head.

"Why would you do this? Which one of Gran's bones told you to ruin my life?"

A sensation ripples up my spine. I think of the day of the

kenning. Of my mother's voice as she cradled the broken bone in her palm. *We've done this before.*

The same words sit on my tongue now—I taste them like bitter medicine. I can feel the echo of a similar moment trembling deep in my bones, and my mother's expression tells me she feels it too. Does this mean she was wrong when she said my timelines were different? In another reality, could we both be sitting in this same place having this same conversation?

I touch her wrist just above the love tattoo that has only grown darker since my father's death. "You matched me with a criminal. You put my life in danger. Don't you think you at least owe me an explanation?"

Silence stretches between us—dense with a lifetime of half-truths, and lies, and things left unsaid.

My mother sighs. "What is it you want to know?"

"The truth."

"It isn't as simple as that—not when it comes to bone reading. There are many truths, some more likely than others, all of them changeable, constantly shifting. Today's truth might be tomorrow's lie."

"Don't speak in riddles. You're not surprised that Declan was selling stolen bones. Why?"

"You forget that I've been performing readings on Declan since he was born. I know his character. He's a follower, not a leader. A boy who was always standing on the cusp between good and evil. He could have tipped either way."

I wonder what that must be like, peering into the same people's future over and over again, knowing what they're capable of, what they might do. What they could have done but didn't. Does she judge each person in town on choices they never made? Like she judges me for breaking Gran's bone when I didn't? Not this version of me, anyway.

"So why did you pair me with him?" My voice sounds soft and small. Like a plea.

I want her to say the bones showed her Declan and I could have had some great, sweeping love story, that he would have made me happier than anyone else, that I was the person who could pull him away from that cusp and fashion his life into something honorable and good.

But that's not what she says.

"Pairing you with him led to this moment, didn't it? To finding your father's bones? To uncovering the truth?"

"You used me to get the outcome you wanted?"

"No," she says, "it wasn't like that." But it was. I can see on her face that it was.

Sorrow blooms inside me. I was so worried at the kenning that my mother would match me as a Bone Charmer, nervous that she wouldn't care about my wishes. It hadn't occurred to me that she would give no thought to my safety, when safety was all I really wanted.

"Declan could have killed me," I tell her. "He still could."

"We'll report him to the rest of the town council. They'll either sentence him to death or send him to Fang Island. He won't be a danger to you."

"It won't work," I say. "Someone on the council is helping him."

231

Her brows arch. "What makes you think that?"

"The truth serum. He lied after he took it. He was selling Papa's bones on the shadow market. Obviously he knew something about how they disappeared from the bone house."

Her features rearrange themselves as understanding washes over her. Someone in that room must have made sure Declan's *keras* was full of something else, something harmless. She presses a hand to her forehead. "None of my readings implicated anyone on the council."

I stand and drum my fingers on the mantel. The fire in the hearth crackles and one of the logs tips, sending sparks flying. I think how the warmth of the flames comes at a cost—they consume and consume without ever being sated. A hunger that never goes away.

"It seems as if the truth has shifted," I say. "Now we're out of options."

"No," she says. "I can fix this."

"Forgive me if I'm having trouble trusting you right now."

"Saskia." She closes her eyes. Her jaw tightens. "Please don't be angry with me. The decisions I have to make are impossible. You had many paths. I chose the one that would produce the best results for the most people."

"Just not the best path for me."

"The kenning doesn't take away your choices. It's meant to give you direction."

Her excuses and platitudes scratch at the back of my mind. This is the fate I wanted, so I should be angry with myself. But she's not only the Bone Charmer, she's my mother. She should have protected me.

"You did a *matchmaking* reading on me, Mama. Paired me to someone you knew couldn't be trusted. And now I'll live my life alone. How does that leave me choices?"

She stands and takes a step toward me. "I didn't know he couldn't be trusted." Her voice is high and thin. "I said I wasn't surprised. Declan's future has always been challenging to read no matter how expensive and well prepared the bones. He's always had more potential paths than other people—"

"And did his paths at the kenning show he'd apprentice as a criminal?"

She bites her lip and a shadow passes over her face. Realization snatches the breath from me like an icy gust of wind.

"He didn't *have* a clear kenning, did he? Declan is a leftover." I can see from her expression that it's true. "You matched me to someone whose future you couldn't see?"

"I saw him on one of your paths," she says. "It was enough."

"Obviously not."

"You broke the bone, Saskia!" she shouts. "You left me no options!"

"No," I say, "I didn't. And like you said, we all have choices."

She sighs and catches one of my braids in her fingers, twisting it around her palm. "You won't live your life alone, sweetheart. Those convicted of crimes aren't allowed to remain matched. If we can't trust anyone in Midwood, we'll report Declan to the Grand Council. You won't have to see him again."

"I have no intention of breaking things off with him," I tell her.

She lets go of my braid and rears back as if slapped. "That's ridiculous. Of course you will."

"My life will be in danger the moment he knows I'm suspicious of him. I have to keep seeing him."

"Unacceptable," she says. "I'll send you somewhere far away until this is resolved. I have an old friend who lives in a village not far from the capital. You'll be safe there."

"I'm not leaving," I tell her. "Whoever Declan is working with killed Rakel. They could kill you next."

"I'll be fine." Her voice is steady, but her eyes call her a liar. Her earlier tears left crooked paths down her cheeks and they shimmer in the firelight. "It's you I'm worried about."

I give a brittle laugh. "You weren't worried when you spoke Declan's name at the kenning."

"Saskia—"

I hold up a hand to stop her. "You said yourself that I have choices. I'm making them now. I will keep seeing Declan. I will use him as he's used me—for gathering information, for getting closer to whoever did this. And once we know the full scope of his crimes, and who else is involved, then we'll report him to the Grand Council."

"Saskia, please . . ." Her voice trails off as she follows my gaze to Gran's finger bone.

"Maybe it doesn't matter if my life is in danger," I say. "Maybe we'll both get lucky and this reality won't be the one to survive."

Ami and I are sitting at the edge of the Shard, our toes tracing patterns in the water when Declan ambles toward us, grinning. His face is a picture of innocence.

I knew seeing him again would be difficult. But even so, I'm not fully prepared for the raw, blistering anger that pushes up my throat. For how painful it is to swallow this rage that burns like a flame. But I know even the smallest error right now could put me in danger, so I force my fists to unclench, my mouth to curve into a smile.

"I've been looking everywhere for you," he says, leaning down to drop a kiss onto my forehead. His lips are dry and chapped. Their texture makes me think of shedding snakeskin.

"Well, here I am." My voice sounds all wrong to my own ears—high, strained.

A crease appears between Declan's brows. He hears it, too. It's as if I've stepped too close to the edge of a cliff and I can feel the ground giving way beneath me, the rocks shifting and tumbling into the chasm beneath. I have to regain my footing, make him believe that I'm exactly as I was when he last saw me.

But I don't know if I can.

How can I pretend to be friendly toward him when I know what he's done? When my whole body is aching with the need to hurt him as badly as he's hurt me?

I think of my father's palms on my cheeks. Of the way he used to look at me when I did something to make him proud. Of his bones displayed for sale in the shadow market.

My resolve hardens into something shaped like a blade.

"Don't be a stranger," I say, patting the ground beside me.

"Sit with us."

A grin spills across his face, and my stomach lurches. I glance at Ami. Her expression is soft and warm—like melting butter. I haven't told her about Declan—I didn't want to put her in danger—and now I'm glad. I focus on matching my expression to hers. I offer Declan an apple and a few slices of cheese from the picnic basket beside me.

"Thanks," he says. "So what have you girls been up to this morning?" I take a bite of bread the moment the question leaves his mouth. I want Ami to speak first—I know what her answer will be, and I want to see Declan's reaction.

Ami sighs. "Master Oskar and I have been working on preparing Rakel's bones. It's so sad what happened to her."

Declan's eyes spark with interest and I grind my teeth together. "It's a tragedy," he says. "I was in the Forest of the Dead paying my respects a few days ago and saw that her family tree is empty again. It must be so difficult to be in contact with her bones day in and day out after what happened. I'm sure you'll be relieved when you're finished."

Declan has artfully wrapped a series of statements in a blanket of sympathy, and though nothing he said contained an actual inquiry, the comments practically beg for answers. I have a feeling he'll get them.

"It *has* been really hard," Ami says. "I keep imagining Rakel's last moments—how scared she must have been—and it makes me feel like crying every time I touch one of the bones. But we should finish in a week or two, and then the bones will be turned over to her family, and I won't need to relive it every day."

236

My fingers curl around a fistful of grass. I need to change the subject before he gets any additional information.

"How about you, Declan?" I ask. "How is your new apprenticeship going?"

He runs a finger down my arm, and gooseflesh ripples across my skin. "Boring. You're definitely the most interesting part of my day."

How many times has he done this before? Carefully avoided my questions with sweet words? Gently pulled my attention to something besides how he spends his time? Suddenly I'm so proud of my bare wrist, so happy that my heart is wiser than my head.

Ami stands and brushes the crumbs from her pants. "I better get going," she says. "I've been away too long and Master Oskar is probably wondering where I am."

I climb to my feet and wrap Ami in an embrace. The thought of her leaving me alone with Declan fills me with trepidation, and I wonder if she can feel the pounding of my jackrabbit heart. But she must not, because she leaves without looking back.

I sit beside Declan again. "So we were talking about how the trading is going."

"No," he says, wrapping a lock of my hair around his finger. "I think we were talking about how beautiful you are."

I frown. "Why do you keep doing that?"

"Doing what?"

"Changing the subject. You won't tell me anything about your life."

His expression shifts. I've knocked him off balance and now

I just need to give him a gentle push. I trace the faint pink tattoo around his wrist. If he can lie to himself this well, then I can at least pretend long enough to get the information I need. "You know, it makes it hard to fall in love with you when you won't let me in."

Alarm flashes across his face—just for an instant—but it's enough for me to realize there's something at stake for him. That he needs to keep me close for some reason.

And I intend to find out what it is.

"I'm sorry," he says. "My work is just so dull that I find it more interesting to talk about other things. Like you." He grins, but my expression remains stony. I think of when he first told me about his apprenticeship—how he left out the fact that his kenning didn't produce a clear result. He knew my mother would never break a confidence, and he used her discretion against me like a weapon. But it's a weapon I can use, too.

"Tutoring isn't exactly riveting," I say softly, "but I share stories with you all the time."

He runs his fingers through his hair. "True. So what is it that you want to know?"

"Everything," I say. "Where do you go every day? What do you do?"

"I've told you all of this before," he says. "I find rare artifacts for people with plenty of coin to spend."

"What kind of artifacts?"

He swallows. "All kinds of things. Last week a man asked if we could find him a gaming board made of bone."

"A *gaming* board?"

He gives me an odd look. "Yes. What's wrong with that?"

"It doesn't bother you that people waste bones on something so trivial? When so many other things could be done with them?"

He gives a humorless laugh. "I never took you for an idealist. The gaming board already existed, Saskia. I didn't make it; I just helped find it."

I want to argue with him. To point out that if he finds and sells these items, he's helping to ensure there's a market for them, guaranteeing Bone Masons will continue to make them. But then I remind myself I'm not here to change him; I'm here to discover his secrets.

"I guess that's true," I say, keeping my tone light. "Maybe I am too idealistic. I just wish things could be fair for everyone, you know?"

His fingers close around mine and I resist the urge to pull away. "Your good heart is one of the things I love most about you."

I nearly laugh. Because right now my heart is full of so much darkness, it feels as if it's been dipped into a vat of ink and emerged black and dripping.

Declan's thumb strokes a delicate pattern on the back of my hand. "What are you thinking?"

My gaze drops to our intertwined fingers. And then a flash of color catches my eye. A single trickle of red on the cuff of Declan's pants. Just one drop at an angle that would be hard for him to see. It looks sticky, like dried blood.

I let the darkness in my heart spill out and spread until

it overtakes me. I give Declan a lie of a smile—sweet and flirtatious. "I was just thinking about how I haven't been to your house since we were matched. And I'm wondering if you're ever going to invite me?"

"You have to stop seeing him," my mother says one afternoon when I walk through the front door.

It's not the first time she's made the request and I'm certain it won't be the last. I've spent every spare moment of the last few weeks with Declan. Taking long walks with him in the meadows and forests that surround Midwood, letting him tuck blossoms behind my ear, pretending to fall for him as I attempt to piece together the details of his life. How often he goes away. The possible towns and villages he could have visited based on how long he's gone. Whether he seems happy or disappointed when he returns.

But I'm not much closer to finding out who is helping him and why.

I take in my mother's drawn expression. The hollows under her eyes. The spell book lying open on the floor next to a cloth scattered with bones.

"Why?" I ask. "Did you see something important?"

"No," she says. "I can't see *anything*." She massages her forehead. "This is too dangerous. We have to think of another way."

I touch her arm. "There isn't another way."

Her glance falls to my wrist and the pale pink tattoo there.

She wrinkles her nose. "That is an abomination."

I smile. It took me weeks to figure out how Declan had managed to trick his heart into falling in love with me. Every day, I stared at the tattoo with equal parts wonder and revulsion, watching it grow darker and darker and willing even a faint line to show up on my own wrist in response to the lies I told myself.

My mind kept circling the problem, looking at it from every angle, trying to find a solution. Tattoos always show up with emotionally intense experiences. Maybe I needed to have an emotional moment with Declan, something that would convince my body and my heart I was falling for him, even if my mind knew it was a farce.

But I couldn't shake the feeling I was missing something. Like looking for a lost object, and knowing you've seen it somewhere recently, but not being able to think of precisely where. And then one day, I remembered the blood on Declan's pants. My mind snagged on that drip. I thought of sitting at my father's elbow and watching him mix colors on his palette—how a few drops of white paint could turn a shade from deep sapphire to cerulean, and a few more from cerulean to the pale blue of the sky right where it meets the horizon.

What if that drip wasn't blood? What if it was paint? Maybe Declan spilled it as he was getting ready to blend two colors—many drops of white mixed with bloodred for an early love tattoo, fewer and fewer drops of white each day, so that the tattoo looks as if it appears gradually.

"It may be an abomination," I tell my mother. "But it's a clever one."

It was my father's final gift to me. A set of his paints and his most delicate brush—one with bristles so fine, it leaves a line that is barely detectable, perfect for painting a single blade of grass or a fake love tattoo.

The pure look of triumph on Declan's face the first time he saw my painted wrist was worth the hours of experimentation to get the color and line just right—pale enough to be brand-new, yet dark enough to be seen. And thin enough not to feel raised when touched.

"You're playing with fire, Saskia," my mother says.

"Maybe," I say. "But fire provides warmth and food and life. Sometimes fire is the only way to survive."

She swallows. "We could try something else."

I shake my head. I've had this conversation with her too many times to count. "We can't go to the town council. I've haven't figured out who helped Declan avoid the truth serum yet."

"No," she says, "that's not what I meant."

I tilt my head and bite the inside of my cheek, sure she's about to offer up some variation of me leaving town.

"I could teach you to read bones."

The sentence is like a goblet dropped from slippery fingers. It lands with shattering surprise and stuns me into silence. I must have misheard. "What are you talking about?"

She crosses her arms and cradles her elbows in her palms like she's trying to stay warm in a chilly room. "The kenning doesn't change your natural abilities," she says. "You could still learn."

"You said it was impossible for me to be a Bone Charmer in this life. You said the kenning was final and I could never have a binding ceremony."

"And all of that is true. But those are legal restrictions, not physical ones. The Grand Council will never recognize you as Bone Charmer. Teaching you would violate my code of ethics—I could get in a lot of trouble if anyone finds out—but you still should be able to learn. And it's a safer plan than this one." She waves a hand toward the painted tattoo on my wrist.

Safer? I think of the prisoner killing those three innocent people because I trusted my blossoming magic. Of the months afterward, when I tortured myself by imagining their bodies hanging in a faraway Forest of the Dead. Of their names tenderly carved into the trunks of their family trees. Of their families grieving because of me.

"You have Second Sight, Saskia," my mother says, her voice more urgent now. "I'm almost sure of it. Think of what that could mean."

I could spy on Declan. I could see what he's doing without getting close to him.

There's nothing safe about me learning bone charming. But maybe there's nothing safe about me rejecting my power either. Maybe my fear is not so very different from Audra's. We're both trying to avoid pain by controlling fate—her by obsessing about the power of the bones and me by shunning it. But rejecting magic hasn't protected me. Rakel is dead. Declan is a traitor. My life is in danger of disappearing entirely.

My gaze slides to Gran's bone. It's nearly healed.

"We're running out of time," my mother says softly, as if she can see the thread of my thoughts. A lump forms in my throat.

She must not think this reality will be the one to survive. I press a hand to my forehead. If there was ever a time to take a risk, to embrace my power, it's now.

"All right," I say, "how do I start?"

Her shoulders relax and the tension drains from her expression. She sits on the floor near the bones and pats the space beside her. "Come," she says, "let me show you."

Saskia
The Bone Charmer

I stand on the dock, waiting to board the ship that is supposed to take me back to Midwood. The pier is full of just as much color and life as the first time I was here—the rich, mouthwatering aroma of roasting meat, vendors brandishing merchandise and shouting out prices, seagulls shrieking overhead. And yet it feels different than it did a few months ago, in the same way that the tree house Ami and I built when we were children felt different when we slept in it again years later. It's the sensation of realizing that the place is just as it always was, and you're the one who changed.

For years I've dreaded becoming a Bone Charmer, hoped against all odds that my mother would say something different at the kenning. But now the magic feels part of me, and the loss of that identity is visceral. Like a flower just beginning to bloom when a storm breaks apart the petals and scatters them on the wind. I've been unmade.

A throat clears behind me and I turn.

Bram.

"What are you doing here?" Shock hardens my voice, and the words come out with more bite than I intended.

"You didn't show up for the evening meal, and Tessa said all your belongings were gone. I couldn't get any of the instructors to tell me anything except that you were headed home." His jaw is tight. "Is it true?"

I swallow. "Half true. I'm not going home."

"Tell me what happened."

Shame climbs up my throat at the thought of admitting I was expelled. Despite our history, I hate the thought of Bram's opinion of me diminishing even more.

I watch as a small girl in pigtails kneels at the edge of the dock and sets a little wooden sailboat into the water. She drags it along, turning it in slow circles, making it fly above the water before plunging it beneath the surface. And then she lets go. The little boat drifts out of reach and she starts to cry. The girl's father leans over and plucks the sailboat from the water, and sets it dripping into her eager fingers. She sniffles and wipes away her tears with the back of her hand.

I think how nice it must be to have someone to fix your mistakes, to whisk you away from the brink of heartbreak. To reach out with strong hands and give you back the things you've lost.

Bram is still watching me expectantly, waiting for a response.

"I got kicked out," I tell him, frustrated by how hard the words are to say aloud. "One of the instructors set me up. He wanted me to get expelled from Ivory Hall. I have to find out why. So I can't go home. I need to find someone who practices dark magic."

His head jerks back. "Wait. What? Have you lost your mind?"

His comment makes me feel small and naive. My blood spikes with fire. "Goodbye, Bram." I spin on my heel and storm toward the ship as fast as my feet will carry me.

He runs after me. "Saskia, stop."

I don't.

He catches my wrist and spins me around. At first I think he's about to yell at me—his eyes are wild and angry—but something about the look on my face makes his expression change. The hard lines around his mouth soften. His eyes go liquid. "Just tell me what's going on."

My heart picks up speed. A war rages inside me—I don't know if I dare tell him the truth. If even Master Kyra—one of the most fair-minded people I know—didn't believe me, why would Bram? I haven't exactly earned his trust. But I feel utterly alone, and it makes me braver than I might be otherwise. "Master Kyra claims I was using dark magic. It's what helped me reach so far into the future when I saw you get hurt."

"What do you mean she claims you were using dark magic? Either you were or you weren't."

I tell him about Latham. About the practice bones and the larger intensifier. I explain that Latham made me believe he was helping me, convinced me that he wanted me to succeed. I wait for Bram's expression to harden in disgust or suspicion. But it doesn't. He only listens intently, brow furrowed and lips pursed in concentration.

"Do you think Latham is out for revenge?" Bram asks. "For something that happened between him and your mother?"

"That's what I assumed at first," I say, "but now I think it's more than that. If he only wanted revenge, he could have set me up without taking so much time to tutor me. There's something else going on. I feel it in my gut."

Bram taps his fingers on his leg. It's a gesture I've come to recognize—something he does when he's mulling things over, as if his thoughts are searching for a rhythm to shape them.

One of the ship's crewmen lowers the gangplank and shouts out the boarding call. I touch Bram's arm lightly, and his eyes lift to meet mine. "I have to go now. Will you tell the others I said goodbye?"

He doesn't answer, so I turn and hurry up the walkway. But his footsteps are right behind me.

I spin to face him. "What are you doing?"

"I'm coming with you."

I shake my head. "No."

He gives a hard laugh. "No?"

My gaze flicks toward the gangplank. The crewmen will raise it soon and it will be too late. "You have to go back to Ivory Hall. If you disappear, they'll terminate your apprenticeship."

"I might be able to help." His hand closes around my elbow and I freeze. He tracks my gaze, and his eyes fall to the tattoos on his knuckles. "Or are you afraid I'll murder you in your sleep the moment we're alone?"

My cheeks prickle with heat. "That's ridiculous. I'm not afraid of you." But I don't want to tell him the rest of the truth—that for once I'm not focused on his tattoos, but at the way my skin sparks under his fingers.

He moves toward me and I back away until I'm pressed up against the railing with nowhere to go. He puts one palm on either side of me, his fingers curled around the silky wood. He's so close, I can feel his breath on my face. My pulse races.

"I'll tell you what," he says. "If you promise to hear me out, I promise not to kill you without a good reason."

His eyes, I realize, are more hazel than brown. His irises are flecked with gold, like the inside of a rock that's been split open.

I swallow. "What would be a good reason to kill me?"

One corner of his mouth lifts. "I'll let you know."

The ship begins to move away from the dock. It's too late for Bram to return to Ivory Hall. "Fine," I tell him. "I'll hear you out."

"I think I know someone who can help us."

My mind snags on the "us." Something flutters softly in my stomach, like wings unfolding. But then I take in the rest of what Bram is saying. "I don't know. After everything that happened with Latham, I need to be careful who I trust."

"If you're going to go searching for information on dark magic, you're going to have to trust someone. And most of your options will be bad ones."

He's not wrong.

"Her name is Esmee," he says in a rush, as if he can sense an opening in my hesitation. "She's a friend of your mother's."

This pulls me up short. I study him warily. It's exactly what Latham said to get me to trust him. Why does everyone assume invoking my mother will earn my confidence?

Bram shakes his head as if he can sense the tenor of my thoughts. "I'm not trying to deceive you. Your mother trusts Esmee. At least she did once. And I trust her now."

I chew the inside of my cheek. I need to find out more about the dark magic Latham was using, and this seems like as good a plan as any. "Where does she live?"

"Not far from here. We could get to her home in a day or two." Bram tugs on the back of his neck. "There's only one problem."

I raise my eyebrows in a question.

Bram sighs and points behind us. "She lives that way."

Our first chance to disembark comes the next morning in Calden. The day dawns bright and cool. Bram and I dress in plain gray cloaks. We carry my belongings in a basket stolen from the kitchens, with a layer of fruit tossed on top. Hopefully it will make us look like traders—simple farmers going from village to village, selling the food we've grown.

But no one gives us a second look as we disembark. Perhaps the ship's crew hasn't been warned to watch us. Perhaps it wasn't necessary, because someone else is watching us. Someone who doesn't need to be close. Someone who can observe from the comfort of Ivory Hall.

A shiver goes through me.

Bram and I combine the last of our coin and scrape together just enough to hire a small boat to take us back upriver. After we sail past the capital, it's another day's journey south to the harbor at Grimsby. As we travel, Bram tells me about Esmee— how she's a historian, knowledgeable about all the bone magics, but an expert on Bone Charming in particular. He doesn't say how he met her, and I don't ask. The earlier tension still vibrates between us like the moments just after the clash of cymbals—not quite noise, but not silence either.

It's late in the day by the time we arrive. The sky is tinged with soft light that is slowly melting toward darkness. The town casts a spell over me the moment I step off the boat, captivating me with its charm. Brightly colored buildings with vivid green roofs press together like wool-hatted children huddling in the cold, and cobblestone streets dip and rise over the hilly terrain.

Bram leads me past all the shops—an apothecary with rows of glass bottles, a bakery with a half dozen pies in the window, a toy shop that spills children's laughter from its open door.

We don't speak as we move through the quieter part of Grimsby, past all the homes, to the very outskirts of town. The sun has disappeared by the time Bram leads me deep into the woods.

My steps slow. A flutter of unease ripples through me.

"Still not planning to murder you," Bram says over his shoulder.

I bristle. "I didn't think you were."

He tosses a glance in my direction. "Are you sure?"

A flash of annoyance goes through me. "Stop saying that."

He turns. "Stop asking if you're sure?" He's being purposely obtuse and it makes me want to take off a shoe and throw it at him.

"I don't think you're going to murder me."

He quirks one eyebrow.

"Though if you were," I say, under my breath, "this would be the perfect spot."

The corners of his mouth lift. And then he laughs as if he can't help himself. As if the sound tumbled from his mouth, unexpectedly, surprising even him.

Something in my chest loosens, like a fist unclenching. Or a tightly closed flower bud bursting into bloom. It makes it easier to breathe when we start walking again.

Gradually the day stretches and the light fades.

"It's not much farther now," Bram says. The sun disappeared long ago, and the moonlight glimmers through the leaves on the trees.

After the long trek through the dense forest—branches brushing the top of my head, twigs snapping underfoot—I'm expecting to find a rough-hewn hunter's lodge or a little hut made of straw. But Esmee's home is just as lovely as the rest of Grimsby. The cottage is tucked in the middle of a clearing of wildflowers. The windows glow with candlelight.

Bram puts a hand on my forearm. "One more thing you should know about Esmee . . ." He swallows. "She wasn't bone-matched."

I'm hit with a wave of cold shock. It freezes the hope inside me. "But you said she was an expert. . . . You said . . ."

"And she is," Bram says. "Everything I told you is true."

"You trusted my fate to a *leftover*?" The panic is slick inside my veins. I put my palms on his chest and shove him as hard as I can, but he doesn't move, doesn't even shift his weight. "You tricked me." I push him again, frustrated at his strength. At my weakness.

He catches both of my wrists and holds them against his chest. "Well, I suppose this an improvement over you being afraid of me."

"You're a liar." I spit the words at him.

"I didn't lie to you."

"You withheld the truth. It's the same thing."

"Just because Esmee wasn't bone-matched—"

But I don't want to hear anything he has to say. I wrench out of his grip and turn away.

"Saskia." Bram's voice is gruff, angry. "You're a leftover now, too."

The words pin me in place. They steal the breath from my throat and make it impossible for me to speak for several long moments. "It's not the same."

"Isn't it?"

I've been so focused on finding out what game Latham is playing that I hadn't considered what getting expelled from Ivory Hall meant for the rest of my life. "My mother can protest Norah's decision. She'll fix it." My eyes flick to his. "For both of us."

He rakes his fingers through his hair. "Maybe Esmee didn't

have anyone to fix it," he says softly. "Does that really make her any less than you?"

"I didn't say she was less than me. I just . . ." But the words die on my lips. As much as I've resented the bones, I've also always trusted them as the best source of knowledge. But getting expelled from Ivory Hall hasn't erased what I've learned any more than having well-prepared kenning bones made me more suited to bone magic than someone who was poor. My mother taught me better than this. But still, my first instinct is to mistrust anyone who isn't bone-matched. The pinprick of realization stings and hot shame courses through me.

"Give her a chance," Bram says.

I nod and follow him to the door. Esmee answers right away. She's at least a hand-width shorter than I am, with a pleasant, heavily lined face and a shock of white hair that she wears piled in a bun at the back of her head.

I expect her to greet Bram, but instead she turns her gaze on me. "Saskia Holte," she says, "I've been expecting you."

Saskia
The Tutor

I sit in front of a velvet cloth scattered with a dozen metacarpal bones. For the last seven days, I've done little more than eat, sleep, and attempt to learn Second Sight Bone Charming from a Third Sight Charmer. I've had some success in performing readings on my mother, because I have access to her blood, but I've failed to see more than fuzzy outlines of anything else.

My temples throb as I try to focus on Declan and give myself over to the tug of magic I feel low in my belly. But it isn't working.

I take in a deep breath and open my eyes.

My mother watches me with such a hopeful expression that it hurts to shake my head and admit that I failed again. Her eyes dim as her optimism bleeds away.

"I'm sorry," I tell her. "I keep getting so close, but I can't make out anything more than shadows."

She stands and goes to the window. Her fingers curl around the wooden frame. Her knuckles turn white. "We need Declan's blood," she says.

Her irritation sparks against my own. "Why didn't you just say so?" I ask. "I'll run on over and ask him for some."

She presses her lips together. Her eyes flutter closed as if she's summoning patience from some inner reserve. "I know you're doing your best, Saskia. But it's not enough."

"Then I'll start seeing Declan again. He won't believe I'm ill forever." My mother has kept Declan at bay—and Audra, too—by telling everyone that I've contracted a stomach bug.

"No," she says, "unacceptable."

"Do you have a better idea?"

"Maybe." Her gaze grows faraway. "There is a species of bat that feasts on blood. Their saliva contains a numbing agent so they can bite a sleeping animal without waking it, and lap up its blood in peace."

My stomach turns at the image. "So what? We find a Watcher who can control a vampire bat?"

"I don't trust any of the Watchers enough to ask," she says, "but Gran once had a customer who was especially sensitive to pain, so she commissioned a special needle made from the bone of a bat wing. It was infused with the animal's saliva. Gran could draw blood without the customer feeling a thing."

"I don't suppose Oskar keeps needles like that in stock at the bone house?"

She smiles for the first time in several days. "No," she says, "but I think I can get one."

My mother returns with the bone needle the next evening. She's been gone for hours—so long that my optimism gradually transformed into worry. And then my worry became anxiety. By the time I hear her key in the lock, my anxiety has caught fire, blazing into irrational anger.

I meet her at the door, a flood of questions pooling on my tongue—biting and bitter—but the moment I see her face, I swallow them one by one. She wears an expression I've never seen on her before. It's raw and vulnerable. Guilty.

Her trembling hands carry a small box. It's not the kind usually used for bones—silver or gold, velvet lined . . . expensive. It's made of plain, cheap wood and looks like it could hold fishing supplies.

"Are you all right?" I ask.

Her eyes don't quite meet mine. "I'm fine, just tired. It was more challenging to get the needle than I thought; I had to resort to buying it from a less than savory trader. Not ideal, but I was out of options." She tucks the box into the top drawer of her desk. "I'll find Declan tomorrow and get enough blood for you to have plenty of practice."

The tenor of her voice makes me uneasy. "How? You can't just walk up to him and stab him with it."

She gives me a tired smile and rests the backs of her fingers against my cheek. They feel like ice. "I'll figure it out. Now get some sleep. You'll learn better if you're well rested."

She kicks off her shoes and pads down the hallway. Her bedroom door closes softly behind her.

I stare at the empty space she left behind. The void feels as if it has a pulse—as if whatever stress she experienced to find the bone has grown into a living thing.

I pull the wooden box from the drawer and remove the lid. The needle rests on a bed of soft fabric. Gingerly, I pinch it between my thumb and forefinger to examine it. It's made from a thin, sharp bone and it's practically weightless, so delicate that it could snap in two with the barest amount of pressure. The hollow tip has a chamber inside to catch the blood. I press it to the pad of my finger. I feel a gentle pressure, but nothing more. It isn't until I move the bone away and notice a faint smear of blood on my skin that I realize the needle pierced me. I turn it over and gaze inside the hollow. A few drops of my blood fill the chamber.

My heart races. This could actually work. But I can't imagine any scenario where my mother gets close enough to Declan to use the needle without arousing suspicion. I have to be the one to do it. If I wait until morning, I'll never convince her to let me go. Not without a fight. She refused to let me play in the Shard with my friends until I was ten years old because she was convinced I wasn't a strong enough swimmer yet. This time, her desire to protect me might ruin us both.

I go to my bedroom and riffle through the box under my bed until I find my father's paint set. I haven't refreshed my tattoo since I saw Declan last. I mix the colors and add one less drop of white than last time. If I were really falling in love, the long absence might have warmed my heart toward him. Once the paint is dry, I find the bone-carved hair clips he dropped off when he heard I was ill—a treasure brought from one of his trading stops that I haven't been able to look at.

But tonight I will need every advantage I can get.

I gather two sections of hair—one above each ear—then twist them together and secure the style with the bone clips. Then I grab my cloak from the hook on the wall and slip into the night.

Chilly air bites at my cheeks as I walk along the bank of the Shard. Only the barest sliver of moon lights the sky. The box in my pocket feels as heavy as a brick, even though it weighs almost nothing.

I tried Declan's house first—shinnied up the tree outside his window and tapped the glass with a branch—but either he was sleeping so deeply that he didn't hear me or he wasn't there.

My next stop is the trading ship. Declan often spends the night onboard if he has a late night or an early morning. When I spot the vessel in the distance, moored alongside the dock, I'm torn between wanting Declan to be there and hoping he's not.

I make my way to the water's edge and pull a pebble from my pocket—I've been gathering stones of various sizes since I left Declan's house—and toss it into the water on the side of the ship where I know he sleeps. I wait, but the night is still. The soft light of an oil lamp glimmers off the water. I throw a larger pebble. Water splashes against the ship. Nothing.

I toss three stones in quick succession. They smack against the water with a crack that reverberates through the night. But still, there's no movement on the ship.

My chest tightens with equal parts disappointment and relief. I turn away.

"Saskia?"

I spin to find Declan, barefoot and shirtless. His hair is messy and his expression is dazed and sleepy.

"You're here," I say.

He rubs his eyes. "Yes, but what are you doing here?"

Blood rushes in my ears. I feel nauseous. "I missed you," I say. He shivers. "You're cold. I'm so sorry." I rub my palms along his arms and think of the anatomy books my mother has forced me to pore over for the past week. I take both of his hands in mine and trace my thumbs along the veins above his knuckles. But he'll see if I try to use the needle there.

He pulls me closer. "Don't be sorry. I missed you too." He laces his fingers through mine. I trace the artery above his wrist, but then quickly dismiss the thought. An artery will bleed too profusely. "Are you feeling better?"

"Much," I tell him. My gaze falls to the vein that runs under his clavicle. "I wanted to thank you for the hair clips." I turn my head so that he can see I'm wearing them.

He smiles. "Do you like them?"

"I love them." I stuff my fists into my pockets and nudge the box open with my thumb. I curl my fingers around the needle.

Declan's eyes drop to my hands and my heart seizes. "Is everything all right?"

My mouth goes dry. "Of course. Why?"

He tucks a stray hair behind my ear. "You went from touching me to shoving your hands into your pockets."

I swallow. Declan is fully awake now and paying attention. This is going to be even more challenging than I thought.

"I got cold." I take my hands from my pockets, making sure to keep the bone nestled in the crook of my palm.

His arms slide around my waist. "I'm more than happy to warm you up."

A shiver goes through me that has nothing to do with the temperature. I trace my thumb against the contours of Declan's throat, feeling for the gentle give of a vein. He sighs into me, his breath warm against my neck. I still can't find a suitable blood vessel. And even if I could, he's still not distracted enough for me to pull this off without him noticing.

Gravity is working against me, making his veins too flat. I need them to swell. Which means I need him on his back.

Nausea threatens at the back of my throat again, but I smile as I tug on Declan's hand. I lead him from the dock to the riverbank, where we sink onto a patch of cold grass. His wide pupils glimmer in the lamplight.

"Where's all this coming from?" His expression hovers somewhere between wonder and doubt.

I slide my hand behind his neck, the needle still tucked into my palm. "I'm in love with you," I say.

His eyes go soft. He's already seen my ever-darkening tattoo, but it's a different thing to say the words aloud. More vulnerable. More intimate. He moves closer to me. I know what needs to happen next, but my heart squeezes in protest. This is a moment I will never get back. A moment I'm about to throw away.

I tip my face toward him and our lips meet.

My mind goes blank. It's my first kiss and it's nothing but a sham. The loss is like a swift kick to the gut. Declan pulls away and studies my face. "Are you all right? You got faraway again."

No one can spot a lie like a liar.

I need to do a better job of selling this or I'm going to spoil everything. "You made me forget where I was for a moment," I say, making sure I sound a touch breathless. "Maybe I'll remember better if we try again."

This time I kiss him. I pretend he's nothing more than a vessel to hold my anger, my worry, my fear. I pour every negative emotion I have into him until I feel like I'm on fire. I let my hands sink into his hair. I push him onto his back and let my fingers roam over his neck. He meets each kiss with hungry intensity.

There. The squishy sensation of a vein. I've finally found his jugular. I press all my fingers against his throat at the same time I plunge the needle into his vein. He moans and deepens the kiss. I wait until I'm sure I have enough blood and then I remove the needle and press a thumb against the vein to stem the bleeding. Declan's fingers roam over my face, but I continue to keep pressure on his neck.

Finally, when I'm sure it's been long enough, I slip the needle into the pocket of my cloak and pull away.

"Come back." Declan pulls me toward him, but I lay a hand against his chest.

"My mother will wake up soon. I don't want her to know I snuck out."

He groans and sits up. "I'm sure she'll sleep a little longer."

I dip my head toward the horizon, which has obliged me by revealing a stripe of deep pink light. "She's an early riser. Besides"—I nudge him lightly in the ribs with my elbow—"we have our whole lives, right?"

He clears his throat. "You have a point." But I didn't miss the dark shadow that crossed his expression before he could sweep it away.

No one can spot a lie like a liar.

Saskia
The Bone Charmer

ram and I sit across from Esmee in the cozy main room of her cottage. A fire blazes in the hearth and on the low table between us is a plate of half-eaten treats—spun-sugar creations that look like bits of lace—along with a kettle of tea that has long since gone cold. I've tried to ask Esmee several questions since we arrived, but she's made a *tut-tut* sound each time. "Let's not talk until you've been fed and fussed over, little lamb." Her tone, while friendly, left no room for argument. She's tiny, but commanding.

Bram knows her best, so I try to follow his lead, but he's done nothing since we got here except eat and gush over how delicious everything is. Finally I can't stand the polite conversation anymore, and I work up the courage to broach the subject again. "So, you must have Third Sight," I say.

Esmee gives a bell-like laugh that makes her sound years younger than she probably is. "Oh, skies no! I have First Sight. Not officially, of course. I didn't have a binding ceremony. Whatever would make you think I had Third?"

I bite my lip, confused. "When we first arrived, you said you were expecting me. So I just assumed . . ." I trail off.

"Ah," she says, licking a bit of sugar from her thumb. "That's because of the letter your mother sent for you."

Both Bram and I inhale sharply. "My mother sent a letter?" I say. "When? What does it say?"

Bram's response is more forceful. "Esmee! Why didn't you tell us right away?"

Esmee gives him a reproachful look and the tips of his ears turn pink.

"I'm sorry," Bram says, dropping his gaze to his lap. He clearly cares about her opinion—I've never seen him look so sheepish before.

Esmee turns toward me. "I don't know what it says. I'm not in the habit of reading correspondence that isn't addressed to me. Wait here and I'll fetch it for you."

She sets off toward the bedroom at the back of the cottage. Bram turns to me. "Your mother knew you'd come here," he says. "What do you think that means?"

"I don't know." I chew on my thumbnail. A tight fist of fear has settled in my stomach.

Esmee returns with the letter a few moments later. Both she and Bram watch me expectantly as I break the wax seal and unfold the creamy paper. A necklace is tucked into the crease—a pendant with three overlapping circles carved from bone—and I set it down on the table next to me. The sight of my mother's small, careful script makes my throat feel thick.

Dearest Saskia,

I hoped you would never need to receive this letter and my heart aches that you're reading it now. During your kenning, I chose the path that I believed would bring you the greatest possible happiness. That main path branched off dozens of times, and each of those paths diverged into even more. Small changes in your future that led in different directions. Almost all of them were equally lovely. But a few of the branches led to danger—a danger that I could never fully see beginning but could always see ending in tragedy. Each time something terrible happened, the branch point was Esmee's cottage, so I'm sending this letter to you there in hopes that it reaches you in time.

Whatever choices you make from here forward, it is essential that you don't return to Midwood. Not until I contact you and let you know that it's safe. Please promise me that you'll honor this wish? No matter how tempting it might be to come home, I need you to stay away.

I'm enclosing a shield to protect you. Esmee can explain how it works. I believe someone is watching you, Saskia. Someone who has access to defensive magic. Maybe you know who it is by now, but I don't yet. Be careful whom you trust.

I love you, bluebird. Don't ever forget that.

—M

The letter flutters from my fingers and lands on the floor. It's as if all the air has been squeezed from my lungs. Did my mother see my death? She doesn't explicitly state it, but I can't help but read into her words. I'm especially disconcerted that she called me bluebird—a nickname usually reserved only for my father. Her heart must have been in a tender place to use it herself.

"What did it say?" Esmee's voice is gentle. I open my mouth and then close it again. I can't find the words to answer. She picks up the letter. "May I?"

I nod. As Esmee reads, a crease forms between her brows. "Oh my," she says once she reaches the end. She scoops up the necklace from where I left it on the table. "Better put this on now, little lamb."

But her voice sounds like it's coming from a tunnel. I stare at her without really seeing. I feel detached—as if I'm watching both of us from a distance. Esmee shares a look with Bram. Without speaking, he stands and takes the necklace from her. He steps behind me and gently moves my hair aside. He settles the slender cord against my collarbone and fastens the clasp. His thumb brushes the nape of my neck.

Suddenly I'm fully present again, aware of my heartbeat. Of my breath.

I shift so that Bram's hands fall away. But still, it takes me a moment to find my voice.

"What is this?" I say, lifting the pendant.

"It's a shield," Esmee says. "It will prevent any Bone Charmer from seeing you while you're wearing it."

"Even my mother?"

She frowns. "Even your mother."

The implications make my mind spark with fresh worry. My mother is concerned enough about this that she's willing for me to be hidden. Even from her.

"Do you know who she means?" Esmee asks, glancing at the letter. "Who might be watching you?"

I tell her about Latham. The story unwinds from me like a tangled ball of yarn, thick and clumsy. Esmee listens quietly, her eyes filling with sympathy and shock. Bram, too, is hanging on every word, even though he's already heard some of the details. By the time I finish speaking, Esmee's mouth has gone thin. "This is certainly about more than petty revenge from your mother's training days, but I'm afraid I don't have any more insight about what it is about than you do."

I swallow. "I heard you knew about dark magic."

Her gaze slides to Bram and then back again. The silence is thick. And then, finally: "I know something about it."

"Will you tell me?"

She sighs. "A little knowledge can cause a lot of grief."

"Yes," I say. "I know. A little knowledge is all Latham was willing to give me."

Her lips purse. She taps them with two of her fingers. "Very well, then."

She stands and goes to a bookshelf on the far wall. She pulls down several volumes and sets them in my lap. "See if you can find what you're looking for in there. But remember that magic always comes at a price. And dark magic is particularly costly."

"I don't want to use the magic. I just want to understand what Latham is doing."

Her hand drops softly to the crown of my head and I'm reminded forcefully of my mother. "I know that's not your intention," she says. "Just be careful."

I pore over the books by the light of a low-burning lamp. Bram sits beside me, his head resting on the table, snoring softly. He lasted longer than Esmee, who turned in hours ago.

Reading through the pages fills me with a slick sense of shame. It's as if the words are living things—shadowy and sinister, and they cling to me like the threads of a spiderweb. Despite all my studying, I can't find anything that explains the interest Latham showed in me. He didn't take samples of my blood or hair to put a curse on me, he didn't destroy my memory, or scoop the voice from my throat. I can't figure out what he gained from tutoring me, or why he would be watching me now—if it even is him. What if my mother saw a different danger?

A noise behind me makes me spin around.

"I didn't mean to startle you," Esmee says. Her expression makes me realize that my hand is pressed to my chest. My heart races beneath my palm. I take a deep breath and try to convince my body that I'm not in danger.

"Did I wake you?" I ask.

Esmee pulls her shawl more tightly around her shoulders. "I'm a restless sleeper." She goes to the cupboard and pulls out two teacups. "How about a break?"

"Yes, please," I say, suddenly desperate for a reprieve from curses and murder.

Esmee puts a kettle over the heat. "So, what's the story here?" She waggles her fingers, indicating the space between me and Bram.

A ripple of unease goes through me. "There's no story." Her skeptical expression looks so much like a reprimand that heat races up my neck and into my cheeks. "We were matched at the kenning, but I don't think . . ." I can't find the words for the restless feelings that rustle inside me. My opinion of Bram has changed, but he still sees me as the girl who ruined his life. "Neither of us intends to accept it at the end of the year."

She pours tea into the cups. Steam curls in the air. "Are you sure about that?"

I tug on the edge of my sleeve. "So, how do you know Bram?"

She laughs. "You need more practice sidestepping a question, lamb. That was artless." She sets a cup in front of me and hands me a spoon. "But I'll indulge you. Bram was born in Grimsby. I was friends with his parents before the accident."

The shock that goes through me must show on my face, because Esmee stops stirring her tea. "You must be aware of Bram's story?"

I shake my head. "I knew he moved to Midwood when he was young. I didn't know . . ." I trail off, unsure how to ask all of the questions teeming in my mind. "What accident?"

Esmee drizzles honey into her tea. "A fire. One of the villagers got Bram out, but both of his parents died. Afterward, Bram's magical abilities made him . . . hard to place, so he stayed with me until your mother helped me find a couple in Midwood willing to take him in."

My mouth goes dry. The story is like a familiar nightmare and it presses against me so firmly, I can scarcely breathe. How did I never realize his parents had died in that fire? All this time, I've been terrified of the rage I saw in Bram's heart that day. But now it makes perfect sense. I think of my own father's death. On the day Oskar carved father's name into our family tree, I took a stack of fancy plates from the kitchen and threw them one by one against the side of our house just for the satisfaction of watching them shatter.

I wanted to destroy everything around me so the whole world would be as broken as I felt.

But my father was still alive when I saw Bram's memories, so I didn't realize then how much anger and grief can overlap. How they can be almost impossible to untangle once they've merged.

It takes me a long time to find my voice. "Bram had magical abilities that young?"

"All children who have bone magic show early signs," Esmee says. "My guess is that your mother knew you'd be a Bone Charmer long ago, am I right?" I shift my weight and the chair creaks. Esmee nods as if my discomfort is answer enough. "The kenning doesn't create truth; it only reveals it."

"What made him hard to place?" I ask, glancing at Bram. His breathing is deep and even. I probably shouldn't talk about him without his knowledge, but my curiosity is stronger than my guilt.

"He was confused and angry," she says. "Any child would

have been. But Bram was powerful. So occasionally, when he lashed out, people got hurt."

"Got hurt how?"

"Broken bones mostly," she says.

I gasp. "But how did he have access to bones at that age? And without any training?"

"He didn't *need* prepared bones—he can pull magic from the bones inside a living body. That's why people were afraid of him."

A chill goes through me. "I was afraid of him, too. I thought maybe he was violent."

Esmee's eyes narrow. "Bram isn't violent. You never threw a tantrum when you were young? You never lashed out in frustration? He was a small child. One who was grieving."

A tear slips down my cheek and I wipe it away with the back of my hand. "I know that now, but it's too late. I ruined everything between us." I tell her about the prison boat in Midwood. About seeing inside the prisoner's mind and then inside Bram's. I tell her about their faces blending together. About the broken cage that allowed the prisoner to escape. About the three people who died.

"Oh, you poor dears," she says, as if Bram were awake and we told the story together. "That must have been terrible. What did your mother say about it?"

I shake my head. "I never told her. I was so ashamed that my vision was wrong, that people died because of me."

"You didn't kill them; the prisoner did." Her eyes cut to Bram. "I'm sure Bram felt the same."

"I should have asked him about the fire. But when I saw those tattoos . . . the same ones the prisoner had . . . I was a coward."

Her hand drops to cover mine. "You were a child," she says, echoing how she described Bram earlier, "one who had been traumatized."

Suddenly a thought sparks in my mind. "The bones on the cage were intensifiers. That's why my abilities were so magnified." I think of the broken bone cage. Bram didn't intend to help the prisoner escape any more than I intended to see the man's thoughts. "And Bram's, too."

Esmee stands and touches my shoulder. "You're probably right. Maybe it's time both of you left your old hurts in the past, where they belong."

She takes her teacup and walks toward the bedroom. My gaze falls to the spell book. I've been studying it for hours and getting nowhere. Between that and everything I just learned about Bram, I feel so defeated, I want to curl up and cry.

"Esmee, wait."

She stops. Turns.

"The First Sight Charmer at Ivory Hall said she couldn't see Latham in my past, but what if she wasn't telling the truth? She could have been protecting him." Esmee tilts her head and waits for me to finish. "I can't stop wondering if I could see my interactions with Latham again, knowing what I know now . . ."

"Are you asking me to do a reading on you?"

I swallow. "Would you?"

Her expression softens. "I have an even better idea."

Esmee and I sit on her bedroom floor in front of a basin filled with bones. The faint scent of vanilla hangs in the air.

I blow a stray lock of hair out of my eyes. "I don't understand how this will work."

"It's simple," Esmee says. "I'll use the bones to do a reading on you—on your past—and you will simultaneously use them to do a reading on me in the present. To see what I am seeing in your memories. If it works, it will be as if you have First Sight and are performing a reading on your own past. You can look for clues in your interactions with Latham that you might have missed when you experienced them the first time. Does that make sense?"

"In theory?"

She pats me on the arm. "We'll use my blood along with yours so you can see me more clearly." She hands me a needle. "You'll need to take off your shield. It will block your magic."

I slide the pendant from my neck and set it beside me.

"It may take some time for me to find the memories you're looking for. Focus all of your thoughts on me and on your interactions with Latham. Not anything else, understand?"

I press my lips together and nod. My mind has been consumed with Latham for hours. It won't be difficult to keep him at the forefront of my thoughts.

Esmee pricks her finger and speckles the bones with blood. Then she sets them alight. Smoke curls from the basin. The bones crackle and snap in the heat. Finally she covers the basin with a heavy lid and extinguishes the flame. Most of my training didn't involve flame—it's a more advanced technique—but I've seen my mother perform this ritual dozens of times and it gives me a pang of homesickness.

Esmee tips the bones onto the cloth between us. I close my eyes. The use of fire makes it unnecessary to be in contact with the bones, so I expect the reading to be more difficult, but I feel the pull of the magic right away.

I'm plunged into a vision.

My mother's face comes into focus, younger than I've ever seen her, and so near that I can see the delicate peach fuzz on the sides of her cheeks. My small hand closes around her nose. She laughs and kisses my baby-sized palm.

The vision changes. I can feel Esmee's effort to drag it forward and I follow her. This time I see a fair-haired toddler, chubby fingers gripped around the edge of a low wooden table. She pulls herself into a standing position. My father sits nearby and claps as he watches. "You did it, bluebird!" She turns toward him and gives him a nearly toothless grin, save for four baby incisors—two on the top and two on the bottom.

Another shift. A lurch that drags us ahead through time.

Hundreds of other scenes from my childhood flash by, too quickly to catch more than passing glimpses. And then I'm sitting across from my mother at the kenning. I watch myself snatch Gran's bone from my mother's fingers, and I feel sick as it snaps.

Esmee pulls the vision forward again—my journey to Ivory Hall flies by, then the binding ceremony, until we arrive at my first day of training with Master Kyra. This was the first time I met Master Latham. I inhale sharply as Esmee's tug slows the reading. In the vision, I hear the explosion from across the hall and watch as the room fills with smoke. Master Kyra throws open the windows. *Let's take a break,* she says before leaving the room. Latham should arrive any moment.

But he doesn't.

I watch myself sit near the window for a bit, breathing in the fresh air. And then I stand and leave the room, alone.

I wrench out of the vision, breathless. Esmee's eyes fly open and she extinguishes the flame. "That explains a lot," she says, wiping a bead of sweat from her brow.

My fingers curl around my knees. "It explains *nothing*. Latham was there that day. He showed me the practice bones. I did a reading with them." I press my palms to my cheeks. "You have to believe me."

Esmee's eyes are soft. "Of course, I believe you. Your mother said you were in danger from someone who had defensive magic, and that's the strongest protection spell I've ever seen."

My breath catches. "You saw Latham?"

Esmee shakes her head. "No, but I saw hints of the magic he used to erase himself."

"To *erase* himself?"

"It works a bit like cutting a strip of fabric from the middle of a cloth and then stitching the remaining two pieces back together. If you look very carefully, you'll always be able to spot the seam. But this—it was masterfully done—almost undetectable. If I hadn't known to look, I would have missed it." She tilts her head and studies me. "Would you like me to show you?"

"Yes," I say, "please."

"This time pay attention to the exact moment you remember Latham entering the memory. You won't see him, but looking for where he should be will help you spot the imperfection in his spell."

She relights the bones and I'm swept up in another vision. The workshop. Norah has just finished a lecture and we're about to compete in a bone race. Frantically, I search for the exact spot where I saw Latham. I remember him finding me to say hello. Offering to give me extra lessons. But I can't find even a hint that we ever spoke. Before I know it, Bram and I are assembling the *Bradypus* skeleton.

Esmee pulls us forward in time. I see myself walking away from the dining hall, headed toward Latham's office. And then everything slows, as if Esmee is deliberately giving me a few extra moments to look more closely. *There*. The vision blurs at the edges, just a little. And instead of going to Latham's office, I turn toward my room instead.

A knot wedges beneath my sternum. No wonder he was able to make me look like a liar. My focus wavers, and I'm about to pull away when the vision shifts again.

Latham. He walks along a dark cobblestone street past an apothecary and then a bakery and then a toy store. He freezes. Touches his collarbone. Curses. He turns around and retraces his steps, watching the ground as he walks. A relieved sigh as he bends to pick up the bone clasp that usually holds his cloak closed. It's shaped like a bear claw. He brings it up to his neck and slides it back into place.

And then he disappears.

My eyes fly open. Terror swells inside me and makes it impossible to breathe.

"You entered your own vision," Esmee says. "I lost you." Her gaze roams over my face. "What is it?"

"We have to go," I say.

"Saskia, calm down. Tell me what's wrong."

"Latham is on his way here. We have to go *now*."

Esmee's expression floods with alarm. "You saw him?"

"As soon as my attention wavered, I saw him walking through the streets of Grimsby."

She digs her fingers into her white hair and massages her scalp. "It makes sense. You've been intensely focused on him all evening. But maybe—"

I tell her about the bone clasp Latham dropped. It must function the same way the necklace does. And for just a moment, both of us had them removed.

Esmee's face goes ashen. "I shouldn't have let the two of you stay so long. I didn't think . . . Yes, lamb, hurry."

I pull the necklace over my head before I race into the main room of the cottage. Bram sits up, rubbing the sleep from his eyes. "What's going on?"

"Latham is on his way here," I say. "We have to leave."

"What? How do you know?"

"Don't ask questions. Just move."

He gives me an odd look, but he stands up and starts gathering his things.

My mother's words scroll through my mind. *Each time something terrible happened, the branch point was Esmee's cottage.*

I've been so foolish to stay here and rely on the safety of the shield. Latham must have seen Bram and me coming before I ever received my mother's letter.

I grab Esmee's books. "May I bring these?" I ask as I shove them into my bag.

"Of course," she says, "take them."

Something about the phrasing makes me pause. "You're coming too, right?"

She gives me the tight smile of someone who is trying hard to conceal worry. "I'll stay and stall Latham. It will buy you some time."

Bram's jaw goes rigid. "Esmee, no." There's something in his expression I've never seen before—something vulnerable and young. I don't know if the shift is real or if I'm letting the vision of him as a child obscure reality. "Come with us. Please."

Esmee stands on her tiptoes and cradles his face in her palms. "You need to go now. Get as far away from here as possible." Her gaze slides to me and then back to Bram. "Protect her."

Bram nods once and then pulls Esmee close and rests his chin on top of her head. "It's been too long since I've been here. And this wasn't enough time."

"Good," she says.

He pulls away and studies her with amusement. "Good?"

"When you love someone, it's never enough time." She smiles at him. "I love you, too. Now get out of here."

Bram and I leave the cottage and hike into a darkness so complete, it feels as if the night has swallowed us in a single gulp. We move in the opposite direction of Grimsby, deeper and deeper into the woods. Cold fear trickles down my spine. I startle at every snapping branch, at every rustling leaf. Latham could be anywhere. What if he saw us leaving Esmee's cottage? What if he knows where we'll end up before we do? I press a palm to the pendant at my throat to reassure myself that it's still there. That my mother can somehow protect me through space and time.

I stumble over a fallen tree limb and a yelp escapes from me before I can help it. I nearly go down, but at the last moment, Bram grabs my elbow and steadies me.

I think of that first day in Ivory Hall. Of how he kept me from falling. But also, how abruptly he let go of me, as if he hadn't meant to help me at all.

But he doesn't pull away so quickly this time. His fingers still graze my elbow. They brush down the length of my arm. He slides his hand into mine.

My breath catches and I'm suddenly grateful for the privacy of darkness, glad I don't have to think about my expression, about what it might reveal.

Bram's skin is rough against mine, but his hand is strong, and it makes me walk with more confidence.

A loud noise splits the night. Both Bram and I freeze.

"What was that?" I whisper.

Before he can answer, a flash of light illuminates his face. We both turn. Esmee's cottage is engulfed in flames. It's so far in the distance that it looks no bigger than a flickering torch. Bram makes a strangled sound at the back of his throat.

"We're never going to be able to run fast enough," I tell him. "We have to find a place to hide."

He doesn't answer. His face is a frozen portrait of horror.

I shake him. "Bram? We have to go now." Nothing.

I step in front of him and take his face in my palms. Force him to look at me. "Esmee wasn't in there," I tell him. "She got away." His eyes begin to focus. "Bram, she got away."

He must realize that, without bones to read, I have no way of knowing whether Esmee is actually safe. But he needs this lie right now if he's going to survive. We both do.

Bram swallows. He gives me a single nod. And then we run.

Saskia
The Tutor

My mother is livid.

"Do you have any idea how dangerous this was?" The bone needle trembles in her fingers. The vein at her temple pulses.

"Not as dangerous as it would have been if you'd attempted it," I say.

"Saskia!" Her face is pale, but for two bright splotches of red on each cheek. "Why do you have to make everything so difficult? For once in your life can you just cooperate?"

"I'm assuming by cooperate you mean obey, right? You don't want me to think for myself?"

She sighs and sinks into a chair. "No, that's not what I mean."

I think of all the times my father used to sit on the edge of my bed and console me after I'd fought with my mother. "That's not what she meant, bluebird," he said once, after she'd called me "pigheaded." The word had sliced through me—an insult that seemed to attack both my looks and my character in one convenient package.

"It's what she *said*."

"Well, sometimes people don't say exactly what they mean. Sometimes they say something else because they're too afraid to say the truth."

"That doesn't even make sense," I told him. "You're just trying to protect her."

He patted my ankle. "It doesn't make sense now, but someday it will. And I'm trying to protect both of you."

I folded my arms across my chest. "So you're saying 'pigheaded' is code for something else? She really meant to say that she finds me intelligent and charming?"

He laughed, a full-bellied sound that pulled up the corners of my mouth in spite of myself.

"I'm not sure I'd use the word 'charming,'" he said, his eyes twinkling, "at least not tonight. But maybe it's code for the fact that the two of you are a lot alike. And imagine how frustrating it would be to have an argument with yourself. You'd always lose."

By the end, I had grown soft around the edges, like ice that's just beginning to melt. That was how my father communicated: He framed each person in their best possible light, judged them by their intentions and not their mistakes. When he died, my mother and I didn't just lose the relationships we had with him but also the glue that held us together.

I sit down next to her. The bone needle is still squeezed tightly in her fist. "What's the *real* reason you're angry?" I ask gently.

Her gaze meets mine and her expression softens. Maybe she's thinking of my father, too.

"You scared me," she says. "I didn't know where you were. I assumed the worst."

I lay my head on her shoulder. "I'm sorry," I say. "I was scared, too. I thought I had a better chance getting the blood from Declan than you would have."

"How *did* you get it from him?"

My cheeks flood with heat and my mother's eyes widen as if my expression has just revealed more than she cared to know.

She curls her hand around mine and squeezes. "Maybe some things don't need a discussion."

At least on that we can agree.

Declan's blood changes everything.

It's as if, until now, I've been trying to find my way through a maze blindfolded, and so when I can finally see clearly, bone reading feels effortless. Familiar. As if I'd already mastered it long ago and I only needed to be reminded. It's as easy as slipping into a warm bath.

But as the day wears on, watching Declan quickly goes from exciting to tedious.

"I can't believe you matched me to him," I tell my mother. I've just pulled out of a vision of Declan eating a bowl of soup with less grace than a still-toddling child. Liquid dripped down his chin and onto his chest and he didn't even bother trying to wipe it away. Still, it was preferable to watching him scratch his hindquarters last night. "He's a buffoon."

My mother ignores my complaints. "Why did you stop watching?"

"He's not doing *anything*," I tell her. "He hasn't moved in hours."

"Saskia, we need to—" Her expression changes. She grabs my elbow and pulls me closer, examining my upper arm.

"Ouch," I say, "what are you doing?"

She lets go of me. Her hand covers her mouth.

I lift my arm toward my face. A faint tattoo has blossomed on my skin—a network of interlacing almond shapes with a circle threaded through the center. The result is an intricate knot design with three corners.

"What is it?"

"I think . . ." She looks unsteady, as if she's just been knocked off balance. "I think it's a mastery tattoo."

I laugh. "That's not possible. I only just started learning."

Her gaze drifts to Gran's bone. "The two halves of the bone are knitting together."

My amusement evaporates. "But my two paths can't affect each other. Can they?"

"I didn't think so. But I don't know how else to explain this."

My shirt is damp. It clings to me. I rub a thumb along the paint at my wrist. I think of the grim satisfaction of the last few weeks, of finding a purpose despite all the pain, of feeling like myself for the first time since my father's death. But this life is as much a lie as this tattoo.

It's a life destined to disappear.

My voice, when I find it, is shaky. "Does this mean I'm a good Bone Charmer in my other life?"

The thought of another version of myself—a happier one—existing once I'm gone is the only thing I have. It's a flicker of hope that I hold close to me, like a flame behind a cupped palm.

My mother's eyes lift to mine. The raw pain there makes me flinch. "I don't know, Saskia," she says. "I don't know what any of it means."

Smoke burns my eyes, curls up my nose. Sticks to me like sand on wet toes. I place the lid over the basin to extinguish the flame, and then spill the bones onto the cloth in front of me. The magic pulls me into a vision, and I smile. The air is clean here. Fresh.

Declan stands on the deck of a ship, surrounded by a small group of people. A bright spark of shock travels down my spine as I take in the man beside him. He's dressed in a red cloak. A Bone Charmer. The man is much older than Declan, probably close to my mother's age. His hair is long and dark, with a hint of gray at the temples. He wears it pulled back and tied at the nape of his neck with a leather cord.

"Everything is in place," Declan says. "We'll have Rakel's bones in our possession by the end of the day." He playfully nudges a girl beside him. "And then, with Bette's help, we can take out the next council member." The name slices through my memory. Bette. Rakel's journeyman. That must be how Declan avoided the truth serum: Bette filled his *keras* with something harmless. She would have had unfettered access to Rakel, too—helpful when planning a murder. The girl giggles and Declan plants a kiss on her neck. Nausea pushes up my throat and I have to force myself to stay in the vision.

"Excellent," the Bone Charmer says. "And how is our other project coming along?"

"It couldn't be going better," Declan says. "Saskia is exactly where I want her."

"She suspects nothing?"

He laughs and shakes his head. "No. She's clay in my hands. She'll be ready in time, I promise."

The Bone Charmer narrows his eyes and Declan's smile falters, then dies. "You're quite arrogant for someone with so much to lose. Do you know what I do to people who disappoint me?" He nods to a man standing beside him, and suddenly Declan yelps and clutches his shoulder. The Bone Charmer leans in close. "I break them."

Declan gasps. "Did you . . . ?" His face is a mask of pain.

"Did I have Lars here break your shoulder? No, he just tweaked it a little as a warning." Sweat beads on Declan's forehead. He looks like he might be sick. The Bone Charmer puts a hand on Declan's uninjured shoulder. "Make sure that girl falls in love with you. Do you understand?"

"Yes." The word comes out as a whisper.

"And make sure we have Rakel's bones by sunset. I'll take what I need to make more intensifiers, and you can keep the profits from the sale of the rest."

"Intensifiers"? The unfamiliar word rolls around my mind. Is that what my father's bones were intended for? But that can't be right. I was able to recover the full set, so obviously this man didn't use any. Why bother to steal them only to let Declan sell them on the shadow market?

The Bone Charmer turns and stalks away. The others follow him—all but Declan and Bette. The two of them disembark from the ship. Declan's expression is still pinched with pain.

"Are you all right?" she asks once they're back on land.

"Do I look all right?" he snaps.

Bette flinches. Her mouth turns to a pout.

Declan sighs. "I'm sorry," he says. "I'm just in pain. It's not your fault."

She rubs his back with the heel of her hand. "That man is horrible," she says. "I don't know why you put up with him."

"Because he's going to make me rich," Declan says. Then he sees her expression and puts an arm around her shoulders. "*Us* rich," he amends.

"When I apprenticed at Ivory Hall last year, I never guessed that one of the Masters was into trading on the shadow market. Or having people murdered. I wonder what his story is."

"Don't know, don't care," Declan says. "As long as he keeps

his side of the bargain."

"But it doesn't really make sense—"

Declan slides a palm behind her neck and lowers his lips to hers. Whatever argument she was about to make fades away.

I suck in a sharp breath as I come out of the vision. My heart hammers in my chest.

"We have to get to the bone house to warn Master Oskar and Ami," I say. "Declan is planning to steal Rakel's bones tonight."

"Wait," my mother says, "slow down. Tell me what you saw."

"Get your cloak. I'll tell you on the way."

Thick clouds race across the sky. I stuff my hands into the pockets of my cloak.

"We'll be lucky if we make it to the bone house before the rain starts falling." Inwardly, I cringe at how wrong my voice sounds. How false. But I want to fill the silence with something other than the truth.

Dread worms inside me.

"Saskia," my mother says softly. "What did you see?" Her words ring with a note of sorrow, as if she's bracing for the worst. As if she already knows it on some level.

"There was a Bone Charmer with Declan," I say.

I don't look at her face, but I can feel her tense beside me. "Do you know who it was?"

As I describe the man, her breathing shallows.

"And there's another thing," I say. "He's a Master at Ivory

Hall." She sucks in a gulp of air as if someone kicked her in the stomach. "You know him?"

"His name is Latham. We trained together at Ivory Hall."

"What was he like?" I ask, desperate to make sense of what I saw.

"When I first met him, he was friendly. Likeable. He was bone-matched with a girl named Avalina. She and Latham were from neighboring towns, and from all appearances they were deeply in love. But halfway through the year, she abruptly left Ivory Hall, and no one ever saw her again. After that, Latham was different. He kept to himself and seemed to resent everyone around him."

"Do you know what happened to the girl? Why she left?"

"Not for sure," my mother says. "There were rumors of scandal. Some said that Avalina's family had bribed the Bone Charmer into giving a false reading, and when the Grand Council found out, their match was nullified. Whatever happened, Latham was clearly heartbroken. And furious with the council, along with anyone who supported them." She sighs. "Still, that doesn't explain why he would be involved in stealing bones in Midwood."

A soft rain begins to fall. It speckles our cloaks. My mother's cheeks shimmer in the gentle light. The rest of what I have to tell her weighs on me like a stone around my neck. "It was Rakel's journeyman—Bette—who helped Declan evade the truth serum." This is the easier part of what I have to say. The other part moves restlessly inside me. I don't want to lie to her. But I don't want to hurt her either.

My mother's hand goes to her throat. "Tell me the rest."

"I'm part of their plan. This man—"

"Latham," she says, her voice a hoarse whisper.

"Latham. Part of Declan's work for him is to court me, to make me fall in love. I think he intends . . ." I swallow. "I think Latham plans to kill me."

My mother is silent. It's the kind of silence that's more than just a lack of sound. It's a hungry silence, one that consumes everything around it—the things said, the things unsaid, all the things that will be said in the future. A silence so full that it bulges at the edges.

"No." She says it softly, but with enough power that it shatters the stillness around us. The wind picks up and whips through our hair. The rain comes at us sideways, lashing, drenching.

"What?"

"No," she says again. "He won't kill you." She turns to look at me and the fierce expression on her face makes me feel as if I've unleashed a beast. "I won't let him."

The bone house is still guarded by Watchers. Several flocks of birds fly in formation overhead. Dogs circle the building. A prowler paces in front of the door. My mother signals to a woman in a green cloak who is standing at the tree line with a large bone flute pressed to her lips. The woman makes eye contact. Her fingers move swiftly across the instrument, and the prowler drops to its belly and closes its eyes like a cat napping in a patch of sunlight.

The Watcher jogs over to us. "How can I help you?"

"I need to speak to Oskar," my mother says.

The Watcher's mouth thins. "May I ask why?"

My mother straightens her spine. Her head cocks to one side. "I am the second-highest ranking member of Midwood's town council and a Third Sight Bone Charmer. That should be reason enough, don't you think?"

The Watcher's eyebrows disappear into her hairline. "Of course," she says. "Forgive my impertinence."

We step carefully around the prowler, who has begun snoring; it's a ferociously wet sound that makes the ground tremble.

Ami looks up from her work when we enter the bone house, and her face melts into a smile. It's one of the things I've always loved about her—the way her expression is always an instant away from radiance, as if she's lit from within.

"Hey," she says, "you must be feeling better."

The lie slides between us like a wedge. But I couldn't tell Ami the truth. If I wanted Declan to believe I was ill, the whole town needed to believe it as well.

"Yes," I tell her. "Much better. How have things been here?"

Her gaze slides out the window, to the dogs patrolling the grounds. "Quiet," she says, "and a bit lonely."

Oskar pokes his head in from the back room. When he sees us, his expression darkens. "Della. What are you doing here?" His tone is decidedly less welcoming than Ami's. He and my mother haven't spoken since she discovered my father's missing bones and the council questioned all of us. Oskar is clearly still harboring some resentment.

"You need to move Rakel's bones," my mother tells him. "Today."

Oskar's face purples. "Excuse me?"

"Rakel's bones need to be moved to another location." She enunciates more deliberately this time, which makes me realize she's holding on to some resentment, too. Her sardonic tone seems to enrage Oskar further. His hands twitch at his sides, and I wonder what revenge fantasy is playing out in his mind.

"Where did you get this information?"

I try to keep my expression calm. But I can feel the heat creeping into my cheeks. I'm sure Oskar would delight in reporting my mother for breaking the law by teaching me bone charming.

Her gaze grows pointed. She arches an eyebrow. "From a vision, Oskar. With bones *you* prepared."

He gives a derisive laugh. "It would take an entire regiment of the Ivory Guard to make it past the Watchers. Did your vision show how anyone could possibly slip by them?"

She shrugs. "And yet I managed just fine." Now she's just provoking him for the fun of it.

"There's not a safer place in the entire town," Oskar says. "I find it a little suspicious that you'd ask."

She rolls her eyes. "Blaming your failings on me is getting a little tiresome, don't you think? Move the bones. Don't move the bones. It's up to you. But if anything happens, I'll make sure the council knows we had this conversation." She turns to me. "Let's go, Saskia."

Ami and I share an uncomfortable glance. We barely got to say hello before things got awkward. *Sorry*, I mouth. She gives me a comical smile, eyes wide, and lifts one hand in a wave as my mother ushers me out the door.

The rain has slowed to a drizzle, but the ground is still soggy. I can barely keep up with my mother as she stomps across the grounds. Our boots squelch in the mud. She mutters under her breath as she walks, but I can hear only snatches of her tirade— individual words that float behind her on the wind. *Arrogant. Condescending. Fool.*

"Della! Wait!" Oskar runs in our direction, struggling to gain purchase on the slick grass. By the time he reaches us, he's mud-spattered and gasping. "I checked on Rakel's bones," he says, "and they're already gone."

Numb shock needles over me. "But that's impossible."

My mother cuts a sharp, silencing glance in my direction.

Oskar turns to me. "Why, Saskia? Why is it impossible? Isn't this precisely what you came to warn me about?"

I press my lips together, afraid of saying the wrong thing.

"What *I* came to warn you about," my mother says. "Saskia wanted to see Ami."

But Oskar's expression says he's not convinced. "What's going on?" His gaze bounces between the two of us.

"I don't know, Oskar," my mother says. "But it's something you should figure out before the council comes calling."

"You know more than you're saying."

"You're wrong. I tried to help, but I was too late. You, on the other hand, have been at the bone house the whole time."

He throws his hands up in the air. "I had nothing to do with this!"

"Then maybe you should spend your energy on finding out who did." A flurry of activity erupts around the bone house as the Watchers pull their animals inside the perimeter and consult with one another in heated tones. "It looks like you're needed," my mother says.

Oskar rakes his fingers through his hair. "This isn't over."

"Yes, that's exactly what I'm afraid of."

A chill seeps into me as we walk through the Forest of the Dead, a slow kind of horror that turns my blood to ice. I'm supposed to have Second Sight. But Rakel's bones are already missing. With a sinking certainty, I realize I didn't do a reading of the present.

I did a reading of the past.

Saskia
The Bone Charmer

The forest is on fire.

Bram and I run until our lungs burn, tripping over tree roots and stones. Clinging to each other to keep ourselves upright. And then a huge rock formation rises in front of us, jutting from the ground like a sleeping beast, and illuminated only by the flickering light of far-off flame.

"The Giant's Foot," Bram says, his tone full of both recognition and surprise. "Come on. I know where we can hide."

He tugs me forward and starts climbing. Does he mean to have us scale the stone column and take refuge under the plateau's overhang? "We'll be too easy to spot up there."

"No," he says, "that's not where we're going. Just trust me."

And so we climb.

I follow him, scrabbling over sharp, uneven rock, trying my best to match his pace, until, finally, he stops at the base of the formation. A small cave is tucked behind a cluster of plants and small trees. A sigh of relief sags out of me.

"After you," he says, holding aside the branches so I can crawl inside. He follows me and we're plunged into utter darkness.

I'm covered in scrapes and cuts. I can't see them, but I can feel their raised contours, and the blood that trickles down my elbows and palms.

Carefully, I lower myself to the ground and Bram sits beside me.

"Are you sure he won't be able to find us?" I ask.

"Yes," Bram says. His breath is so close that I feel it gently lift the strands of hair that have escaped from my braid. "I used to play here when I was small. You'd never know there was a cave unless you were looking."

"But Latham will be looking."

"He'd have to climb over the same rocks and branches we did. We'd hear him coming long before he got to us."

I don't point out that even if we do hear him coming, we'll have nowhere to go.

We don't speak for several minutes, each of us shifting to find a comfortable position, but bumping into each other instead. The cave has barely enough room for both of us.

The silence grows heavy.

"I'm sorry," I say finally.

"For what?"

"Esmee. This never would have happened if you hadn't brought me into her home. I don't . . ." I swallow. "I hope she's safe."

"Yes," he says softly, "me too."

I desperately wish there was enough light to see his expression. To see if I would find resentment there, or understanding.

"We can stay here until morning," Bram says, "and then we'll figure out what comes next."

"We." The word settles against my heart, warm and comforting. I tuck my bag under my head and try to sleep.

When I open my eyes the next morning, Bram is gone.

Disappointment slices into me, swift and sharp and cold. He must have decided not to stay after all. I had a foolish image of the two of us figuring this out together. Of Bram helping me find the loose stitches that have made my life come apart. Of him helping me piece it back together.

I sit up and pull my knees to my chest. My eyes burn with unshed tears. I've never felt more alone. I can't go back to Ivory Hall. I can't go back to Midwood. I don't have a friend in the world who can be a safe harbor right now. I allow myself a moment of despair—just one moment to feel the sadness that wells inside me, thick and consuming—before turning away and ignoring it completely like a misbehaving child. I don't have the luxury of feeling sorry for myself. Not now.

If there is no *we* anymore, then I need to make a plan.

Soft, speckled light trickles into the cave. It should be enough to read by. I move closer to the entrance and pull one of Esmee's books from my bag, balancing it on my knees. If I'm going to escape from Latham, I need to know what exactly he wants.

I flip to the page I was studying last night. My eyes glaze over as I search through more dark-magic spells—all of them full of sacrifice and suffering. They make me feel filthy as I read them. I hate the way Latham has forced me to confront dark magic. To immerse myself in its horrors for hours at a time. And then I come across a phrase that makes my heart stop: *Three generations of Bone Charmers.*

My blood turns to ice as I read.

Complete control of fate is the most powerful of all dark magic and nearly impossible to obtain. The spell requires the bones of three generations of Bone Charmers—one with First Sight, one with Second Sight, and one with Third Sight. All three must be killed violently so that their bones are, in effect, intensifiers. The power of the bones is directly related to how long the three have lived, longer lives producing more powerful magic. At a minimum, the youngest Charmer should have all three essential tattoos before being murdered. The lucky mage who achieves this difficult spell will have the ability to see past, present, and future with perfect clarity. A gift that grants extraordinary power.

All the air leaves my lungs. Latham wants me dead. And not just me, but my mother, too. Realization prickles over my skin as I think of Gran's final days. Of her paranoia. But she wasn't delusional; she was afraid. Latham killed her. He must have. Bile rises in the back of my throat. Did he purposely frighten her in the weeks before her death so that her murder would be more violent?

I think of the kenning day, of my mother seeing each of my paths. Did she see me laughing with Latham, accepting his advice when I never listened to hers? Did she know he wanted to kill her? That he killed Gran? Did my relationship with Latham feel like a knife sliding between her shoulder blades?

I push the thoughts away. Her letter said she didn't know who was watching me. If she knew about Latham, she never would have let me leave Midwood.

A rustle outside the cave brings me to my feet. My pulse goes wild. When the branches part, I'm ready. I lift Esmee's heavy book over my head and smack the assailant hard in the face. He screams. Loses his footing. Hits the ground with a thud. But it's not Latham.

It's Bram.

My chest constricts. I kneel down and take his head in my hands.

"I'm so sorry," I say, my fingers traveling along the contours of his face, trying to assess the damage. Nothing seems to be broken, but his nose is bleeding and one eye is already starting to swell shut. His cheek is turning an alarming shade of purple.

He groans. "Remind me never to sneak up on you again."

I grab my cloak and press the hem to his nose to stem the bleeding. "I thought you were someone else."

"Another guy snuck into the cave last night?" he says. "I knew it was too much to hope that it was you cuddling me."

I give something halfway between a laugh and a cry. "I feel terrible."

"Well, you should. I have very strong feelings about curling up with strangers."

"I thought you left me."

"No," he says, all the playfulness gone from his voice.

He lifts himself to sitting position. His expression is different now. Like some armor has been stripped away and now he's unprotected. "I went to check on Esmee's cottage. I thought it would be safer without you—just in case Latham was still there."

"And?"

His face drops into his hands, and I wonder if he wants to hide his expression from me. If he's afraid of showing his pain.

I touch his knee and his hands fall. "Esmee is dead," he says flatly. "Latham is gone."

A deep well of sympathy opens inside me. I think of my vision of Bram standing outside the charred home of his parents. To have Esmee die the same way is a cruel twist of fate. Or maybe Latham knew Bram's story. Maybe he did it on purpose.

"Bram . . . I'm so sorry. . . ." But I don't have the words to comfort him, and trying to find them makes me feel as if I'm diminishing his sorrow, trying to make it smaller so that it fits into a container I can understand.

So I take his hand in mine instead, lean my head on his shoulder. "Latham won't get away with this," I say. "We won't let him."

"We're not even sure what he's after yet."

"Actually," I say, "I think we are."

Bram's face changes as he reads Esmee's book. A slow dimming. From dusk to darkness. From curiosity to horror.

"Oh, Saskia." He says my name in one anguished breath. Like a funeral cry. Like I'm already dead.

"It explains why Latham wanted to tutor me. Why he was so anxious for me to learn Bone Charming. He hoped I'd get a mastery tattoo so my bones would be more powerful when he killed me. Thank the stars I didn't."

Bram flinches. His eyes widen.

"What?"

"Saskia, I don't . . ."

I follow his gaze to my upper arm and a tremor goes through me. A tattoo has blossomed on my skin—a network of interlacing almond shapes with a circle threaded through the center. The result is an intricate knot design with three corners.

"How is this possible? There was *nothing* there yesterday."

"You said Esmee did a complicated reading with you," Bram says. "Maybe it was enough to achieve mastery?"

I worry my bottom lip with my teeth. Master Kyra did say I was close. But could one reading—even an advanced one— make the difference? And did mastery tattoos just show up like this? Overnight and full of color?

"At least I'm not in love." The words slip out before I think them through. My cheeks flame. Bram coughs. Clears his throat. Looks away.

An awkward silence stretches between us. It's Bram who speaks first. "So what do you want to do?" He motions toward the book. "About this, I mean."

"I don't know," I say. "I wish I had access to bones."

His eyes spark. "You do." He steps out of the cave and scans the ground. And then comes back with a large satchel over his shoulder. "I brought it back from Esmee's," he says, "but I forgot all about it when you attacked me."

I take the bag from him and peek at the contents. It's full of bones, carefully separated into sets sized for readings. In the bottom are several pieces of flint, a small stone, and a velvet cloth. There are also two flasks of water and a bit of food.

My throat gets thick. "You had the presence of mind to gather all of this?"

"No," Bram says. "Esmee left them for you."

"What? Where?"

"In a storage bench by the back door. It was my favorite hiding place when I was small. Esmee probably knew if I came back I'd look there." He rubs a hand over his face. "The outside was charred, but nothing inside was destroyed. It was a good hiding place."

I run my fingers along the bag, tracing patterns in the rough fabric. "I'd feel guilty using these."

"Don't," he says. "Esmee lived without regret. She chose to give up her life so we could escape. She'd be angry if you didn't use her gift wisely."

I smile. "I would never want to make Esmee angry."

Bram grins back—a swollen, misshapen thing, shaded with

grief, that pricks my heart. "No," he says, "you really wouldn't."

Ash falls from the sky like gray snow. The blaze died out long ago—after it burned a path all the way to the Shard—but now the wind plucks the ashes from the forest floor, and they flutter in front of the cave's entrance as a grim reminder of everything we've lost.

A handful of bones is scattered on a cloth in front of me. My head is lightly throbbing. I've been trying to see Latham for nearly the entire day, without any success.

"I think we need a backup plan," Bram says. "If Latham is wearing a shield, you might never see him again." His eyes flick to the limited food and water Esmee left us. "We can't stay here forever."

I rub my eyes with my thumb and forefinger. I feel like a wrung-out cloth. "He'll take it off eventually. If he wants to kill me, he'll have to find me first."

Bram's hand falls to my knee. "But if you don't see him soon . . . ?"

I sigh. "Then we'll go back to Ivory Hall and try to get a meeting with the Grand Council."

Bram doesn't point out how impossible that will be. The Grand Council doesn't simply grant an audience with every apprentice who might have a grievance—especially one who has been expelled. We're far more likely to be detained than to get a meeting with anyone who can help us.

I think of Tessa, Talon, and Linnea back at Ivory Hall. I imagine them sitting under a tree, quizzing one another on anatomy and gossiping about the instructors. I wonder if they think of us, if they miss us. My eyes sting. I long for simpler times, when my only worries were if I was learning bone charming fast enough and questioning if I was matched to the right person.

"You look exhausted," Bram says. "Maybe you should take a break for a little while?"

I shake my head. "No. I'll keep trying."

He watches me carefully, searching my face. "All right," he says, "but at least drink something first." He hands me one of the water flasks. I didn't realize how thirsty I was until I bring it to my lips. The cool liquid sliding down my throat is a relief.

"Thank you," I say, handing the flask back to him.

And then I place my hands over the bones, close my eyes, and try again.

Latham stands on the grounds outside Ivory Hall, framed by the soft light of early evening. A gentle mist leaves flecks on the shoulders of his red silk cloak. His gaze sweeps across the rolling hills dotted with apprentices—studying, eating, a few of them walking arm in arm, the pink flush of new romance in their cheeks.

An apprentice in a blue cloak jogs up to Latham, her dark curls bouncing behind her. Tessa. "Pardon me," she says. "I wonder if I could ask you a question?"

"Of course." Latham gives her the same genuine-seeming

smile that made him seem so trustworthy when I first met him.

"Since you're one of the Master Bone Charmers, I wonder if you might be able to tell me what happened to my friend? Her name is Saskia Holte."

Latham glances toward the sky as if he's searching his memory.

"She was the Second Sight apprentice," Tessa prompts, "and she left recently without saying goodbye."

His eyes spark with recognition. "Ah yes, I know who you're talking about now. I'm sorry, but I can't discuss the results of disciplinary hearings with other apprentices."

Tessa's mouth falls open. "She was disciplined?"

Latham looks chagrined. "Oh no. I've said too much. Please don't spread that around. I'm sure Saskia would be terribly embarrassed."

"Of course not," Tessa says, "but it doesn't make any sense. What could she have done?"

"I've already told you that I can't say."

"Can you at least tell me if she's coming back?"

Latham gives a small, sad shake of his head. "I'm quite certain she is not."

Tessa's face falls. He puts a hand on her shoulder. "I'm headed to Midwood tomorrow morning for some business. Would you like me to find her and ask her to write?"

Tessa presses a palm to her heart. "Yes," she says, "yes, please."

Latham tugs at his collar and the vision fades.

My eyes snap open. Bram is lying next to me, curled on his side, eyes closed. His hair has grown longer since we left Midwood, and now it flops across his forehead. I watch him for a moment. The gentle rise and fall of his chest. His full lips, slightly parted in sleep. The green vine tattoo that curls over the top of his foot. The sight of him tugs at something inside me, and I'm filled with sadness.

I put a hand on his shoulder and shake him gently. He startles.

"What is it? Is everything all right?"

"We have to go back to Midwood," I tell him.

He lifts himself into a sitting position. "It worked? What did you see?" As I tell him, his expression darkens. "Didn't your mother's letter say not to come back?"

"He's going there to kill her, Bram. We have to warn her."

I start gathering our things—Esmee's spell books, the bones, our water flasks—and shoving them into our bags.

"Hey," Bram says, touching my wrist, "slow down. What if this is a trap?"

"Of course it's a trap," I tell him. "Latham didn't just forget to wear his shield. He wanted me to know he's going to Midwood. But here's the thing—now I know he's going to Midwood."

Bram's eyebrows inch up. "I don't follow."

"Latham's not the only one who can lay a trap. I know he's trying to lure me out of hiding so he can kill me. But maybe we can outsmart him. Maybe we can throw him off the trail long enough to warn my mother."

"Saskia, I don't think—"

"If it were *your* mother, what would you do?"

It's a terrible question to ask him, when I know how guilty he feels that he couldn't save his parents, but I need him to understand where I'm coming from. I can't do this without him.

"Well?"

He sighs and rakes a hand through his hair. "I'd go. But how are we going to throw him off the trail when he can't even see us?"

"That depends," I say. "How good of an actor are you?"

Saskia
The Tutor

The walk home from the bone house feels surreal—as if someone has picked up my life and tipped it over and now I don't remember how any of the pieces fit together.

Questions bubble up inside me, but when they reach my throat, they pop and fizzle away.

I'm not sure what my mother could say, what answers she could provide, that would lessen the seeping defeat that is overtaking me. I've spent weeks learning Bone Charming only to interpret the vision incorrectly, to read the wrong moment in time. And now Rakel's bones are gone.

"Your mastery tattoo has three corners," my mother says. Her voice splits through the silence like the toll of a bell at dawn. Sudden and startling.

"Does that mean something?"

Instead of answering my question, she asks one of her own. "Did you know that there weren't always binding ceremonies?"

"No," I say, "I didn't."

"It used to be that magic was allowed to develop naturally, without so many boundaries. Without such specialized training. But some apprentices were skilled in many different areas of magic, and others were only gifted in one. The Grand Council felt it created a power imbalance. So they attempted to even things out with the binding ceremony. If the kenning identifies an apprentice who has bone magic, they are assigned to specialize in one small area. And through the binding, they agree to confine their magic to the boundaries of that specialty. It's like pruning a garden. The magic is directed and confined. And eventually the potential in other areas withers and dies. And the nurtured magic grows stronger."

"But most people don't have magic at all," I say. "So there was already a power imbalance."

She gives me a small smile as if my response has pleased her. "Yes, you're right. Long ago, magic was considered something that belonged to everyone. Not everyone wielded magic, of course, but everyone had access to it. Much like a woman with a beautiful voice—she might be the one singing, but everyone gets the pleasure of hearing the music. And a baker might bake a delicious loaf of bread, but everyone gets to eat."

She sighs. "But now bones are bought and sold. Magic comes at a price. And we all suffer for the loss."

I think of her argument with Audra a few weeks ago: *Have*

you ever thought of the hundreds of children who could have avoided being leftovers if you had done something less foolish with your excess? I always wondered why the town assumes we're wealthy when we're not. We've always been comfortable, but other than the constant readings my mother has performed on me, we haven't lived extravagantly. Now I realize, maybe we've had enough coin to be considered wealthy, but my parents used our excess on something other than luxuries for ourselves.

Sudden warmth flares in my chest. "But what does any of this have to do with my tattoo?"

"You didn't go through the binding ceremony," my mother says, "so your magic hasn't been pruned. It's growing like a plant in the wild, spreading roots and going wherever it pleases."

"So I have First Sight instead of Second?"

"I think you might have both," she says. "And maybe Third Sight, too."

The irony isn't lost on me. I have more power than I ever imagined. Yet in the eyes of the country of Kastelia, I have no power at all.

The next morning I wake to someone pounding on the front door. It's a loud, persistent noise that drags me up through the gauzy layers of sleep. I get up and pad down the hallway, but my mother is faster. I hear the gentle creak of the hinges as she opens the door.

"Valera," she says, her voice full of concern. "What's wrong?"

I round the corner. One of the non-magical members of the town council stands at our threshold. Her mouth is set in a grim line. Her eyes are crinkled with sorrow. Maybe she's heard about Rakel's bones? Gran used to say that bad news travels faster than a storm cloud.

"It's Anders," Valera says. Her voice is raw and it catches on his name. Time slows. Stretches. I don't want Valera to say another word. I want to live forever in this moment between not knowing and knowing. But I can't. "He's dead."

My mother grips the edge of the door. Her knuckles turn white. "When? How?"

"He was murdered last night," Valera says. "His throat . . ." She takes a shuddering breath. "Just like Rakel."

A buzz grows in my ears. Anders was a Healer—his life's work was to alleviate the pain of others. If anyone deserved to die gently, it was him.

Valera puts her palm on my mother's forearm. "Della, you're the ranking member of the council now. You need to decide how you want to handle this."

My mother gives a dark, half-wild laugh. "How I want to handle each of us being picked off one by one?"

Valera frowns. "We need to stop whoever did this so it won't happen again."

My mother's face changes. Like curtains falling closed. "Assemble the rest of the council." Her voice is detached and lifeless. It makes a cold knife of fear slide down my spine. "I'll meet you at Midwood Hall in an hour."

If my mother were home, she'd be horrified by what I've done to the house. It looks like we've been robbed by a gang of thieves. Cupboard doors are flung wide. Drawers slid open in varying degrees, like a mouth full of crooked teeth, furniture that's been moved just enough to be noticeable.

I've been searching for hours, but I finally found it—a small box of Gran's bones hidden in the bottom drawer of my mother's bureau. The box is beautiful—delicately gilded, with a lioness on the lid. It was well concealed, wrapped in a length of blue silk and tucked under a stack of blankets.

My mother will be furious when she realizes I used Gran's bones for a reading. But I'd rather see her angry than dead.

She told me at the kenning that she infused the bones with extra magic so they would allow her to see my future more clearly. I'm hoping they will help me flesh out the details of Declan's plans so we can stop him.

I gather all the supplies together and light a bit of cinnamon incense to increase my concentration. Then I sit on my mother's reading rug and tip Gran's bones into the basin. The bone needle rests on the floor at my knee, but I haven't decided if I'll need it. I'm not sure where to look. Another reading of Declan? Of my mother?

A knock at the front door pulls me from my thoughts. I'm tempted to ignore it, but it could be news about Rakel's missing bones or a messenger from Midwood Hall.

I open the door to find Declan waiting on the front porch. The sight of him freezes my feet to the floor.

"Well, hello there," he says, leaning to brush a kiss against my cheek. "I've missed you." He pushes past me without waiting for a reply.

Panic blooms inside me. The incense is still burning. The basin is filled with Gran's bones. A needle full of his own blood is resting on the rug.

Declan's confident step falters when he sees the room prepared for a reading. He trades one false expression for another—affection for casual curiosity. But his true feelings are hidden under a thin veneer, and his suspicion is showing through.

"Oh, is your mother here?" The way he asks makes me realize he came here knowing she was gone. His eyes flick from me to the bones and back again as if he's trying solve a puzzle.

I blink. My frozen shock begins to thaw. I have to handle this carefully. "She's not," I say, motioning toward the basin. "She had to leave in a hurry."

I break off the glowing tip of the incense stick and drop it into a small bowl of water.

"Is everything all right?" Declan asks. He comes behind me and snakes his arms around my waist. The muscles in my shoulders tense.

"No," I say, gently disentangling from his grip, and spinning to face him. "We just got some bad news. Anders is dead."

His eyes widen. "Oh, Saskia, I'm so sorry. Your mother must be devastated."

I imagine myself with a blade in my hand. *Not as devastated as I'm about to make your mother.* Not yet. For now he must believe I'm in love with him. That I think he's on my side. Still, I can't resist a small provocation.

"She's heartbroken," I say, "but the council has a strong lead on a suspect, so hopefully whoever did it will be caught soon."

He flinches. A tiny movement, barely perceptible, but it fills me with pleasure. His face quickly smooths. "I hope so, too." He circles my wrists with his fingers, and I'm suddenly grateful I reapplied the paint on my wrist before we left for the bone house yesterday. "Is there anything I can do?" His palms travel up the length of my arms, leaving my sleeves bunched at my shoulders. I try to pull them down, but I'm not fast enough. His gaze settles on the mastery tattoo.

Something sparks in his eyes. "This is new."

My mind goes blank.

I feel as if I've been swept up in a vision of the future. A series of images flash through my mind. This moment—Declan finding me in the house alone with a basin of bones and a burning stick of incense; him making the connection to my new mastery tattoo; a report to the Grand Council; a trial; my mother stripped of her status, and possibly imprisoned.

It would take so little to destroy us both.

But then I think of my father. Of the way he used to dole out little nuggets of wisdom like they were candy. "The most likely explanation is usually the true one," he told me once when I kept trying to guess his strategy in a game of Winds and Currents. "When you hear wings flapping, assume birds, not dragons."

The most likely explanation for the bones is that my mother was preparing a reading before she left. My mastery tattoo most likely came from my assigned apprenticeship. Declan has no reason to mistrust me unless I give him one.

"If I'd known a tutoring tattoo would be so large, I would have wished for a different specialty," I say lightly.

"But it's so early to have achieved mastery. Especially when you haven't spent that much time with Willem."

I widen my eyes in mock outrage. "Thanks a lot," I say. "Do you have any idea how difficult it is to teach him when he has a mother like Audra? I'm surprised the tattoo took this long to appear."

He laughs and the knot in my chest loosens. He runs a thumb across the design. "I wonder why it has three points?"

"Body, mind, and spirit. The three cornerstones of a well-rounded education."

He makes a small noise of appreciation. My answer seems to have convinced him, because the suspicion is gone from his expression. He pulls me close and plants a kiss on my forehead. I will myself not to recoil. "I have to get going," he says.

"So soon?" I ask, even as relief floods through me.

"It's a delivery that can't wait," he says. "But I promise I'll see you later."

It's a promise I hope he never has a chance to keep.

Gran's bones wrench me into a vision with more speed and force than ever before.

But it's like trying to swim in a turbulent sea. Waves of images crash over me, one after another, leaving me breathless and disoriented—my mother standing on the riverbank, gazing out over the water; Declan and Latham sitting at a corner table in a dimly lit pub; Ami biting into a ripe apple. I'm not sure if I'm seeing the past, present, or future. I'm not sure of what I'm seeing at all. My stomach spins dizzily.

I decided to use my own blood for the reading. It might be a close enough match to mother's that it'll allow me to see her in the council meeting, or maybe even stretch further into the future to see what danger might be there.

Slowly, a single image begins to crystalize—a pear-shaped face softened with wrinkles, wise gray eyes, a crooked smile that promises mischief and love in equal measure. My heart stills. It isn't my mother I see—but Gran.

I suddenly feel powerless. I long to fling myself into her arms and rest my head against her shoulder, curl up with her on a patch of grass and pepper her with questions, hold her forever. Something inside me splits apart, and two feelings twine together in the chasm like clasped hands. Joy at seeing Gran's face again and sorrow that it's not real.

Gran sits at her dressing table, unbraiding her hair. It spills down her back like a trail of freshly fallen snow. She's humming to herself, a tune I recognize from an old lullaby she often sang to me when I was young. A soft knock sounds at her door.

"Come in," she calls, her voice raspy with age, and so familiar, it makes me ache inside.

I watch as a version of me—a recent one—enters the room, drops a kiss on the top of her head, and sits at her feet.

"What's on your mind, love?" Gran asks.

"Do you think the bones are always right?"

Outside the vision, my stomach clenches. I remember this discussion. It happened the night Gran died. I can't bear to watch. I can't bear to pull away.

Her hand drops softly on the top of my head. "Well, that's a tricky question. I think the bones always tell the truth, but how accurate they are depends on the reading."

"What do you mean?"

"First Sight is the most accurate—the past is a rigid and unchangeable thing. Second Sight is usually correct as well. Sometimes people make last-minute decisions that deviate from a reading, but that's more about the Bone Charmer's range than the accuracy of the bones. It's Third Sight that often proves more thorny."

In the vision, I lean into her. In my memory, I can smell the delicate lilac scent of the oil she used to keep her skin from becoming dry.

"So Third Sight can be wrong?"

Gran laughs. "I feel like this is a trap you're laying for your poor mother. No, it's never wrong. It's just more open to interpretation. Third Sight Charmers see many, many potential paths for someone during a reading. They can't possibly wander down each one—it would take years. So they have to choose the most likely paths to explore."

I turn and look at her. "But what about the kenning?"

"What about it?"

"What if Mother doesn't go down the path I would choose?"

Gran strokes my hair. I can nearly feel the ghost of her hand on my head. "Saskia, you're acting as if fate and freedom are opposites."

"Aren't they?"

"No, love, they're partners in the dance of life. Always circling each other, touching and then coming apart again, both made more beautiful by the existence of the other."

My expression falters in the vision. I remember wondering if Gran's lucidity was fading, as it so often did in the evening hours. If what she was saying was wisdom or foolishness.

The vision moves forward. I watch myself hug Gran good night. Watch her stare after me with an expression of uncomplicated love that squeezes my heart.

And then a noise. A shuffle.

"Who's there?" Gran calls. Someone steps out of the shadows. It's the same man I saw in the earlier vision with Declan. Latham, my mother called him. He's wearing black leather gloves and holding a cloth in one hand.

"It's you again," Gran says. "Why are you here?"

"That was a beautiful speech about fate and freedom," Latham says, moving toward her. "I'm here because I intend to control both."

"Get out." Gran's voice is firm.

He laughs, a dark, horrible sound. "Oh, I will. But not until I get what I came for. I've waited years to find three generations of Bone Charmers."

It's Gran's turn to laugh. "Saskia hasn't even had her kenning yet. She could be matched as a baker for all you know."

Latham scoffs. "I think we both know she won't be a baker.

I've been watching Saskia for a very long time. If anyone ever had a natural affinity for bone charming, she does."

Gran's eyes go as hard as flint. She pushes her chair back from the dressing table and takes a step toward him. "You clearly don't know the women in our family if you think you'll get away with this."

She opens her mouth, a scream already forming on her lips, but Latham steps behind her and presses the cloth to her nose and mouth. While she struggles, he whispers in her ear the graphic, terrible way he will kill her daughter and her granddaughter.

I want to shout at myself in the other room. *Do something! Help her!*

But I can't save her. The past is a rigid and unchangeable thing. Gran died knowing the people she loved most would suffer. For her, that would have been the most violent death of all.

I emerge from the vision, trembling. Droplets of sweat bead on my forehead. My stomach lurches and I run outside to be sick, heaving and gagging until there's nothing left. I wipe my mouth with the back of my hand and sink into the grass.

Gran was murdered while I was in the next room. The knowledge ruptures my grief, turns it into a freshly opened wound, a sharp, blistering pain that nearly suffocates me. If only I had known she was in danger. If only I had walked back into her room once more.

And nestled right beside my anguish is confusion. If Latham's goal was to kill all three of us, why didn't he do it that night? We were all in the same place. It would have been so easy. And why does he need Declan to pass him information? To pretend to be in love with me? The unanswered questions swarm my mind like a colony of ants.

I think of Gran's steely gaze as she promised that the women in our family wouldn't let Latham get away with killing us all. I rise from the ground and go back inside to do another reading.

My final gift to Gran will be to make sure she told him the truth.

Saskia
The Bone Charmer

We're going to use Latham's own plan against him.

He made sure I saw him in a vision to draw me to Midwood. So if he sees us in one, perhaps we can lead him somewhere else. It will only work if he doesn't suspect we're trying to trick him.

Bram and I stand outside the cave. My fingers are clutched around the slender cord of the shield, but I have the pendant pressed tightly to my sternum, so the bones don't lose contact with my skin.

"Are you ready?" I ask. "Once I let go, we have to assume we're being watched."

"Ready when you are," he says.

Carefully, I thread the cord of the shield around a branch and let go. Bram and I make a show of gathering small berries from the bushes, trying to act as naturally as possible. We duck back into the cave and pack up our things, and after a suitable amount of time has passed, Bram touches the back of my hand.

"How are you feeling?" It's the signal we agreed on before I removed the shield.

"Nervous," I say. "But I managed to use the bones Esmee left behind to trade for enough coin to purchase a Swift Note to send to my mother."

Swift Notes are messages sent via bird, usually white-throated needletails, though occasionally golden eagles are used as well. The birds are exceptionally fast on their own, but when outfitted with message capsules made of bone and controlled by Watchers, their speeds are remarkable. But they're incredibly expensive.

"Where did you tell her to meet us?" he asks.

"At the pier in Calden." And then, uncertainly: "Do you think that's far enough from Midwood?"

"I hope so."

My fingers fly to my throat. "My shield . . . ," I say, in what I hope is a thoroughly panicked voice. "It's gone."

Bram's eyes go wide, and he leaps to his feet. "It has to be here somewhere," he says. "I'll help you look."

We make a show of searching the cave and then the area outside until we find it exactly where we left it.

"Oh, thank the bones," I say. "It must have snagged on a branch." I slip the slender cord over my neck and breathe a sigh of relief. If Latham believes we're meeting my mother in Calden, maybe he'll go there first to try to intercept us. It will buy us some time to get to Midwood before him.

I can only hope that Latham was watching. And that we were more convincing than he was.

Bram and I stand on the pier in Kastelia City, waiting to speak to the shipmaster of the *Falcon*. It's one of several winged-fleet vessels—small, narrow ships with three masts and square rigs, that are mostly used for transporting tea and spices. They travel with a limited crew and don't generally accept passengers. But they're the fastest ships in the entire country, and I'm determined to be aboard this one when it sails out later today.

I shift on the balls of my feet as we wait. My hands are sweating.

Finally a man approaches us. He's younger than I thought he'd be—maybe in his midthirties—with bright copper hair and a neatly trimmed beard. "What do you want?"

"We need transport to Midwood," I tell him.

"You had my men call me over here for that? Idiot kids. Go buy a ticket." He points to the other side of the harbor. "Ships leave from over there."

"No," I tell him, "we want to sail aboard the *Falcon*."

"I don't accept passengers," he says, "and even if I did, you couldn't afford it." He walks away.

"We have bones to trade!" I call out.

He stops. Turns. "What kind of bones?"

"High quality. A mix of animal and human. Already prepared

for readings." I open the bag and take out one set of bones to show him.

He gives them a cursory glance. "Nice, but no deal. You two would take up space I can use for cargo, and those bones wouldn't make up for the lost revenue."

I swallow. Pull out a second set of bones. "What if I add these?"

His eyes flicker with interest. "How many bones do you have there?"

Bram and I share a glance. We hoped to hold on to at least some of the bones, but I'm not sure we have a choice. I open the bag wide and show him. He gives a low whistle.

"What in Kastelia's name would make you give up all these bones for a ride?"

"We have to get to Midwood as quickly as possible," I tell him. "It's a matter of life and death."

He studies both Bram and me with narrowed eyes, looking us up and down. Finally he sighs. "I can't turn down an offer like that. Hand them over and follow me."

I give him the bag, hoping I'm not making a mistake. Without the bones, I'll be blind.

Bram and I sit side by side on the sun-warmed deck of the *Falcon*. Crew members give us occasional odd looks, but for the most part, they leave us alone.

The wind blows my hair around my face. In any other

circumstance, it might be relaxing, but all I can think about is getting to my mother before Latham does. What if our final moments together were the ones at the harbor before I left for Ivory Hall? I was so angry that I barely acknowledged her. I didn't even say goodbye. What if she dies believing I hated her?

Would things have turned out differently if I'd accepted the kenning? If I'd forgiven my mother for being a servant of fate? Maybe then we would have left on better terms, and I wouldn't have arrived at Ivory Hall already homesick. Maybe then Latham's connection to my mother—the connection he claimed they had—wouldn't have had the power to warm me like it did, to soften my defenses. I sigh.

"Where did you go?" Bram asks. "You seem lost in thought."

"Do you ever wish you could go back in time and choose a different path?"

He's quiet for a moment, and I can tell he's weighing his answer. "No," he finally says, "not really."

I turn to him, surprised. "There's nothing you would change?"

"Terrible things have happened to me, but I wouldn't change my own choices, no. They made me who I am, mistakes and all. And who's to say a different path would have led somewhere better? It could just as easily turn out worse." He nudges my shoulder gently. "Of course, maybe I'd feel different if I were a Bone Charmer."

"So you believe in freedom over fate?"

"I believe in both. Fate is the ability to see the choices people will likely make. It doesn't rob freedom."

The words have a familiar ring. "Where did you hear that?"

Bram's mouth is soft, as if he's recalling a pleasant memory. "Your mother."

His tone is like a key in my mind. It turns over and lifts my ignorance like the lid of a box. One filled with vivid and glittering insight.

"You *know* her. As more than just the Bone Charmer."

"She always watched out for me. I think she felt she owed it to Esmee. Before I even moved to Midwood—when Esmee was still trying to convince me to go—Della came to the cottage and gave me a reading."

"What did it show?"

His mouth curves into a gentle smile. "She didn't tell me. She just put her hand on top of mine and said, 'I've peeked into your future, Bram, and I promise there's a lot of happiness there.' It was enough to sway me."

Sorrow swells in my throat. What if my mother saw me in that future? What if I was supposed to be part of that happiness? Instead I've spent the last several years pushing Bram away and accusing him—in my own mind, at least—of being a monster.

Gran gave me a blanket when I was a little girl. It was woven on one side with a beautiful summer scene—trees and birds and a golden sun in the sky. But on the other side, the pattern looked completely different, just a jumble of connected threads that didn't make any sense at all. When my mother matched me to Bram, I assumed she was matching me to someone she knew was violent. But maybe she was just matching me to a boy she knew had a future full of happiness.

At midday the shipmaster—whose name, we recently learned, is Gunnar—presents us with a simple meal—hard bread, salted dried meat, and an apple for each of us.

"It's probably not what you're used to, but it's all we've got," he says. "So I don't want to hear any complaining."

But Gunnar didn't need to worry. Nothing has ever tasted better. It eases the gnawing hunger that's been plaguing me since we left the cave. And Bram must feel the same, because he eats eagerly and without small talk.

When we're finished with our food, the crew shows us to our quarters—a tiny cabin with two beds built into an alcove on the wall, one on top of the other. It's so cramped that there isn't room for both of us to stand in the space at the same time, so I slide onto the bottom mattress and sit with my legs crossed at the ankles. Bram follows behind me and settles on the top bunk.

Moments pass. The only sounds are the rustle of Bram digging through his pack and the soft rhythm of his breath.

There are so many things I'm longing to say. All morning I've been on the verge of opening my mouth, yet each time I came close, I lost my courage. This feels different, though—somehow being alone with Bram, but unable to see him, loosens my tongue.

"Before Esmee died, she told me what happened to your parents." I swallow. "I wish I'd known. That day on the prison boat . . . the killer pulled me into a vision of his past when he

331

touched me. He'd done unspeakable things. I was terrified. And then when you grabbed me, I saw the fire in your past. You were so angry. You were both so angry. Later, when I saw your tattoos . . . I was scared and I made assumptions. I was wrong, Bram, and I'm sorry."

He doesn't speak for so long that I'm sure he's fallen asleep. But then I hear him shift above me. Inhale quickly.

"Do you remember the first day we met?" he asks.

The question is so unexpected that I go still. "Yes," I say softly. It was at the Harvest Festival just after Bram moved to Midwood. I spotted him under the shade of an oak tree, braiding vines together into a long chain, so I sat by him and introduced myself. He was shy at first, but with a little prodding, I eventually got him to talk. At the end of our conversation, he twisted the vines into a crown and put it on top of my head. *Keep it*, he said. *It's yours.*

I haven't thought about that day in years.

"I was so broken when I first got to Midwood," Bram says, "and you made me feel like I had a chance for happiness there. Like I might be loveable after all. And for a few years things were good. Until . . ."

I stop breathing. My heart feels like spun glass. Transparent. Breakable. I wait for him to finish the sentence. *Until I tried to help you, but you betrayed me. Until you ruined my reputation. Until you treated me like a criminal.*

But he doesn't. He only sighs. "I wish things had been different between us."

"Me too." My voice catches on the words and I want to say

something more, something that will build a bridge that spans the space between us, but I don't know how. Bram and I were on the same path once. Until I ruined everything.

Until I let my freedom rob my fate.

As the days go by, it becomes clear why these ships are called winged-fleet vessels. They travel so quickly, it feels like we're flying. We sail past towns and villages that would still be a week away or more if we'd been on any other ship.

I stand on the deck, my gaze fixed on the deep purple of the northern horizon. Stars glitter in the distance.

Bram joins me. Rests his hand on the glossy wooden railing near mine. It's so dark that he's little more than a shape beside me.

"We're getting close to home," he says. "Are you ready for this?"

"I don't think I'll ever be ready," I say.

Bram and I haven't discussed our conversation from the other night. It sits between us like a giant boulder in the middle of a trail. We both politely edge around it, but his words are a constant echo in my mind: *I wish things had been different between us.*

Over the last few days something has taken shape inside me. I can feel the contours of it—small. Warm. Heavy. Like a stone that has been worried smooth.

"It's late," I say. "I think I'll head to bed."

"Wait." His hand closes around my elbow and I freeze.

"Our conversation before . . . It's taken me a few days to gather my thoughts." He lets go of me and rakes his fingers through his hair. "You're not the only one who has made mistakes. I hated you for seeing those memories, hated that you looked at me differently because of them, when all I wanted was to leave the past behind. And then, after the kenning . . . you can't imagine how terrifying it was to picture you as the village Bone Charmer. To know that the person I'd need to rely on for readings had looked into my memories once before and found my character lacking." My stomach lurches and my fingers curl around the railing. "The fact that we were matched only made it worse. It felt like I'd never escape you. Like your power would forever shape how people saw me."

Bram's voice stills me, the halting cadence of it, the undercurrent of pain. I feel as if I'm inside a bone reading, watching him at the junction of two paths, not sure which one he'll turn toward. One choice will shatter me and the other will mend my heart.

He clears his throat and keeps talking. "Once we got to Ivory Hall, sometimes I felt like I caught glimpses of you peeking through—that girl I knew before the day on the prison boat. The girl who was my friend. I thought maybe spending time with me again had reminded you of our friendship."

I move my hand so it rests on top of his. "I did see you differently, but not because I remembered who you were then. But because I got to know who you are now. And for what it's worth, I'm not afraid of your power. Not anymore."

"I'm glad," he says. "I would never hurt you, Saskia." His voice is a thread pulled tight.

"I know," I say. "I'm sorry I didn't before."

"I'm sorry, too," he says.

"So, you don't still hate me?"

He gives a small laugh. "No. I don't hate you."

It may be more than I deserve, but it's so much less than I hoped for.

We stand together in silence for a stretch, and then I realize that my hand is still covering his. My cheeks prickle with heat. I shove my fists into the pockets of my cloak.

His fingers slip from the railing and I worry that he'll walk away.

"Bram . . ."

"Yes?"

"I wish . . ." I feel as if I'm stumbling through a room in the dark. Grasping for something I desperately want but can't find.

"What, Saskia? What do you wish?"

I turn toward him. Our faces are finally close enough that I can see his jawline etched in silver moonlight. His eyes hold mine. A silent question. I don't look away.

He slides a palm beneath my hair and rests it in the curve of my neck. My breath catches. Bram's thumb strokes my cheek, and my skin sparks at his touch. I close the narrow space between us and rest my hand against his chest. His heartbeat is wild beneath my fingers. His face dips toward mine.

Then the ship hits a bit of rough water and we lose our footing and stumble apart. I grab the railing to steady myself.

My breath is ragged, and my thoughts spin wildly. I want to go back to Bram's hand against my skin, his lips inches from mine. But the moment was like a butterfly in a cupped palm—delicate, and impossible to recapture once it's flown away.

A group of drunken sailors stumble around the corner, talking and laughing loudly.

Bram sighs, and I hear all of my own frustration in that single sound. "It's late. We should probably get some sleep."

And as I drift off that night, I can't help but wonder if fate will ever work in my favor.

Saskia
The Tutor

he air is thick with the acrid smell of smoke laced with spicy cinnamon incense. A nauseating combination. My head swims as I tip another set of Gran's bones from the basin onto the rug in front of me. I fall into the vision the way one might fall into a swiftly moving river. Easily swept away, but completely out of control.

I take deep breaths and try to center myself. I used Declan's blood this time. As much as I long to see Gran again, I don't have time for self-indulgence. Not if I want to stop Latham before he does something terrible. I need to find Declan, and quickly. I nudge my thoughts toward him, try to see his face in my mind. Images flicker in and out of focus until, finally, I find him.

Declan and Latham stand behind Midwood Hall, their backs

pressed against the stone facade.

"Your girl understands the plan?" Latham asks.

"Yes," Declan says, almost flippantly. "Don't worry about it. Bette has everything under control." Latham's face goes hard. Declan flinches under the weight of his stare. He swallows. "She knows to leave the back door open and to delay Della in the council chamber until we get there."

"We can't afford mistakes," Latham says. "I will hold you personally responsible if this goes sideways, is that clear?"

"Of course," Declan says. "I understand."

"I'm not sure you do." Latham's gaze flicks toward the sky—bright summer blue and cloudless, the sun at its highest point. An orange tabby cat meows from the branch of a nearby tree. "The council meeting should be ending shortly," he says. "Go around to the front and signal me when the members start leaving. We'll go in once they're gone."

I yank my hands away from Gran's bones, and the room snaps back into focus. My heartbeat roars in my ears. Latham is setting up an ambush. I have to get to Midwood Hall before that meeting ends, and warn my mother.

My lungs are on fire and my legs ache. I'm not sure I've ever run so fast in my life. I press a palm to my side to quiet the stabbing pain below my ribs.

Midwood Hall is just on the other side of the town square. I take a deep breath and force myself to make one more hard push across the cobblestones. I let my gaze sweep over the grounds for any sign of Declan, but I don't spot him. Either he's a good lookout, or the meeting is over and I'm too late. I rush inside the building, and I'm greeted by an eerie silence. My footsteps echo as I curve through the corridors. Dread coils inside me like a serpent. I suddenly wish I'd thought to slip a knife into my boot.

A heavy set of double doors hides the council room, and I tug on one of them, relieved to find it unlocked.

But the room is empty.

I turn in a slow circle, confused. I know the council had a meeting this morning—I saw my mother leave with my own eyes. I know Latham and Declan were just here. I was careful to pay attention to details this time, so that I didn't mistake the past for the present. It's the same time of day. The sky is the same shade of blue. I race from the council chamber and through the hallways to the back door. Latham and Declan are nowhere to be found. I must have been wrong.

My gaze flicks upward. A tabby cat studies me from its perch on a tree branch. The same cat I saw in the vision. Did Latham find a way to manipulate my visions to trick me? Is that even possible?

A flash of color catches my eye, and I turn to see an orange cloak.

"Hilde," I call. The Bone Mason turns, and I jog up to her.

"Saskia," she says, "what are you doing here?"

"I'm looking for my mother. Have you seen her?"

"I'd imagine she's back home by now. The council meeting ended a little while ago."

"Did she stay? Longer than everyone else, I mean?"

"No, she left with the rest of us. I'm just coming back because I forgot something." Hilde tilts her head and studies me. "Is everything all right, dear?"

"You saw her leave?"

"Saskia, what's wrong?"

I wave an impatient hand in front of my face. "Did you see her leave or not? It's important."

"Yes, we walked out together. She was headed in the direction of your house when we parted ways and said goodbye. Now, tell me what's bothering you."

But I don't stay long enough to answer. I run toward home as fast as my already-exhausted legs can carry me.

The front door is ajar. The hair prickles at the back of my neck, and blood shudders through my veins. Every instinct screams that something isn't right. But still, I step inside.

And the air goes out of me in one swift motion, like a blow to the stomach that has sent me flying and flailing and careening to the ground.

My mother sits in the center of the room tied to a chair. Declan stands behind her, a knife pressed to her neck. Latham paces back and forth across the room.

"Saskia," he says, "how nice of you to finally join us."

Saskia
The Bone Charmer

The *Falcon* lands in Midwood in late morning. It's a perfect summer day—vibrant green leaves against an azure sky. Just a hint of a breeze coming off the harbor. Warm, but not hot. Bram's hand curls around mine as we disembark. My whole body is still in bloom with the newness of him. The miracle of coming together—of finally seeing each other—in the midst of despair, like two candles flickering in the darkness. His palm against mine is both a comfort and a reminder of everything I could lose.

I woke up today with a delicate pink line around my wrist, so faint, it was barely visible. A wave of bittersweet irony washed over me. The tattoo that marks me as a girl falling in love is the same one that makes my bones more useful to Latham. The moment I finally feel alive is the moment I'm more valuable dead.

341

"Welcome home," Bram says once we're on dry land. His voice sounds exactly like I feel—heavy with worry, but shot through with one slender, golden glimmer of hope.

"You too." I lean into him, longing to say something reassuring, but we both know it would be a lie. I won't feel better until I've seen my mother.

Every time I think of her letter, unease ripples over my skin: *. . . it is essential that you don't return to Midwood. . . . Please promise me that you'll honor this wish . . . No matter how tempting it might be to come home, I need you to stay away.* But she didn't know what she was asking when she wrote those words. And I won't honor her wish if it puts her in danger.

Walking through Midwood with Bram feels surreal. Everything seems smaller, transformed somehow by my travels, as if the town now exists only in juxtaposition with every other place I've been.

A young boy runs past us—Audra Ingersson's son, Willem—chased by his harried-looking tutor.

"Willem, come back here!" she calls out. "Stop right this minute, young man." I don't recognize her—she must have been matched from another town. A pang of sympathy goes through me. Willem doesn't look like an easy charge.

"Did I ever tell you I hoped to be matched as a tutor at the kenning?" I ask.

Bram's lips curve into a gentle smile. "Really?"

"It's true," I say, watching Willem crest a hill, and then spin toward the tutor and stick out his tongue. "Though now I can't remember why."

Bram laughs. And then, in a serious tone: "It would have suited you."

"More than bone charming?"

He considers this. "Maybe not. But still, I'm sure you would have been good."

"What did you hope for at the kenning?"

"I wanted to use my skills to help people. To be considered an asset and not a liability."

"Is that all?"

"Pretty much."

"So you got exactly what you wanted?"

He doesn't miss the flirtatious tone in my voice, and he playfully nudges his shoulder against mine.

But as my house comes into view, my muscles tense and my desire to try to lighten the mood fizzles away. Bram's hand tightens around mine. "Everything will be all right." We climb the porch. "And, Saskia?"

I tip my face toward him and his eyes go soft.

"Yes, I got exactly what I wanted."

A tangle of emotions churns inside me. Most of all, sadness that I can't freeze time and hold this one lovely moment in the palm of my hand. I long to bask in uncomplicated joy.

But that's not the path in front of me.

The door creaks as I ease it open. We step over the threshold. The air is heavy and still.

I move through every room, calling my mother's name, but only silence answers. She could be anywhere. The market. The bone house. Midwood Hall.

Wherever she is, it's not at home.

I wander into my bedroom. It's tidier than I left it—the quilt pulled smooth and tucked in, the pillows fluffed, the furniture free of dust. A pair of too-small shoes sits neatly beneath the bed as if they're still worn daily. As if they might be needed at any moment.

A lump forms in my throat. My mother misses me. She's never been good with words—my father was the more demonstrative parent—but this bedroom feels like reading a love letter.

I sit on the edge of the bed and Bram sinks down beside me.

"We have to find her," I say. Urgency pulses through me like a drumbeat.

Bram threads his fingers through mine. "We will. Let's start searching."

When we get to the town square, I spot Hilde leaving Midwood Hall. Her orange cloak is a bright spot in the distance. Relief leaps in my chest.

"There must have been a council meeting scheduled this morning," I tell Bram. The sun has risen in the sky. It's nearly midday.

"Hilde," I call, "wait!"

The Bone Mason turns and her eyes widen in surprise. "Saskia. What are you doing here?"

"Visiting," I say. "Have you seen my mother?"

Her eyes narrow in suspicion. "Does she know you're back in Midwood?"

"It's a surprise. Have you seen her?"

"Yes," Hilde says, "the council meeting just ended, but your mother stayed behind. Bette asked to speak with her alone."

It takes a moment to pluck the name from my memory. Bette is the journeyman who is studying under Rakel. She finished her Mixer apprenticeship in the spring and arrived shortly before Bram and I left for Ivory Hall.

"Thank you," I tell Hilde.

We hurry up the path. A tabby cat saunters along the cobblestones, stopping to examine us before moving along.

Midwood Hall is nearly empty. Our footsteps echo as we twist our way toward the council chamber in the center of the building. When we reach the double doors, Bram and I each take a handle and pull them open at the same moment.

Time freezes. The world goes silent. I can feel each slow beat of my heart as I take in the scene before me. My mother, tied to a chair in the center of the chamber. Latham holding a large knife. A man I don't recognize stands nearby, his huge arms crossed over his broad chest. He's wearing a black cloak. A Breaker.

Latham got here first. I thought I could beat him at his own game, but I should have known better. He's been one step ahead of me the whole time.

But it's my mother's expression, the sinking disappointment on her face, that finally breaks me.

Time snaps back into place. Blood roars in my ears.

We're all going to die in this room.

Saskia
The Tutor

The walls feel like they're closing in around me. I was so sure I would find Latham and Declan outside the council chamber, so certain that I would be able to warn my mother in time. Gran's bones are powerful—the visions I had while using them were so vivid. But I trusted them too much. Maybe if I'd stayed home, things would have been different. Maybe if my mother and I had been together, we could have prevented this.

"Well, don't just stand there," Latham says. "Come join us." He smiles as if we're at a ball and he's inviting me to dance. I take another step farther into the house, my mind scrambling for how to get out of this. But I'm not sure I can.

"Saskia, think—" my mother starts. But Latham holds up a finger and Declan presses the knife more firmly against her throat.

"Let's not get chatty, Della. We really don't have time."

"What do you want?" I ask. I'm stalling. My mind is teeming with random bits of information, like an unfinished puzzle in a box. I pick up each piece. Examine it. Discard it when it doesn't fit. What was my mother trying to tell me when I walked in? *Think what?* And what does this have to do with the vision I saw? Nausea pushes up my throat as I think of the prison boat. I've been wrong about magic before—so wrong that people died—what if it's happening again? What if I put my mother in more danger by trying to warn her?

"Isn't it obvious?" Latham says. "I want your mother. I want *you*."

"You want us dead, you mean?"

"Unfortunately, yes. Your bones are only useful to me if you're gone. Nothing personal."

I hear my father's voice in my head. Find your opponent's weak spot.

"You didn't get enough money selling Rakel's bones in the shadow market? Now you need ours, too?"

Declan's eyes go wide and he casts a guilty look in my direction. The blade in his hand trembles. A rush of clarity. It bothers him that I know what he's done. *He's* the weak spot.

Latham laughs. "You've been doing some detective work. How charming. But no, I wouldn't dream of selling your bones or Della's. They're far too valuable for that."

If he doesn't want to sell our bones, what *does* he want with them? Why are my mother and I different from the others? Were my father's bones—along with Rakel's and Anders's—just an incentive for Declan? A way to turn a profit in exchange for helping Latham get to me?

Something about the vision I saw dances at the edges of my mind. Something I catch in flashes but can't quite reach.

My mother makes a small noise—a subtle shift in her seat—and my eyes find hers. She's trying to tell me something, but I don't know what.

"Does Declan really need to hold her at knifepoint?" I ask. I need a reason to keep looking at her without drawing Latham's suspicion.

"Oh, is this taking too long for you, sweetheart? Would you like him to slit her throat right now?"

My mouth goes dry. I need to think.

"You told my gran that you wanted to kill all three of us yourself. Now you're going to let some lackey do it?"

Latham's eyes narrow. And then he laughs.

I steal another glance at my mother. She looks pointedly at my hand. I touch my wrist and her eyes spark. The painted tattoo. But what does she want me to do?

"Someone's been learning Bone Charming on the sly, and I must say, I'm delighted. To find you have an affinity for all three Sights is a special treat." He turns toward my mother. "You're such a straight arrow, Della. I didn't think you had it in you. But thank you. Saskia's mastery tattoo was the last piece I needed."

His mention of the tattoo can't be coincidental. Is my mother telling me to get rid of the fake tattoo? I lick my thumb and scrub at my wrist. Her shoulders relax slightly, which makes me think

I understood correctly. But the tattoo isn't budging.

"What do you want with our bones?" I ask as I continue working on removing the paint.

He smiles like a cat with a mouse between its paws. He's enjoying this.

"Della didn't tell you what the bones of three generations of Bone Charmers can do? Oh, that's right. She doesn't believe in using dark magic. Except when it comes to protecting you, of course."

My stomach goes cold. "What are you talking about?"

"Della? Do you want to tell your daughter what you did or shall I?" He motions to Declan to lower the knife. Once her throat is free of the blade, my mother takes a deep breath.

"Saskia already knows that I infused the bones with extra magic."

Extra magic. The thoughts that have been darting in and out of my mind crystalize. Maybe the vision I saw wasn't inaccurate. Gran's bones are more powerful than normal. Maybe the vision was from my other timeline. A slow pulse of dread goes through me. If that's true, it means my two paths weren't so very different after all. I must have stayed in Midwood in both. Declan was working with Latham in both. The small flicker of hope I'd had for a different future, a better one, snuffs out.

"Oh, now don't be modest, Della," Latham says. He turns back toward me. "Your mother used a bit of forbidden magic to make your gran's bones especially potent. Which was brilliant, really. I'd always planned to turn your bones into intensifiers by violently killing each of you. But having the bones actually *prepared* with blood from all three generations—that was a stroke of genius. One I intend to replicate."

Intensifiers. It's the same word he used in the vision when he was talking to Declan about stealing Rakel's bones. Suddenly the recent murders fall into place. Latham has been killing people to amass a collection of especially powerful bones. Maybe that's how he knows so much about our family: He's been using the intensifiers to read our future paths. But what did he want with my father's bones? Papa wasn't killed violently, so they couldn't be used as intensifiers.

"We're not so very different, your mother and I," Latham continues. "It's just that I need her dead to work my magic. And you too, I'm afraid. But once I have your bones, I'll be able to see anything I want, control anything I want—past, present, or future."

"It won't matter," my mother says calmly. "You can't change the past no matter how much power you have. What happened with Avalina—"

"Don't say her name." Latham's face twists with rage. "You have no idea what I can do."

My heart strains against my ribs. We're running out of time. I need to put pressure on the weak point. I turn to Declan. "What did he promise you? Money?"

Declan flinches. He looks a little ill, and I wonder if he didn't know the full extent of Latham's plan until now. Does any part of him still care about me? If so, I might be able to use that to my advantage.

"Was our entire relationship a lie?" I ask. "Did you actually have feelings for me before Latham got to you, or were you acting the whole time?"

He doesn't answer, but he shifts his weight. Licks his lips.

"Enough chatting," Latham says. "Declan, hand me the knife."

But Declan doesn't move.

"He's using you," I say. "Do you really think he'll let you live after everything he just confessed?"

Declan's gaze flicks to Latham. He adjusts his grip on the knife—the blade is slick with sweat. He blinks. He's almost there. He just needs another push.

"You've given him everything he needs, Declan. As soon as we're dead, he'll kill you too."

Latham holds out a hand, palm up. "Hand it over."

Using Declan's moment of hesitation, I ram him in the side, knocking him off balance and away from Latham. The blade flies from his fingers. I pick up a large vase and smash it over Declan's head. He slumps to the ground. I scramble for the dropped knife, curl my fingers around the handle. A surge of victory swells inside me.

But behind me, I hear the chilling sound of laughter.

Saskia
The Bone Charmer

*O*ur plan failed. Latham arrived before us—far enough ahead that he was able to capture my mother. My chest tightens at the sight of her tied to a chair in the middle of the council chamber, at the knife in Latham's hand. Bram steps in front of me as we enter the room, shielding me with his body. "Stay behind me," he says.

Latham's chuckle echoes through the room. "Saskia brought her own Breaker. Isn't that charming, Della?"

My mother ignores him. Her gaze is fixed on me. "You didn't get my letter?"

"I got it," I tell her.

"And you showed up anyway? Saskia, I *told* you to stay away." Her eyes are bright with betrayal.

I've imagined seeing my mother again a hundred times. The thought of it was like a coin in my pocket that I couldn't resist reaching for again and again just to make sure it was still there. It wasn't supposed to be like this, though. I've risked everything to get here. To warn her. I hoped she would be grateful, proud of me at least. But I didn't expect the anger in her expression that slides beneath my skin like a sliver.

"Your daughter came all this way to save you and that's how you thank her?" Latham's voice is thick with outrage. False, of course. But it's as if he knew exactly how to reach into my heart and pluck the string that would make the saddest sound. It gnaws at me how easily he can see through me when my own mother can't.

"This is madness, Latham," my mother says. "No matter how much power you amass, you can't change what happened with Avalina."

I look back and forth between them. His fingers curl into his palms. The name clearly affects him. I think of the faded red tattoo around Latham's wrist and what he said during our training: *I loved her, but the rules of the Grand Council didn't allow us to be together.*

"Oh, Della, let's not pretend you and I are so very different. Look at the lengths you went to to change Saskia's fate. And yet here we are."

"Untie her." Bram's voice trembles with rage. His hands are curled into fists at his sides, his knuckles white. "Now."

Latham's eyes go wide, startled. His leg crumples at the knee. He has to grab the back of a chair to remain upright. "Don't you dare, little Breaker. That's a game you're going to lose. Lars?"

The older Breaker dips his fingers into the pouch that hangs from his waist and snaps one of the bones. One of Bram's ribs breaks with a sickening crack. His face goes pale. He presses a hand to his side, but his expression stays focused. Lars grunts in pain.

"Saskia," my mother says, her voice a low, urgent hiss, "run."

I shake my head. "I'm not leaving you." My eyes flick to Bram, who is still trading breaks with Lars. "Or him."

"Please," she says, "*please* go now while they're distracted."

Instead I edge closer to her, trying to get a better look at the knots around her wrists. If I can untie her, maybe we'll have a fighting chance of escaping.

Lars crashes into the dais. Bram advances on him, rips the pouch from his belt, and tosses it aside. Latham's gaze flicks between them. And then to me. He has to retrieve his Breaker's bone pouch, or Bram will overtake him.

Latham points a finger in my direction. "Don't you move."

But the moment he looks away, I run to my mother. The ropes around her wrists have left angry welts. Blood trickles down her hands. She's clearly been trying to wriggle the rope loose on her own.

Bram lets out a sharp cry and I risk a glance at him. He's clammy, but he's still on his feet. I keep pulling at the knots.

"Leave me," my mother says. "Please, Saskia. Do this one last thing for me."

One last thing. The words are a tight band of fear around my heart. I keep working.

Suddenly I'm yanked backward by my hair. A cold blade presses against my throat.

"Stop or she dies," Latham says.

Bram freezes. His expression transforms from concentration to horror. "Let her go." More a plea than a command.

Latham sighs. I can feel his breath, hot against my neck. A wave of nausea rolls over me. "You've really left me no choice, little Breaker. I'd hoped to draw this out a bit. Her bones would be more valuable if she died slowly. But alas, you're too talented, and I can't have you ruining everything."

I struggle against Latham, but his grip is tight. His knee might be injured, but his arms are strong. When I try to land a kick, he digs the knife into my skin. A warm trickle of blood creeps down my neck.

"Please." Bram's voice is small, broken. "Don't do this."

"Do you love her?"

Bram hesitates, a dozen emotions flickering over his face.

Latham holds me more tightly against him, and I press my lips together to keep from crying out. "Do. You. Love. Her?"

"Yes!" Bram snaps.

"Good," Latham says. "We should all be loved before we die." His mouth bends into a cruel smile. "It makes us so much more powerful."

His knife slides between my ribs. One swift moment of intense pain followed by a numbness so complete, I think I must have imagined the blade. Latham lets go of my shoulders and I stumble forward. I look down. Blood blooms against my shirt, but it feels like a dream. There should be more anguish if I were really dying.

I put my fingers to the fabric and they come away sticky.

Someone is screaming.

Bram rushes to me. Agony twists his features. I try to ask if he's all right—ask where he's hurt and what's broken, but the words come out garbled. He lifts me into his arms and we slide to the ground.

Is it my mother screaming?

Bram presses a palm against my stomach, but I can still feel the blood seeping. "Stay with me," he says. "Please stay with me." I'm not going anywhere. I try to tell him, but I can't breathe properly. I touch his face. His cheeks are wet with tears.

"Saskia?"

I realize my eyes have slid closed and I fight to reopen them. Bram's face hovers above mine, fuzzy. I know this expression. It's the same one he wore in the vision as he watched his home burn. Bleak despair.

"Bram?"

"Yes?" He smooths my hair away from my face. My cheeks are wet, but I think maybe it's his tears falling and not mine.

"Tattoo." The word comes out weakly, but I think he understands. He lifts my arm and a sob chokes his throat. His thumb feathers along the thin pink line. He brings my hand to his lips and kisses the soft inside of my wrist. I cup his chin in my palm and he leans into me. His fingers trace the contours of my face as if he's trying to memorize every detail. Then he inclines his head toward mine, kisses my temples, my cheeks, the spot just below my ear.

Finally his lips find mine. The kiss is slow and gentle and

salted with tears.

Love melts through me. There are so many things I want to say to him, but I don't know if I can find the strength. "Do . . . you . . . ?" I'm too breathless to finish.

Bram lifts his arm and pulls back his sleeve. A bright red tattoo circles his wrist, vibrant and alive. "It's not the first tattoo you've given me." His fingers softly stroke my forehead. His tears keep falling. I think of the tattoo on the top of his foot—the teardrop-shaped leaves dangling from a slender vine. Of Bram twisting the same kind of vine into a crown and offering it to me. I can hear the end of his sentence even though he doesn't say it. The love tattoo wasn't the first I gave him. But it will be the last.

I lift my fingers to his lips and try to speak. ". . . love . . ."

Black spots rush into my vision. And the world goes dark.

Saskia
The Tutor

*D*eclan lies on the ground surrounded by broken glass from the vase I smashed over his head. A slender rivulet of blood trickles down his temple. He gapes at me—my hand now curled around his knife—as if I'm a stranger. But the laughter coming from the other side of the room is anything but afraid.

I turn to find Latham with my mother in his arms—her back pressed against his chest, another, larger knife at her throat. His laughter slides down my spine like ice. "You didn't think I'd give that stupid boy my only weapon, did you?"

"Let her go," I say, "please."

My mother doesn't even struggle against him. Her gaze is fixed on me. Pleading for something I can't decipher.

"Better," he says, "let's have more of that."

"More of what?"

Latham smiles, but it's a wicked, feral expression. "More begging."

Why isn't she fighting? This isn't the woman Gran described when she told Latham he'd never get away with killing all three of us.

"*Do* something," I say. This time my begging is for my mother, not for Latham. Still, it seems to please him.

"Della isn't going to do anything, sweetheart. She knows I intend for her to die violently, so she's trying to slip away peacefully. It won't work, but I admire the effort."

Bile rises in the back of my throat. My fingers tighten around the knife in my fist. I take a step toward Latham. Maybe I can get close enough to do some damage. I have to at least try. My mother gives a subtle shake of her head.

Latham makes a disapproving noise. A sharp pain shoots through my leg and I cry out. Frantically, my gaze darts around the room. I spot a man in a black cloak skulking in the hallway. A Breaker.

"Thank you, Lars," Latham says, and the man melts back into the shadows. "Consider that a warning. Now, then, where were we?"

"Stop playing games, Latham," my mother says. "Leave her alone. My bones will provide more than enough power for one person."

"Ah, but I'm not just doing this for one person. I'm doing it for every Charmer whose power has been limited by the council. Every Charmer who has lost someone they should have been able to save. Every Charmer who has been prevented from controlling fate by the ridiculous rules of the council. I would think you of all people would understand, Della."

"I'm the last person who will *ever* understand," my mother says.

Latham's voice goes soft, as if he's whispering in the ear of a lover. "Didn't you always say that the kenning should be free? That the council's rules favored the privileged instead of the most talented? You were right, Della. Avalina and I would be together if not for the council. And perhaps your husband would still be alive if you'd been willing to break a few rules, too."

I feel the blood drain from my face. *Could* she have saved my father?

"Even if you're right, this isn't the way to go about changing things." She swallows, and her eyes flick to me. "And I couldn't have saved Filip. Some things can't be altered."

"With enough power, *anything* can be altered. You have no idea the marvelous things I have planned for Kastelia. Think of this as a worthy sacrifice for your country."

"You don't care about anyone but yourself. You never have."

Latham's blade bites into her flesh. A trickle of red runs down her neck, bright against her pale skin. "I won't tell you to be quiet again."

"You don't have Gran's bones yet," I say, grasping tightly to this fact, like a slender branch arching over a vortex. "If you kill us, you'll never find them."

"Don't I?"

His tone makes my gaze cut to my mother. Her expression

is stony.

"I don't have *all* of them, it's true," he says. "Della used a few in the kenning." He waves a hand toward the basin on the other side of the room. "And it appears one of you used a few more recently. But the rest of them? They're mine."

"How?" I ask. "When?"

He gives a dark laugh. "Della didn't tell you? I've had your grandmother's bones since the handlers finished preparing them. Except for the few Della held back and had prepared on the sly, but I'll get those in time."

"You're lying," I say. "Oskar would have told us they were missing."

"Oskar is an incompetent fool. He *still* doesn't know they're missing," Latham says. "So, when I took your father's bones, I made sure to make it obvious enough that even he knew they were gone. I needed something personal to get you involved, dear Saskia."

I think of the open, empty box in the middle of the floor at the bone house. Of my mother speculating that someone wanted her to know what they'd done. Latham was taunting her. But why? I try to remember what he said about my mastery tattoo. Something about it being the last piece he needed. My father's missing bones, along with Anders's and Rakel's murders, led my mother to train me. Latham must have known exactly what series of events would lead to the tattoo on my arm. He's been planning this for months. Maybe for years.

And I played right into his hands.

If the bone hadn't broken, if I'd just accepted my fate,

maybe we wouldn't be here now. Maybe I wouldn't feel so powerless.

But I'm not powerless. I may not be matched as a Bone Charmer, but I'm trained as one. And that has to be good for something. Still, it's not as if I can pull out a set of bones and do a reading right here and now. *Find your opponent's weak spot. Nurtured magic grows stronger.* My father's and my mother's wisdom echo in my mind and melt together. I think of the first time I was successful reading the bones. Of Latham's words to Declan—*make sure that girl falls in love with you.*

My thoughts spin around my mind like a child's toy.

And then they slow.

Tip.

And go still.

Latham needs me to have the mastery tattoo, but he needs me to have the love tattoo as well.

And I don't.

My plan to trick Declan into believing I'm in love with him is Latham's weak spot. I can use what Latham doesn't know against him. *That* is my power.

I scrub at my wrist more vigorously. Finally the tattoo begins to smudge.

"Latham, don't do this," my mother is saying, "please."

She's trying to buy me more time. I lick my thumb and smear the paint along my skin.

"Avalina wouldn't want this for you. She'd hate what you've become."

Latham sucks in a sharp breath. He turns to me and I freeze.

His head cocks to one side. Birdlike. Inquisitive. "How about a small mercy, Saskia? Would you like to embrace your mother one final time?"

My mind goes blank. I know the question is a game, but I can't understand the strategy.

He drops the knife to his side. "Well?"

"Yes," I say, my voice tight.

He gives my mother a little shove. "Go on then. Say your goodbyes."

She takes a step toward me. And then another. Her expression is resigned, sad. She gives me a small smile as she reaches for me. And then, suddenly, her eyes go wide. She looks down at her chest, at the blood that seeps through her shirt.

I was only a moment away from falling into her arms, when Latham stabbed her in the back.

My vision goes red. I scream. "Mama, no. Please, no!"

My mother falters. I catch her, and we sink to the floor. Her breathing is ragged. Her eyes are glassy. I press my hands against the wound, but blood oozes through my fingers. Tears flow down my cheeks.

Latham grabs me by both arms and yanks me backward. My mother tumbles away from me, still gasping.

I struggle against Latham, elbow him hard in the nose. He grunts and tightens his grip. My shoulder blazes with pain. Latham flips me onto my back and presses the knife to my throat. I rear up and punch him in the face.

He flips the knife around in his fist so the blunt end of the handle is facing me, and then he brings it down hard on my temple. Pain explodes in my head. Warm blood trickles down my cheek.

"My love tattoo is a fake!" I cry out.

His expression falters. "What?"

"I could *never* love someone like Declan."

He whips his head in Declan's direction. "She better be lying."

Latham uses his knees to pin my shoulders down. He catches my wrist and twists it viciously, bending my entire arm at an unnatural angle. Agony makes nausea rise in my throat. He brings my hand close to his face and examines my wrist. I can only hope I've done a good enough job of smearing the dark paint.

Declan makes a noise that sounds like a frightened animal. His eyes are trained on me and full of dread. Latham spits on my wrist and scrubs at my skin. Quiet fury chisels his features. Then, abruptly, his expression changes. He smiles. Begins to laugh.

He drops my hand and sits back on his heels. I examine the tattoo and my heart ices over. Beneath the smeared paint, a faint pink line has etched itself around my wrist.

And I have no idea where it came from.

I push the hair off my forehead and scoot away from him. If I can just get to my mother . . .

"Don't bother," Latham says quietly. "She's already dead."

He's lying. He has to be. I crawl toward her even though my head screams in protest. She lies prone in a pool of blood. Her eyes are open and vacant.

"No!" The word scratches from my throat. "Please, no."

I reach for her, take hold of her cold hand in mine. My vision blurs. Hot tears roll down my cheeks and I don't bother to wipe them away. For months I've worried about this reality winking out of existence, but simply disappearing would be a far more merciful end.

"Lars," Latham says, "tie her up. We're going to kill her slowly."

The Breaker yanks my hands behind my back and secures them with a rope. I try fighting him off, but it's no use. I've lost too much blood and he's too strong.

Latham stalks toward the kitchen, and I hear cupboards and drawers opening and slamming closed. My stomach seizes. He's probably looking for things to torture me with.

I turn toward Declan. He sits motionless in the corner, still surrounded by broken glass. But his expression is haunted and full of regret. He's been my ruin, but he's also my last chance for survival.

"You never answered my question," I say softly. "Did you ever care about me at all?"

He flinches. His eyes are uncertain as they fall to my wrist. Is he wondering if the tattoo means I'm in love with him after all? Can I use that to save myself?

"We've been through so much together. Declan, please."

His gaze darts to Lars, who is sorting through his satchel of bones. Declan's fingers close around a shard of glass. I give him an encouraging nod. If he can incapacitate Lars, we'll have a much better chance of escaping. Latham won't be nearly as powerful without his Breaker.

In one fluid motion, Declan springs to his feet. But instead of attacking Lars, he races away from the Breaker and toward the front of the house. The last of my hope bleeds away and white-hot hatred burns through me. I should have known he'd abandon me and save himself.

Declan throws open the door. "Help!" he screams. "Somebody help! We—" His words strangle off and he slumps to the ground. Lars stands at the threshold, his bone pouch gaping open, a broken frog vertebra between his thumb and forefinger. I gag at the thought of Declan's spine snapping.

Latham runs from the kitchen, his face twisted with rage. He holds a mallet in one hand and a long needle in the other. "You idiot!" he shouts at Lars. "How did he get outside?"

The Breaker's face goes stony. He dips a hand into the pouch at his waist and lets the tiny bones tumble through his fingers. "This town is crawling with Watchers." His eyes flick to me. "You better kill her now."

Latham glances out the window and his jaw goes tight. "Too late. The Ivory Guard is almost here."

He bends and scoops my mother's lifeless body into his arms. I ram my shoulder into his leg to try to stop him, but he aims a foot at my temple and kicks me away. Pain shoots through my head. I taste salt and I don't know if it's from blood or tears or both.

Latham heads toward the door, cradling my mother close to his chest, and I sob. "Please," I say. "Please don't take her."

He turns to me and smiles. "I'll see you soon, Saskia. You can count on it." He leaves, and I'm left alone to wonder how it is that a broken heart can continue beating.

Saskia

I swim through layers of darkness, trying to reach the surface, but sleep tugs at me. Pulls me under. Holds me captive.

My skull is heavy with hammering pain. Throbbing and relentless. Distantly, I'm aware that something needs my attention—my mind stretches for it, but it's out of my grasp. The pounding is too loud to focus. Images pull me up toward the surface—my mother braiding her hair, expert fingers darting between pale strands; Ami lying in the grass on the bank of the Shard, her toes digging into bright green grass; Gran pulling me on her lap for a story. And then other images thrust me deeper into the darkness—the glint of a blade against a throat; wide, shocked eyes; acid fear.

I instruct my eyes to open, but they won't obey. It's too much effort. And so I give up and let the darkness swallow me, let it

369

sweep me away to a place where pain doesn't exist and hearts can't be broken.

A scream punches through the heavy silence that envelops my mind. My eyes fly open. I try to sit up, but my head pulses with pain. My limbs feel slow and heavy.

"Saskia?" Ami's voice perches on the razor edge of hysteria. She kneels beside me. "Can you hear me? What happened?"

I flinch away from the memories that swarm my mind. Nightmares. Only nightmares. Except . . . the thoughts don't float away when I try to hold them, like dreams do. They grow more vivid. More real. Grief pushes against my rib cage. I make an involuntary noise.

Ami loosens the knots at my wrists and then dabs at the blood on my forehead with the edge of her sleeve. "There's a dead Watcher outside"—her voice wobbles—"and Declan . . ." She trails off. "Sas, who did this?"

I squeeze my eyes tightly closed before opening them again. "I want . . ." It's so hard to speak. The words feel like gravel in my throat. "I want my mother."

Ami bites her lip. Her eyes fill with tears.

"You need a Healer," she says. I can hear the forced calm in her tone, like she's struggling to hold herself together. She squeezes my shoulder gently. "I have to leave for help, but I won't be long. You're going to be fine, I promise."

But she's wrong. I will never be fine again.

The door closes behind her and I try once more to pull myself into a sitting position. My head throbs and a wave of dizziness washes over me. When my eyes finally focus, I wish I'd never opened them. My mother is gone, but the pool of blood remains, a reminder that it wasn't just a bad dream. Sorrow pushes up my throat, so thick that I can scarcely breathe.

My gaze flicks to Gran's bone on the shelf. I'd been so worried about this life disappearing, but now it's my only tendril of hope. I long to wink out of this existence and live in a world where my mother survives. Carefully, I lift myself to my feet. My head aches. I pull the bone from the shelf. It's still suspended in the nutrient solution. I turn it from side to side. Examine it from all angles.

And then I sink to my knees.

The bone is completely healed. This is the reality that survived.

Gran's words drift through my mind. I taste the bitter truth of them. *The past is a rigid and unchangeable thing.*

My mother is gone forever.

Time passes. The shadows in the room elongate, become distorted versions of the objects above them. Darker, uglier versions of the truth.

Vaguely, I wonder where Ami has gone. And then I remember that Midwood doesn't have a Healer anymore. Anders is dead. Just like Rakel. And Declan. And my mother.

I rub at the paint on my wrist until the pink line underneath is clearly visible. I've waited months to see this—first with the breathless hope that I was actually in love with Declan, and later when I was desperate to trick my body into believing something that wasn't true. But it never appeared. So why now?

Tattoos always occur in response to highly emotional experiences. It's why so few children have tattoos from loving their parents. That kind of love is too instinctual, too gradual. But plenty of people who didn't have love tattoos before they were parents get them the first time they hold their child in their arms.

It's a singular moment of overwhelming love.

But maybe seeing a knife pressed to my mother's throat—realizing what it would mean to lose her—was enough for the tattoo to materialize. It's the only explanation I can think of.

Voices drift from outside and pull me from my thoughts. I yank Gran's bone from the nutrient solution and shove it into my pocket.

The door opens, and Ami comes in, followed by the two non-magical members of the town council—Valera and Erik—along with several people I don't recognize. A collective gasp ripples through the room.

"Oh, sweetheart," Valera says. Something about the tender note in her voice, the raw pain, makes fresh tears fall. "What in the name of bones happened here?"

The story tumbles from my lips like broken glass—sharp and startling, with jagged pieces that cut as they fall. I tell them about everything except Gran's broken bone. I don't know how I would explain it, and even though my mother is gone, I still want to protect her secrets. Besides, maybe my timeline never split at all. Maybe this terrible life was the only one I ever had.

A Healer comes from Brisby the next day. He's an older man with a thick mane of bright silver hair. His hands are gentle as he examines me. The lump on my head is the size of a plum, and still hurts when I move.

"You'll recover, but you should rest for a few days. No running. No swimming. As much sleep as possible." My whole family is dead. All I want to do is sleep.

He lays a palm on my forearm. "You've had to suffer far more than is fair for someone so young. I'm not a skilled enough Healer to ease that pain. It won't ever go away—not completely—but remember that sharp things tend to dull over time."

I turn my face away and stare at the wall. I'm in no mood for folksy wisdom or false promises. The Healer waits for a while before he seems to get the message that I'm not going to say anything more.

"I'll leave something on the bedside table for the pain." He gives me an awkward pat on the back and then leaves, closing the door behind him.

I drain the medicine in one swallow. Bitterness coats my tongue and slides down my throat. I sink back against the pillows and wait for my pain to disappear. It doesn't.

I chase sleep, but I never catch it. Each time I start to drift off, I jolt back awake, breathless. It's as if my mind knows that sleep is a creature with claws. That my nightmares won't fade when I wake.

A gentle knock sounds at the door and Ami pokes her head inside. I've stolen her room, her bed, her peace. "Can I come in?"

"Of course."

She sits on the edge of the bed. "Feeling any better?"

I shrug. The thick feeling of the medicine has started to wear off, and the lucidity that comes with it is unwelcome.

"The Grand Council is sending a team to investigate," Ami says, "and the Ivory Guard is searching for Latham. I thought you'd want to know."

"They won't find him."

She frowns. "They might."

But she's wrong. He robbed the bone house while the Ivory Guard stood outside. While a team of Watchers had their animals circling the building. Whatever magic he has at his disposal is stronger than theirs.

Dawn seeps through the curtains. The hours have trickled by like days. The days like months. I am trapped by time—it moves too slowly and too quickly all at once. I can hardly believe that my mother has been gone nearly a week. And yet she feels so far away, so out of reach, it's as if we haven't been together in a year.

And I still can't bear to go home.

A throat clears—deep, masculine—and I lift my head.

Bram Wilberg stands at the threshold. The sight of him sends a jolt of recognition through me. Since the encounter with the prisoner when I was twelve, each time we've crossed paths, I've felt a combination of guilt and fear that made me want to turn away. But now . . . there's something else. An unfamiliar stirring in my chest that makes me equal parts curious and confused.

"I'm sorry to arrive unannounced," he says. "Can I come in?"

I smooth a hand over my hair, suddenly self-conscious about my messy, day-old braid. "Yes, of course." My voice comes out gravelly, whether from too much crying or not enough talking, I don't know.

Bram comes to my bedside. His gaze falls to my hands and his eyes widen in surprise. At first I think he's looking at the love tattoo around my wrist. But he's not. He's staring at the small black tattoo on my knuckle. Suddenly the full weight of our history sits between us like a barricade. I tuck my hands beneath the quilt.

Bram's expression clears, like a slate wiped clean. "I heard about your mother. I'm so sorry. She was a wonderful woman." It's the same sentiment I've heard at least three dozen times as townsfolk have come to pay their respects.

"Yes," I say woodenly, "she was." Something elusive dances at the edge of my mind, but I'm too sluggish to reach it.

"How are you?" he asks.

"I'm surviving."

His face falls. "I'm sorry. What a terrible question. Of course, you're not well. You'd think after six days on a ship I would have thought of something better to say."

Suddenly the room comes into sharp focus and I realize what I couldn't put my finger on before. Bram got here far faster than should have been possible. If he's spent the last six days on a ship, he would have had to leave Ivory Hall almost immediately after my mother died.

"How did you find out about what happened?"

"Oh," Bram says, "Master Latham let me know."

My stomach lurches. "You saw Latham? He was at Ivory Hall?"

Bram's brows pull together, as if confused by my strong reaction. "Actually, no, he sent a Swift Note suggesting you could use a visit. He's kind of taken me under his wing this year. And since he knew I was so close to your mother . . ." My blood chills and Bram stops talking. "What is it? What's wrong?"

"Bram, Latham was the one who killed her."

His face goes slack. "No," he says, "that can't be right."

"I was *there*. She fell into my arms after he stabbed her in the back."

He sucks in a sharp breath. "That doesn't make any sense. Why would he do that? And why would he send *me* a message?"

I run my palms up my arms, suddenly cold. I don't even know where to begin to explain.

Bram touches my elbow gently. "Is there anything I can do?" Both the expression on his face and the tone of his voice are so hauntingly familiar that I feel a tug low in my belly.

"Actually, yes," I say. "Could you get me the supplies for a bone reading?"

Saskia

$\mathscr{I}$ sit on the floor of Ami's room in front of a stone basin with only a solitary bone in the bottom. Bram paces back and forth across the length of the room. "I still don't understand how you're going to do a reading when you were matched as a tutor."

I'm not sure how much to tell him. Two warring impulses battle inside me—one is an inexplicable tenderness for Bram, a nearly irresistible pull toward him that makes me want to confess everything. But the other is just as strong—I can't help but mistrust him. The last person Latham pushed in my direction betrayed me. What if Bram is the new Declan?

I swallow and settle for a middle ground. "My gran's bone broke in the kenning, and it . . . complicated things. I'm hoping now that it's healed, I can see what my mother saw and figure out what to do."

"But you aren't trained," he says. And then, after a pause: "Are you?"

"I'm trained enough."

I prick my finger with a sewing needle and speckle the bone with my blood. *Gran, wherever you are, please make this work.* I use a rock and a piece of flint to set the bone alight, and then I close my eyes.

Color bursts behind my lids and I'm pulled into a vision. Dozens of paths stretch out before me, splitting off into hundreds more. But a few branches start off brighter and wider than the others. I wander down a well-lit path and see myself waiting at the harbor for the ship that will take me to Ivory Hall. Bram boards along with me. We're matched, but we're both unhappy about it. This path splits into dozens of others. I explore them one by one.

In most, Bram and I slowly come to terms with our past, take down the wall between us, and fall in love. On a few paths, we avoid each other and reject the match. I watch myself get trained as a Bone Charmer, failing at first, but eventually learning. Accepting my power. Becoming gifted. But then I see something that pulls me up short. Some of the paths have gaps in them, short periods of time where I seem to disappear. In each of those paths, I eventually end up at a small cottage in a town I don't recognize. In some of them, I see myself die violently, though the identity of my attacker is invisible. In others, I hold a letter from my mother warning me that I'm in danger. A necklace with three interlocking circles slides from the envelope. I put it around my neck and the path disappears. Not a gap, but an end. I watch myself die again and again. I have no doubt the future my mother selected for me in the first kenning led to a rich and full life—she wouldn't have picked it otherwise. But whatever choices I made afterward must have veered it off toward disaster.

I rush backward and go down each of the paths that start with me staying in Midwood. This time there are no gaps. Sometimes I am matched as a tutor and gain a mastery tattoo very different from the one that now rests on my arm. Other times, I'm matched as a jeweler, a baker, a cobbler. In each, I gain a different mastery tattoo. And every single path fizzles out shortly after it starts. I die violently by the hand of someone who is invisible to me, was invisible to my mother. Latham. He kills me at the end of all of them.

All except one.

One slender, poorly lit path leads to a bone match with Declan. In that path my life plays out more or less how it really did. It's my mother who dies. And I live.

Once she takes her final breath, a thousand other paths widen and blaze to life. And Latham waits in the shadows to kill me at the beginning of all of them. I try to follow the options as they branch off, but they're too hazy too see. I must not have enough bones—or enough range—to keep going.

I pull out of the vision breathless, and sobbing. My mother knew Latham would kill her if she chose this path. She died so I could live.

A hand falls on my shoulder. "Saskia, is everything all right?" I'd forgotten Bram was here. The sound of his voice brings back every tender feeling I experienced as I wandered down my Ivory Hall paths. I stand up and turn to him, my voice urgent. "You have to go back to the capital. You'll be in danger if you stay near me."

I realize now why Latham sent Bram. Bram isn't the new Declan. Not in the way I thought, anyway. Somehow Latham collected enough intensifiers to see both of my paths.

I think of his delight when he mentioned my mastery tattoo before he killed my mother. He needed me to have it before I died, so he must have planned for me to get that tattoo in my other reality, but I got it here instead. And I think of the slender pink tattoo that mysteriously appeared without me falling in love. It must have come from my Ivory Hall path, even though Latham thought I'd fall for Declan and get it in Midwood.

He knew the tattoos would appear across timelines and was scheming to kill me in both. If he's seen my other possibilities, then he knows Bram is the person I'm most likely to end up with. That's why he sent Bram back to Midwood. Latham wants me to fall for Bram in this reality, too.

Because love tattoos—just like love itself—can fade. Things that aren't nurtured eventually wither. And without all three tattoos, my bones will be worthless. Ensuring the tattoo stays intact buys him some time to kill me.

The more connected Bram is to me, the more at risk he'll be, which means I need to stay as far from him as possible.

"What happened?" Bram asks. "What did you see?"

"Latham wants me dead. He has my gran's bones and my mother's, too, and he isn't going to stop chasing me until he kills me." I take his fingers in mine, and they feel familiar in a way that makes my heart crack open. "Thank you for coming, but you have to go now."

"Saskia, what's going on? I'm not just going to leave if you're in danger."

For one brief, glittering moment, I imagine myself clinging to him. Begging him to stay and fight with me. Telling him we could have a great love story, that we did once in another life. But it's time for me to grow up, to be my mother's daughter. I need to be as unselfish as she was. I pull my hand away from his.

"Go," I tell him. "Please."

"No. Saskia, I want to help you."

The earnest expression on his face breaks my already splintered heart in two.

I know what I have to do, but the thought sickens me. I take a deep breath and force a chill into my voice. "Avoiding me is a better path for you. Go back to Ivory Hall. Forget I ever existed."

He cocks his head to one side and studies my face. "You didn't do a reading on me, so how do you know a different path would lead somewhere better? It could just as easily turn out worse."

The words reverberate in my mind. He's said something similar to me before. In another place, another time. I would bet my life on it.

"Bram, please." My throat feels tight. I fight competing urges to embrace him and push him away. "Latham wants me dead. I don't want you to be in danger, too."

"He killed your mother and then sent me here to help you mourn." Bram's hand drops to mine, curls around my fingers. "I think it's already too late."

I should yell at him. Say something so awful that he never wants to speak to me again. Find a way to hurt him so deeply that it keeps him safe.

But I feel hollowed out, empty enough that I could simply drift away, and his hand in mine is the only thing keeping me tethered. I can't bring myself to do it.

"We were friends once," he says. "Remember?"

"Yes," I say softly, "I remember."

"Then let me help. For your mother." He tugs on the back of his neck. "For you."

The thought of having Bram by my side, of not having to face this alone, wraps around me like a warm blanket. Maybe I can be strong enough to accept Bram's friendship without falling in love with him? Maybe the tattoo can still fade away and keep both of us safe?

Or maybe fate has other plans.

Another week passes before I can bring myself to go home. Someone—probably at the behest of the town council—has cleaned the house from top to bottom. The blood has been scrubbed from the floor and the walls, the glass swept away. The sharp scent of wood polish is thick in the air.

I wander through the rooms like a stranger. The house feels like an empty husk. My mother was its soul, and now it's just a collection of things sharing the same space.

I run my fingers along the fireplace mantel. I'm an orphan. I feel myself being remade by this fact, shaped into something harder. Something with fewer curves and more angles. I don't know where to go from here.

"Hello? Is anyone home?" A woman steps over the threshold. Her silver hair is braided and rolled into a tight bun at the back of her head, and she has a yellow half-moon–shaped tattoo on the side of her neck. She sees me and her face relaxes into a smile. "The door was open," she says, extending her hand. "You must be Saskia."

"Yes." I take her hand. "And you are?"

"Norah. I'm Steward of Ivory Hall." She must see my blank expression, because she explains, "I'm in charge of all the apprentices who train in the capital."

"Oh," I say, "nice to meet you."

"I'm terribly sorry for your loss," she says. "Della was beloved by everyone who knew her." By now the sentiment has lost all meaning, and only makes me feel numb.

"Did you?" I ask. "Know her, I mean?"

"Only by reputation. But many of the instructors who have taught at Ivory Hall spoke highly of her."

"One of your instructors *killed* her," I say. These days my patience is a shallow puddle that evaporates quickly.

Norah swallows. "I'm aware of that. We're doing everything we can to find Latham. I'm confident we will. But that's not why I'm here."

"Why *are* you here then?"

"Your mother never reported the results of your kenning to the Grand Council."

My fingers twine together. The room feels too warm. "She didn't?"

Norah shakes her head. "An oversight, I'm sure. I know *her* mother recently passed—"

"My gran. Latham killed her, too."

Her expression falters. "I hadn't heard that part," she says softly. "I'm sorry." She smooths invisible wrinkles on her shirt. "I heard that Della lost her husband—your father—recently too. So much tragedy. She must have had a lot on her mind. Normally we would have another Bone Charmer verify and record the results. But, unfortunately, the bones used in your kenning are missing."

"I don't know where they are."

"No, of course not. I just wanted to know if you could tell me about your kenning? I know you've done some work tutoring, but I can't imagine . . ." She clears her throat. "Was that really your match?"

I wrap my arms across my body, grateful that my long sleeves hide my mastery tattoo.

"You're not in any trouble," she says gently. "We just need to know for our records."

I think of my mother's sacrifice for me. Of the fierce expression on her face when I told her I thought Latham wanted to kill me. *I won't let him.*

And she didn't.

My mother never did anything without a reason. If she didn't report the results of my kenning, it wasn't by accident. Maybe she was able to see further down this path with all of

Gran's bones than I could with just one. Maybe this is what she intended all along.

An idea unfolds inside me like a map to a new land. I can't decide if it's brave or foolish.

I feel as if I'm standing at the edge of a sheer cliff with no idea whether the water below is deep and calm or shallow and turbulent. If I jump, will I drift to greener shores or be crushed against jagged rocks?

"Saskia?" Norah prompts. "Were you matched as a tutor?"

"No," I say. "I was matched as a Bone Charmer." It might be a lie, but it feels like the truth.

Her face registers only a moment of surprise, as if she half expected this answer. "Why didn't you come to Ivory Hall to begin your apprenticeship?"

"My father had just died. And my gran before that. I wasn't ready to leave home."

"I understand," she says. "Normally we wouldn't allow an apprentice to start so late—once the binding ceremony is over, we don't allow new arrivals. But under the circumstances . . ." By *circumstances,* she means one of their own instructors murdering my family. "I think it's appropriate to make an exception. Would you like to come to Ivory Hall and begin your training?"

The idea rolls around inside me—gritty, uncomfortable— but gradually it takes the shape of something luminous and appealing. Like a pearl plucked from an oyster. Other than Ami, there's nothing left for me in Midwood. But Latham worked at Ivory Hall. And even if he isn't there anymore, he must have left clues behind. I can't quiet the echo of his voice inside my head:

You have no idea the marvelous things I have planned for Kastelia. The possibility of finding answers—of having another chance to stop him—is too tempting to resist.

Then there's Bram. Working together from Ivory Hall would allow him to continue his apprenticeship. And if we're going to thwart Latham's plan, we'll both need all the training we can get.

My toes grip the edge of the cliff. I take a breath, let go, and jump.

"Yes," I say. "I'd like that very much."

Norah's mouth curves into a gentle smile. "I think you're going to make a wonderful Bone Charmer. Just like your mother."

I hope she's right. I can't think of a better fate.

Acknowledgments

Writing is often a solitary endeavor, but it takes many people to turn a draft into a book. I'm incredibly grateful to each one of them.

First to my amazing editor, Ashley Hearn: I can't thank you enough for how well you understood this story and these characters right from the beginning. Your brilliant insights not only made this a better book but also made me a better writer. You truly are the Book Whisperer!

To my fantastic agent, Kathleen Rushall, who loved the idea for *The Bone Charmer* from the moment I first told her about it and enthusiastically championed it every step of the way. There really aren't words to adequately express how much I appreciate you! From your sharp editorial insights to your savvy career advice, you never lead me astray.

I also appreciate all the other smart, supportive women at the Andrea Brown Literary Agency; and special thanks go to Jennifer March Soloway, who was kind enough to read early pages and provide invaluable feedback.

I'm so grateful to the entire team at Page Street for helping bring *The Bone Charmer* into the world: publisher Will Kiester; publicists Lauren Cepero and Lauren Wohl; editorial interns Trisha Tobias and Chelsea Hensley; production manager Meg Palmer; production editor Hayley Gundlach; editorial manager Marissa Giambelluca; designer Kylie Alexander; illustrator Mina Price; and the fantastic sales team at Macmillan. I'm so grateful to each one of you for the part you played in making this book happen and making it better than it would have been without you.

Also to Kaitlin Severini: Thank you so much for the thoughtful copyedit, and for making me look smarter than I am.

My heartfelt thanks to Katie Nelson, Kate Watson, Emily R. King, Rosalyn Eves, and Tricia Levenseller. I adore you all, and I'm so glad I have you in my life, both as fellow writers and as friends.

To the authors who join me on writing dates in a variety of cafés: Kendare Blake, Marissa Meyer, Lish McBride, and Rori Shay. Thank you for making the work feel a little less solitary. (And for helping me locate the just-right word when I've been staring into space for too long.)

As I was writing this book—exploring ideas on fate and grief and the love of family—I had no way of knowing that my dad would be diagnosed with esophageal cancer shortly after I finished the final page. Or that he would pass away right before I began editing. It was agony to open the file on my computer and realize that the book begins with a girl who recently lost her father, written before I had any inkling I was about to lose mine. My dad was one of the biggest supporters of my writing career, and as I edited, I felt him with me on every page. Dad, I wish I could have seen you grow old; I needed you in my life for so much longer, but I will be forever grateful you were there in the first place. Thank you for choosing a path that led to me.

To my mom, who survived the worst year of her life, while still managing to be there for the people around her: I love you with my whole heart!

To my children, Ben, Jacob, and Isabella, who are smart and funny, and some of the best people I've ever had the privilege of knowing. I can't wait to see where your paths take you!

Finally, to Justin, who helps me build worlds—both real and imagined—and then holds my hand while we live there. You are my everything.

About the Author

reeana Shields is an author of books for young adults, including *The Bone Charmer*, *Poison's Kiss*, and *Poison's Cage*. She graduated from Brigham Young University with a BA in English. When she's not writing, Breeana loves reading, traveling, and playing board games with her extremely competitive family. She lives in the Pacific Northwest with her husband, her three children, and two adorable, but spoiled, dogs.